THE
CLASS THAT
WENT WILD

Ruth Thomas

RED FOX

Also available in Red Fox by Ruth Thomas

The Runaways
The New Boy
The Secret
Guilty!
Hideaway

A Red Fox Book
Published by Random House Children's Books
20 Vauxhall Bridge Road, London SW1V 2SA

A division of Random House UK Ltd
London Melbourne Sydney Auckland
Johannesburg and agencies throughout the world

First published by Hutchinson Children's Books 1988
Beaver edition 1989
Red Fox edition 1990

14 16 18 20 19 17 15

© Ruth Thomas 1988

Printed and bound in Great Britain by
Cox & Wyman Ltd, Reading, Berkshire

RANDOM HOUSE UK Limited Reg. No. 954009

Papers used by Random House UK Limited
are natural, recyclable products made from wood grown in
sustainable forests. The manufacturing processes conform to
the environmental regulations of the country of origin.

ISBN 0 09 963210 1

Contents

To Tina Greenlaw, with thanks

1

Come back, Mrs Lloyd

The noise was getting worse. There were thumps now, as well as shouting voices. Gillian Rundell put her hands over her ears and tried to concentrate on her work; the trouble was, she had no third hand with which to write. Gillian tried putting the pencil between her teeth, and writing like that, but the result was so illegible she had to rub it out. Just then a well-aimed crayon hit her right on the back of the neck, and Gillian twisted round indignantly, trying to see who had thrown it. 'Stop it, you!' she complained.

'*Quiet*, everyone!' said the supply teacher, for the twentieth time. 'I said *quiet*. And the next person who throws something will stand outside the door.'

'Don't look at me,' called Sean Adams to Gillian, ignoring the supply teacher. '*I* didn't do it.' He was smirking all over his handsome black face though, and he was hiding something in his lap. A load of broken crayons, probably. Sean Adams is the horriblest boy in the world, thought Gillian, furiously. I hate him. I *hate* him.

'Get on with your *work*, all of you,' said the supply teacher. He was a small young man, with glasses and a whining voice.

Waves of mutual dislike flowed between him and the class. This was the supply teacher's third day with Class 4L, and the experience was a battle which he was clearly losing.

'I've finished, sir!'

'I can't work in all this noise!'

'It's boring work. Mrs Lloyd gives us better work than this.'

'What is it we supposed to *do*?'

'You *know* what you're supposed to do. You *all* know what you're supposed to do.' The supply teacher was getting desperate. 'And if you can't remember, it's on the board. *English for Juniors*, page twenty-one, Exercise Ten. Now *do* it. Without talking, without fighting, without falling off your chairs. Do you know, this is the worst behaved class I've ever met in the whole of my life!'

The supply teacher would have been wiser not to say that. Class 4L did not accept criticism from strangers.

'We ain't bad for Mrs Lloyd!'

'Nah – we like our own teacher!'

'Wish Mrs Lloyd'd hurry up and come back! We want Mrs Lloyd!'

It was a real riot now. Fists pounding desks, feet stamping, voices heartlessly chanting. 'We want Mrs Lloyd. We want Mrs Lloyd. We want . . . .

An excitable boy with spiky blond hair, and a rather silly grin, jumped on to his desk. He had a round face which seemed not quite to belong to the skinny body, and spidery legs beneath it. With great enthusiasm he began to conduct the chorus.

The door of the classroom opened, and the din ceased immediately as though someone had cut off the sound track of a battle film. In the doorway stood the awesome figure of the headmistress, come to see what all the disturbance was about.

Mrs White was tall and big-boned, with sloping shoulders and a neck which poked sharply forward. She wore a dowdy skirt and a fawn cardigan which had seen better days. As she advanced into the room, she bared large yellow teeth in a cheesy smile for the supply teacher, but her eyes were cold and unfriendly. Mrs White was displeased with Class 4L for being stroppy, but even more displeased with the supply teacher for being unable to manage them.

'Excuse me, Mr er-er,' said the headmistress; she had forgotten his name. 'Excuse me a moment, will you – I just happened to see – *Joseph Rundell, come here*!'

The fair haired boy on the desk climbed down, sheepishly.

'*Bring me your work*!'

Gillian turned her head, apprehensively. She was a thin, peaky child, with brown curly hair cut short; a little, intense, triangular face, and great big soulful eyes. The pointed face was strained and anxious now. Knowing Joseph, he would have *done* no work. 'Look at *my* work, Mrs White,' she invited the headmistress, pushing it across the desk.

'No thank you, Gillian.'

'I done a lot, Mrs White, I really tried.'

'No *thank* you, Gillian. Not now.'

'I done nearly all the questions, look!'

'NOT NOW, Gillian . . . . She's a nice little girl,' the headmistress continued in an audible whisper to the supply teacher. 'She's only trying to distract attention from her clown of a brother. *That* is Gillian's brother, that buffoon, dancing on the table just now. In case you haven't discovered it, they are twins.'

There was a snigger, from somewhere in the front.

'Who laughed?'

Silence. Then another explosive snigger, loud and uncontrolled.

'Stand up, Grace Johnson.'

9

Grace was Gillian's best friend. Her dark cheeks hardly showed the blush which covered them, but the shining brown eyes spoke her shame, and begged the headmistress's understanding.

'Is there something funny?'

'No, Mrs White.'

'Then why are you smiling? You're smiling now.'

'I'm not, Mrs White. I mean, I can't help it.' She couldn't. The more embarrassed and flustered she became, the more the nervous smile stretched her face.

'How old are you, Grace?'

'Nearly eleven.'

'Isn't it time you developed a more grown-up sense of humour? Does anyone else think bad behaviour is funny?'

Silence.

'Well, let me say that *I* don't find it funny. And Mr er-er, your teacher for this week, doesn't find it funny. There is nothing humorous whatsoever about rude children. Is there, Grace?'

'No, Mrs White.'

'Is there, Joseph?'

'No, Mrs White.'

'Bring me your work, Joseph. I'm still waiting to see it . . . . Is this your work? One line of scribble? Your sister has managed nearly two pages. What have *you* been doing all the afternoon?'

Silence.

'Well?'

'I forget . . . . Oh, I know, I know, I was thinking. I was thinking *hard*, how to do it good.'

'Really? I can't say I'm impressed with the results. Am I to take it that you intend to waste *all* your time like this, while Mrs Lloyd is away?'

'No, Mrs White.'

'I'm very glad to hear it. And while on the subject of Mrs

Lloyd . . . pencils down, eyes this way, this is for all of you
. . . while on the subject of Mrs Lloyd, I may as well tell
you now, I'm sorry to say that I have some rather sad
news.' Pause. What sad news? Everyone listened very hard.
'Mrs Lloyd is not coming back this week. And she is not
coming back next week . . . . In fact, I'm afraid, *she may not
be coming back at all*.'

Shocked silence, followed by dismay, disbelief, lamen-
tations.

'Now – you're big children, old enough to understand
what I'm going to tell you. Mrs Lloyd is going to have a
baby. Did anyone not know that Mrs Lloyd is going to
have a baby? So Mrs Lloyd would be leaving soon anyway,
at any rate for a while. But the doctor says she must stay
home *now*, and rest, otherwise something might go wrong
with the baby. Right, then we have to carry on as best we
can, without her, haven't we? And that means, among other
things, showing proper courtesy to Mr er-er, who has
kindly come to help us out.'

Groups of sullen, depressed faces stared back at Mrs
White. No one displayed the least interest in showing
courtesy to Mr er-er, whose name they also had forgotten.
Well – he hadn't bothered to learn their names, so why
should they bother to learn his?

'The work on the board is to be finished,' said Mrs
White. 'I shall come back at playtime, and inspect everyone's book. You have twenty minutes more, and those
who haven't done enough will lose their play. In fact, from
what I saw as I came into this classroom, most of you have
had your play in any case. Please send any nuisances to me,
Mr er-er, *immediately*.'

The class was subdued now, at least for the moment, but
resentment floated in the air like a cloud of dangerous gas.
You could hear the hiss as it escaped into the atmosphere;
you could smell it, almost. At any moment it might ignite,

11

and there would be uproar again. Mr er-er was deeply unhappy. He had been longing for playtime, but now that the lazy ones were to stay in to finish their work, he would have to stay in with them, to supervise. He would not be able to escape to the sanctuary of the Staff Room, and a lovely cup of hot strong tea.

Would the afternoon never end? How in the world was he going to control this impossible lot through playtime, and for a whole hour afterwards? He wished he had paid more attention last night to planning lessons for today. He wished he had never become a teacher at all. Whatever had made him do it? He didn't really like children very much. Come to think of it, he didn't like children at all, he decided.

A story – perhaps he could read them a story. There was a fair selection of books on the library shelf. Mr er-er picked one out at random and flicked through its pages. This would do – it was called *Tales of Dragons and Witches*; this would keep the little monsters quiet for the last half hour, at least.

When Mrs Lloyd read to the class, she always made it exciting. She spoke in different voices for the different characters, and even if the story was quite ordinary, Mrs Lloyd made it sound as though she couldn't wait to know what happened next. But Mr er-er didn't read like that. His voice trailed along monotonously, without any changes of expression, without any *feeling* at all. It was a good story really, but Mr er-er made it quite boring. Disappointed, the class began to fidget and whisper, and lift their desk lids in search of better amusement.

Sean dropped his head on to his arms and snored. A rude, honking snore. Mr er-er tried to ignore Sean's snore, and Sean did it again, looking straight at the supply teacher this time, his hands covering the lower part of his face.

Mr er-er stopped reading. 'Who made that noise? It was

you, wasn't it? Yes, you, the tall one.'

'Me, sir? No not me, sir. I didn't do nothing, sir.' Sean was a good looking boy but his eyes were cruel, mocking.

'Yes, you did, I saw you. I saw you put your hand in front of your mouth.'

'Just yawning, sir,' said Sean, grinning.

They seemed to be all grinning now. Wherever Mr er-er looked he could see nothing but insolent, grinning faces. 'Sean didn't do nothing, he was just yawning,' one or two others confirmed.

Suddenly there was another honking noise, loud as pistol shot. Joseph, copying Sean, was doing a tremendous snore. He was doing it quite openly.

'It was you!' Mr er-er accused him.

Joseph snored with abandon. The class cheered and clapped, so Joseph went on doing it.

'Shut up, Joseph,' said Gillian. 'You'll get in trouble.'

Joseph snored on, enjoying the applause and beaming round at his audience.

'GO TO MRS WHITE!' Mr er-er was at the end of his tether. That was it, he wouldn't be coming back tomorrow, but let this little brute, at least, get what was coming to him!

'Oh, sir!'

'You heard me. Go to Mrs White.'

'Oh please, sir! Kind sir! Forgive me, sir, I won't do it again. It's nearly home time, sir.'

'Yes, but not for you, I imagine,' said Mr er-er, with considerable satisfaction.

'Please sir—'

'*Just go!*'

Joseph went. Mr er-er picked up *Tales of Dragons and Witches* again, and the class moaned. Finally defeated, Mr er-er slapped the open book face down on the table.

'I like the story, sir,' said Grace, who could not bear to see people unhappy.

13

'Tough,' said Mr er-er, and he began collecting up his belongings. He had had enough of Class 4L, they could do as they liked. Finding themselves ignored, a few people went back to throwing paper darts and bits of crayons around the class. Someone wrote on the board MRS LLOYD IS OUR TEACHER, as though the chalk letters could make the wish come true.

The bell went. Mr er-er put on his coat and made for the door without another word.

'We supposed to put our chairs on the desks,' someone called after him, but Mr er-er did not hear. 'We supposed to line up,' said someone else, but Mr er-er did not hear that either. Pushing and shoving and trampling one another, Class 4L dismissed themselves.

Left in the classroom, Gillian and Grace surveyed the mess.

'Look at all that rubbish on the floor,' said Gillian, severely. 'What's Mrs Lloyd going to say?'

'She's not going to see it,' said Grace, sadly. '*You* know, she's not coming back perhaps.' Even in her sorrow, Grace's eyes were bright as stars.

'Oh yeah, I forgot. I can't seem to believe it really. She been our teacher such a long time. We better pick up all this litter though.'

'And put the things away.'

'And clean the board. That's the best we can do to make Mrs Lloyd happy.'

'Yeah – how will she know we done it, though?'

'I'm going to write her a letter tonight. Are you going to write to Mrs Lloyd, Grace?'

'I dunno. I think I rather do some knitting. I think I shall knit something for Mrs Lloyd's baby. . . . I wish Mrs Lloyd wouldn't have left.'

'So do I wish that.'

It took the girls a long time to bring order to the ravaged classroom. 'Joseph hasn't come back yet,' said Grace.

'Yeah, well, Mrs White got to tell him off, hasn't she! He does do naughty things, you know. He's a *terrible* responsibility.'

Grace privately thought Joseph was a downright nuisance. This term, of all things, he had declared himself to be in love with her. She thought he mainly said it to be in the fashion, and she certainly didn't return his affections; Joseph was so silly after all – nobody could actually be in love with *him*. But Grace didn't want to hurt his feelings by telling him that, so mostly she just giggled and looked embarrassed when the subject came up. 'We got to watch out for him now,' she said, wisely. 'Now Mrs Lloyd ain't here, he's going to get worse.'

'Yeah, I know . . . . Here he comes, Grace. I can hear his footsteps, can't you?'

Joseph burst into the classroom like a tornado. 'She didn't say nothing! She didn't say nothing!' He was enormously pleased with himself; jubilant and crowing he danced across the desks, and a pile of books came toppling to the ground.

'Do you mind?' Gillian scolded him. 'We just this minute put them books back.'

'She must have said something,' said Grace.

'No she didn't, then, she just said she hadn't got time to listen to my stories.'

Gillian sighed. 'So what story did you tell her this time?'

'I said I had sleepy sickness, and I couldn't help snoring. I said I caught it in Southend.'

'Sleepy sickness is in Africa,' said Grace.

'I know, but I only been to Southend. Mrs White said the best cure she knows for sleepy sickness is hard work. She didn't really tell me off. I don't think Mrs White likes sir very much.'

Joseph was at his desk now, rummaging for pens and

15

sweets, and scattering paper everywhere. Gillian stamped her foot. 'Don't put your rubbish on the floor, Joseph Rundell! What you think the bin is for?'

Joseph made a paper dart, and hurled it into the air. 'I made them laugh, didn't I? They were all laughing and clapping. Did you see when they clapped?'

'Yes, and we rather not see it again.'

'Boring old book! Silly, boring old dragons! Is that the silly, boring book on Mrs Lloyd's table?' Joseph picked it up. 'Boring, snoring old book. I'll make it more interesting, shall I?'

'*No!*' said Gillian and Grace together – but before they could stop him, Joseph had flourished the ball-point pen in his hand, and drawn a rude picture, all over the open page of *Tales of Dragons and Witches*.

It was a *very* rude picture. The girls stared at it in horror, and Grace put the backs of her hands against her hot brown cheeks to cool the blush.

'You done it now! Look what you done!' Gillian was not as tall as Joseph; she had to look up at him to scold.

Joseph shifted, uneasily. 'Don't matter.' He rather wished he hadn't drawn in ink, though. You couldn't rub out ink.

'That ain't sir's book, that's a library book.'

'So?'

'What about when Miss Campbell finds out?'

'She won't know it's me.'

'Yes she will.'

'No she won't,' said Joseph. 'How will she?'

'By your face.'

'I can keep a straight face.'

'No you can't,' said Gillian. 'You can't keep a straight face for anything. You can't keep a straight face for a hundred pounds. Miss Campbell's going to find out, and she's going to tell Mrs White, and you're going to get suspended, Joseph!'

'Hide the book then.'

'Why not you?'

'You can do it for me. You hide it for me, Gill, eh?'

'Let's shut it up anyway,' said Grace, primly. 'It's nasty. It's a nasty picture, you didn't ought to have drawn it, Joseph.' She flipped the cover over, so that the book was now closed on Mrs Lloyd's table. And just as well, for at that moment Miss Campbell herself poked her head into the room.

Miss Campbell, who looked after the library, was the most unpopular teacher at Castle Street Junior. Possibly the most unpopular teacher in the whole of England. She was young, but not jolly like most young teachers. She had a face like a dried-up lemon, and a voice of acid sharpness. 'What are you doing here?' she snapped at them. 'Don't you know it's past four o'clock? Haven't you got homes to go to?'

'We was tidying up,' said Grace.

'Well, now you can go home. Go on, all of you! The cleaning ladies will be wanting to come in. Is that your library book, Gillian Rundell? Is it on your ticket?'

'No, Miss Campbell, it's the class's.'

'Leave it where it is then. You can put it on the library shelf in the morning . . . . What are you grinning about, Grace Johnson? I never see you these days without that silly look on your face. There must be something wrong with you.'

'Yes, Miss Campbell.'

'Do something about it then. Go on, now. I'm waiting to go home myself.'

They went. Clattering down the stone steps, buttoning coats as they ran. Spirits dragging, hearts chilled with apprehension for tomorrow, they crossed the draughty playground. It was the beginning of November, and winter already, with a squally London sky, and a spiteful little wind gusting round the corners.

17

Out of the front school gate and across the road by the caretaker's house. Past Dippy Dora's, dead shrubs waist high in the garden, and the curtains drawn as usual. Lingering here a moment, because there was fascination as well as fear, and you never knew when the terrifying old thing might appear. Round the corner into Tower Street, and home. Number 32 for Joseph and Gillian, Number 34 for Grace. Cheery gas fires in both small houses, identical chips and beefburgers frying in the pan, and in each kitchen a mum with a smile as warm as glowing coals.

But later, after tea, Gillian tore a page out of her homework book and began to write, with a very blunt pencil:

Dear Mrs Lloyd,
I hope you are well and I hope your baby is going along all right. Me and Grace cleared up the classroom. Don't worry about the classroom me and Grace will look after it for you while you are away. Mrs White said you might not come back but we all hope you will. We got a nother teacher but we dont like him he does not like us neither. Thats all for now but please say hello to your husband Winston for me.
            Love from Gillian.
        X X X X X X X X X X X X X X X X X

She folded the paper and put it inside her homework book. Class 4L hadn't been given any homework this evening; Gillian wondered if anyone would give them homework tomorrow. Anyway, she would go to the school secretary in the morning, beg an envelope for her letter, and ask for Mrs Lloyd's address. And she would get to school early, and try to get hold of *Tales of Dragons and Witches* before anyone else found out what Joseph had drawn inside it.

2

An accident in the library

There was a very strict rule about not coming into school before the bell without permission. If you were caught doing it you had to go to Mrs White to be told off, and nagged at about why you felt entitled to break the school rules that were there for everyone's protection. And Mrs White had a way of making you tell the truth, even when you were determined to tell a lie, and had the story all ready.

So Gillian was very much afraid of being caught, but very much more afraid of the consequences of Joseph's artwork being discovered. It wasn't just that a teacher might discover it. Suppose Harjit saw it, or that spiteful Sharon? Either of those would be only too pleased to point out the offending drawing to Miss Campbell. Only too pleased to see someone else, not them, getting into trouble.

It would not be easy to get into school without being seen. The back way was impossible. That way you had to go through the hall, and there were always teachers crossing, with armfuls of books and papers and things. The front way was bolder, but less risky; the stairs led directly

19

up from the vestibule, which was likely to be empty. There was still the hazard of the long corridor upstairs, though. The classroom doors would be open, and there would be teachers in some of those classrooms, ready to hear, and pounce, and accuse.

There was one other possibility. Just inside the far back entrance, the one that was hardly ever used, there was a little wooden staircase, forbidden to children because it was steep, and narrow, and twisty; and mysterious and exciting because it was forbidden. Gillian had never been up the little stairs, but she knew where they came out – right by the boys' toilet at the end of the top corridor, almost opposite Class 4L.

Up the little stairs then. If the supply teacher was there already, there would be nothing Gillian could do about the book, but she could probably bluff a supply teacher about being in school. First, though, she had to make sure none of the tell-tales saw her from the playground; so she stood against the wall, by the far back door, bouncing her ball and looking round. No one took any notice of her. It was so early there was hardly anyone in the playground anyway. The anxious frown on Gillian's pale little face re-laxed just a bit.

She reached behind her and found the door handle. Would the door be locked? She turned the handle and pushed. No, it was not locked; well, that was lucky. Gillian slipped inside, and scuttled up the little stairs, her heart banging like a drum. She felt very wicked, doing two wrong things at once. It wasn't the first time she had done wrong things to cover up for Joseph, but this was probably the most disobedient yet, she thought.

Class 4L was empty. Gillian could see, before she crossed the corridor, that there was no one in it. Unless Mr er-er was lurking round the corner. Pinning pictures on

20

the wall, perhaps, out of sight. Gillian gave a quick glance to left and right, and hurled herself through the door. No one! Safe! *Tales of Dragons and Witches* still lay on Mrs Lloyd's table, undisturbed since yesterday afternoon. Gillian grabbed it, and prepared to escape. Down the little stairs again? Better had, she was not out of danger yet.

It was sheer bad luck that Miss Campbell should come out of the library just as Gillian was disappearing down the little stairs.

'Gillian Rundell!'

She had been seen; she had been recognized. Now what? She could turn, and answer the summons, or she could go on and get caught anyway, and punished for not coming back. The book, though! In a panic, Gillian threw the book down the stairs, and watched it bounce against the wall, to slide on round the next corner. Then she climbed again, slowly and with dread, to face the terrible Miss Campbell.

'*What* are you doing in school? You know you're not allowed. *And* using the little stairs. What do you mean by it, Gillian? Who do you think you are? You know those stairs are only for the teachers.'

'Yes, Miss Campbell.'

'You'll have to report to Mrs White . . . . No, not now, she's not in school this morning, she's gone to a meeting. This afternoon. Don't think I'll forget – I'm looking after your class today. For my sins. So I'll have your face to remind me. Go on to the playground now . . . not that way, stupid child, the proper way!'

Gillian, with a sinking heart, trudged along the corridor, and Miss Campbell took the short cut to the Staff Room, down the little stairs. So she would find the book. What would happen now?

Gillian looked for Grace, but Grace was late. Sharon was

21

in the playground though, and Satibai and Minaxi. 'Sir ain't here,' Gillian told them, gloomily. 'We got Miss Campbell.'

'Oh no!' they groaned.

The word rippled along the line as they assembled to go in. 'We've got Miss Campbell for our teacher!' 'What happened to sir, then?' 'It's not fair!' The mutters continued, all the way up the stairs.

Miss Campbell came into Class 4L, loaded with bags which she dumped on the floor beside her chair. *Tales of Dragons and Witches* was in her hand, and Gillian was terrified Miss Campbell might already have looked through it, but she put it on the table and said nothing. Gillian glanced back at Joseph to see if he was frightened too, but Joseph was looking quite unconcerned. Probably he had forgotten all about the rude drawing. He had left it all to her, as usual.

'Answer your names,' said Miss Campbell, sharply, opening the register. She was not at all pleased at having been asked to take Class 4L. Not only were they the worst class in the school, but also Miss Campbell did not consider that she should be asked to take charge of *any* class. Her job was to look after the library, and do remedial teaching throughout the school. It was very annoying that she had to give up her timetable to mind this unruly lot. Especially as, by all accounts, they had already driven out one supply teacher.

'Richard Abbott?'

'Yes, Miss Campbell.'

'Sean Adams?'

'Yeah.'

'Yeah? Where are your manners, Sean?'

'Don't know, miss.'

'How careless of you to lose them.'

The class laughed, cautiously. Sean scowled. Miss

Campbell was trying to put him down, and no one was supposed to put Sean Adams down. 'Cow!' he muttered, under his breath.

'Was that remark addressed to me, by any chance?'

Sean would have liked to say that it was, but he wasn't quite brave enough. 'Just talking to myself, miss.'

'Oh really? Do you know what they say about people who talk to themselves?'

The class laughed again, but only a bit. It wasn't a good idea to get on the wrong side of Sean. Sean was the boss, the king, and he could be very vengeful towards anyone not showing him proper respect. He was extremely angry now, with Miss Campbell. If looks could kill, Miss Campbell would certainly have dropped dead.

The door opened and Grace burst in, breathless and agitated from running, the shining eyes still half dazed with sleep.

'Oh, *you've* condescended to join us, have you? Hurry up, then. What are you smiling about? Take that silly smile off your face, Grace Johnson, it makes you look half-witted!'

Miss Campbell finished calling the register and then said that as there was no Assembly that morning, she supposed they had better get on and do some maths. *Quietly*, since she, Miss Campbell, had some important work of her own to finish. Was there anyone who couldn't find some suitable maths to do? Very well then, and anyone who was *really* stuck could come out and ask, of course.

Gillian opened her maths text book, and tried to understand what it said on the page after the one she had worked from last. Normally, the class did maths in groups, hard work for some people and easier work for others; and Mrs Lloyd went round the groups, helping and explaining. Often they did practical maths, with weighing and measuring, or board games to make it fun. It was hard struggling on your own. Gillian did not think that anyone would actually venture to interrupt Miss Campbell, now poring over catalogues at Mrs Lloyd's table. Whatever difficulties they might be in, all would prefer to stay in their seats, out of reach of Miss Campbell's biting tongue.

Gillian looked at *Tales of Dragons and Witches*, still lying on the corner of Mrs Lloyd's table. She did not think Miss Campbell could have looked inside it yet, since she had said nothing about Joseph's rude drawing, and surely, surely, the skies were going to fall when she found that. Also, she didn't seem to have connected the book being on the little stairs, with *Gillian* being on the little stairs. Probably she thought some teacher had dropped it. Probably she didn't realize the book was part of Class 4L's library allocation for that term. Probably she was going to take it back to the library at playtime, and it would be harder than ever to get hold of it, and hide it.

While Gillian worried, Sean plotted. He wanted, very much, to punish Miss Campbell for being sarcastic to him, but he didn't want to do it himself. Sean did wrong things himself often enough, but why risk trouble, if you could get someone else to do your dirty work for you? So what about using Joseph Rundell? Joseph was always ready to play up, even play up Miss Campbell, given enough encouragement. What could Joseph Rundell be induced to do now, that would annoy Miss Campbell, but not get him, Sean Adams, into trouble?

Amongst the clutter of belongings which Miss Campbell had brought with her was a plastic carrier bag full of orange knitting. Not something for Mrs Lloyd's baby, of course, but a heavy jumper she was knitting for herself. Unnoticed by Miss Campbell, the bag of knitting had tipped over, and a ball of orange wool was unrolling itself across the floor. Sean thought it would serve Miss Campbell right if someone helped the ball of wool to unroll itself a bit more. A lot more, actually.

The double desks were arranged around the room in groups of three, so that there were five or six children in each group. Luckily for Sean's purpose, Joseph was in his group, so it was easy to lean across the table of desks and poke him. Joseph, bored with the silence and the maths, was quite ready to start off something more entertaining. He followed Sean's pointing finger, and got the idea. His face brightened and he sniggered.

'Quiet!' said Miss Campbell, without looking up. 'Get on with your work.'

Joseph sighed; a great exaggerated gusty breath. Nothing happened, so he did it again.

'Stop that silly noise, Joseph Rundell. It's getting on my nerves.'

'I can't do this sum,' said Joseph, plaintively.

'Well, *try*.'

'I *have* tried. I'm stuck.'

'Oh all right, all right, bring it here. Come on then, I haven't got all day.' And, when he stood beside her – 'Stuck on *this*? What are you, Joseph, a dunce?'

'Yes, Miss Campbell, I expect so.' Joseph was grinning amiably. He didn't mind being called names by Miss Campbell. He had his foot under the ball of orange wool, and that was the main thing. He gave the orange wool a little kick, to start it rolling.

'Oh *I* see how to do it, *I* see. Silly me. Silly me, eh, Miss Campbell? *This* is what you do, innit!' He flourished his book in front of her face, so she would not see what was happening to the orange wool.

'Yes, well *think* next time. Use your brains, boy, if you've got any. Go on then – back to your seat.'

Miss Campbell's eyes returned to her catalogue and

Joseph happily began trundling the orange wool towards the back of the class. He kicked it to Sharon, hoping she would help make a tangle by twining the thread round the leg of her desk, but Sharon was afraid of Miss Campbell, and didn't want to be involved. Chandra and Minaxi and Satibai wouldn't play, of course – they never did anything wrong! Joseph offered the ball of wool to Harjit, and then to Stephen, who was Sean's best friend at the moment, and one of the toughest boys in the school. But even Stephen declined the invitation. You didn't play up Miss Campbell; if you had any sense you had a healthy fear of Miss Campbell. Not so much because of what she ever *did* to offenders, as what that sharp voice hinted she *might* do, one of these days, if she so chose.

All by himself then, Joseph busily wound the orange wool round his desk leg, round and round and between his legs. By this time most of the class had spotted what was happening, and little spurts of sniggery laughter were erupting all over the room. Gillian watched her twin brother, aghast.

Miss Campbell looked up. 'What is it *now?*' Then she saw. 'Joseph Rundell, bring me that wool this minute!'

'Yes, Miss Campbell. I can't, Miss Campbell. It's all caught in my legs, miss, I can't undo it.' He was deliberately tying more knots in the wool as he spoke; it was quite obvious what he was doing. 'My legs are like that, Miss Campbell. They're always getting tied up in wool, and string, and cotton, and . . . .'

The class held its breath. What lunacy was this?

'*Now*, Joseph.' There was venom in Miss Campbell's voice now, a real threat. The happy smile faded from Joseph's face. He had gone too far; he was frightened. He struggled, in earnest this time, to free himself from the mesh of wool.

'I'M WAITING.'

He would never do it with Miss Campbell's eyes on him, Gillian thought. No one nearby helped, even Sean who had really started it. Gillian pushed back her chair, and began to go to Joseph's aid.

'Leave him!' said Miss Campbell grimly. 'Let him do it himself.'

Joseph looked trapped, and scared. And, angry with him as she was, Gillian couldn't see him hurt. 'Stop it, you!' she shouted suddenly at Jennifer, who sat at her table.

'I didn't do nothing,' protested Jennifer, who was indeed the most inoffensive child in the world.

'Yes you did, you kicked me!'

'I never,' said Jennifer, indignant and bewildered.

'Stand up, both of you,' said Miss Campbell.

As they stood, Gillian saw that Joseph was still struggling hopelessly with the wool. She grabbed Jennifer's hair and tugged it hard. 'That's for kicking me!'

'I never, I never! Leave me!'

There would have been a fight, but Miss Campbell, exasperated beyond words now, seized Gillian by the scruff of the neck and hauled her to the front of the class. 'I don't know what's the matter with you today, Gillian Rundell,' said Miss Campbell grimly. 'But I know I'm not going to stand for it. Carrying on like a little fishwife! Who do you think you are?'

'Sorry, Miss Campbell.' She *was* sorry now. Sorry for herself, that was, and trembling. It was no small thing to bring Miss Campbell's anger crashing down on your head. But from the corner of her eye, Gillian saw that Joseph was making headway with the wool at last. By creating a diversion she had given him the time he needed. Another crisis passed.

Miss Campbell took the wool from Joseph with no more than a contemptuous glance. Her fury now was all directed at Gillian. 'If it's not one thing it's something else with you. You don't stop, do you! All right, Jennifer, cut out the snivelling, I daresay you'll live! And what are you smirking about, Grace Johnson? Smirking and grinning like a Cheshire cat . . . . There's the play bell, thank goodness! Fifteen minutes' rest from you lot. Line up, no talking. Gillian, since you don't deserve any play, you can help me carry these things to the library.'

'It's on top of the high shelves,' said Gillian to Grace, at dinner time. 'I saw her put it there. You know what I mean – where she puts all the books she don't want us to get at yet.'

'Do you think she saw?'

'Saw what?'

'You know – thingy. I don't like to say. What Joseph drawn.'

'Nah. She just put the book with a load of others. To sort them out later. After school, most likely. Will you come to the library with me now, Grace, and help get it down?'

'I don't like,' said Grace, nervously. 'We're not allowed.'

'I know, but will you?'

'Well . . . all right . . . but, you know something?'

'What?'

'I think Joseph is going to do something worse than that, soon.'

'What do you mean?' said Gillian, alarmed.

'I mean worse than that picture he done in the book.'

'Don't be silly! What could be worse than that? Anyway, how do you know?'

'I just feel it.'

'Oh you just *feel* it,' said Gillian relieved.

The rule about not coming into school at dinner-time was just as strict as the one about not coming in before school.

28

It was something to do with the school's being responsible, if you hurt yourself when no grown-up was supervising. There were even monitors on the door at dinner-time. Mrs White did not like having some children to police other children, but unfortunately there were some people who could not be trusted to discipline themselves; who had so little sense of personal honour, etc., etc. So the door monitors, Richard and Chandra that week, were the first obstacle.

'We got to go to Miss Campbell,' Gillian tried.

'All right then,' said Chandra, believing her.

Well, *that* was easy. But crossing the hall was Mr Davis. He was humming the theme from *EastEnders*, which he often did when he was in a good mood. As he nearly always was.

'We got to go to Miss Campbell,' said Grace.

'Miss Campbell's gone to the bank.'

'Oh—'

'*Out!*'

'Please, sir—'

'OUT, OUT, both of you. Scram. Skedaddle. On the double, one two, one two!'

The girls fled from the hall and hid in the cloakroom. 'What now?' said Grace.

'Make out we're with that lot,' said Gillian.

A group of children from 3K, coming in to put the painting things out for Mr King, trooped past the cloakroom. Grace and Gillian joined them, skulking in their wake.

'You're not our class!' 'What you coming up for?' 'Yeah – what you doing in school?'

'We got to go to Miss Campbell,' said Gillian, and they ran along the upstairs corridor before anyone else could stop them.

The library was empty. Of course – Miss Campbell was at the bank. 'There it is,' said Grace. 'I see it.'

'I can't reach it,' said Gillian, stretching.

'Stand on a chair . . . this one . . . I'll get it for you.'

Gillian stood on the chair and stretched again. On tiptoe, she was just tall enough. *Tales of Dragons and Witches* was almost at the bottom of the pile. Trembling with eagerness, now she was almost there, Gillian grabbed it with both hands and began to tug.

'Not like that!' called Grace, in sudden alarm.

Too late. As Gillian wrenched out *Tales of Dragons and Witches*, the whole pile began to topple, and fall forward. As the heavy books struck her, Gillian lost her balance. The chair legs shot from underneath her and she fell, with a sickening thud, on to the hard parquet floor. Worse still, the sharp corner of one of the books caught her full in the face. There was pain, and shock, and blood.

'I'll get someone,' said Grace, very much frightened. 'I'll get someone quick.'

'No,' said Gillian. 'We'll get in trouble.'

'You're hurt though, Gillian. You're bleeding. You might be going to bleed to death. My best friend's bleeding to death!'

There was blood all over the books and the floor, and trickling down Gillian's neck to soak into her navy blue pullover. Grace was terrified. 'I'm going, I'm going!'

'No,' pleaded Gillian, trying desperately to mop up the blood with her one small tissue. But Grace was gone. Gillian looked round wildly. Where was *Tales of Dragons and Witches*? Oh here it was, here right in her hand still. Could she hide it? Not really – there might not be time, and her shoulder was hurting where it had hit the floor, and there was blood dripping everywhere.

With shaking fingers, Gillian found the offending page and tore it out, and stuffed it into the pocket of her skirt.

Actually Gillian was not much hurt. She was bruised, of course, and there was a small cut on her cheek, but most of the blood was from her nose. The worst thing was the fear she felt, after she had been patched up and left sitting outside the headmistress's room to meditate on her sins while waiting to explain herself to Mrs White. No, Grace could not stay with her. Grace could go to her class and be sent for later, if required. Gillian waited, in misery. She knew she ought to be making up a story for Mrs White, but somehow she couldn't think of one.

'It won't do, Gillian, will it?' said Mrs White. 'The school rules are not there for nothing. They are not there for my amusement, nor Miss Campbell's amusement, nor for Gillian Rundell to ignore if she feels like it. The rules are for our safety. We all need rules.'

'Yes, Mrs White.'

'Why did you come into school at dinner-time? You and Grace Johnson?'

'No reason.'

'People don't do things without a reason. Miss Campbell tells me you came in before school as well. Why did you do that?'

'I dunno.'

'You do know, Gillian. And you are going to tell me.'

Gillian began to cry.

'Now stop that! I'm not an ogre. Am I an ogre, Gillian? No, look at me, look at me! Am I an ogre?'

Gillian would have liked to say that yes, Mrs White was *rather* an ogre, but she didn't like to. 'No, Mrs White.'

'Right. Now, there's a time and place for all things, Gillian, and the time to come into school is not when you have been told to stay in the playground. And the time to come to the library is not at dinner time, when the teachers are too busy to supervise you. Look what happens when you break the rules that have been made for your safety. So you are going to tell me why you did it. Aren't you?'

Gillian's tears flowed faster. Great sobs shook her shoulders.

'Well?'

Sob, sob.

'*I'm waiting.*'

Gillian's arm seemed to have developed a will of its own. Certainly she hadn't meant to give in so easily, but she found herself doing so, nevertheless. Blowing her nose with one hand, and fumbling in her pocket with the other, Gillian brought out the crumpled, bloodstained page of *Tales of Dragons and Witches*.

'What's this?'

Gillian handed it over wordlessly and then waited, cold with shame, for the appalled reaction that must surely follow.

'Did you draw this?'

'No, Mrs White.'

'No, it doesn't look like *your* artwork. Who, then? No, no, look at me, who did this – er – unusual drawing?'

Gillian felt her gaze drawn upwards, to meet the headmistress eye to eye. She thought suddenly that Mrs White had a face like a horse, long and bony and with great big teeth, on the end of the poky neck. Even the short, grey hair hung coarse and straight, like the mane of an elderly Dobbin. And this horse was trying very hard not to laugh. Could it be that Mrs White actually thought Joseph's rude picture was *funny?*

All that worry for nothing? But Gillian was quite shocked. It was wrong for Mrs White to *laugh*. She should have been scandalized, like a proper grown-up.

'Well now, for a start, *we don't tear pages out of library books*. Do we, Gillian?'

'No, Mrs White.'

'*Nor draw in them*, so next a word with the artist, I think,' said Mrs White, quite gleefully, as though she expected to get some fun out of the interview.

'Oh it wasn't *Joseph*, Mrs White. Joseph never done it. It wasn't *him*—'

'Don't bother, Gillian,' said Mrs White, showing the yellow teeth right up to the gums. 'You know, I was a teacher before you were born.'

Gillian dawdled back to the classroom where 4L, under Miss Campbell's beady eye, were busy making get-well cards for Mrs Lloyd. Most of the girls had done brightly coloured lopsided hearts on the front of their cards, with patterns of flowers around the edge. The boys had mostly drawn space-men, or robots; one or two had drawn aeroplanes with bombs coming out of them. Miss Campbell was walking round, when Gillian entered the room, inspecting the class's efforts, and making remarks like, 'Not bad, not bad.' 'What's this rubbish?' 'Do it again – you can't send that mess!'

When she came to Joseph she paused. His work was different from the rest. He had drawn a beautiful picture of a baby angel, with little feathered wings, flying down from Heaven to a waiting Mrs Lloyd. The baby angel and Mrs Lloyd had their arms stretched out to each other, and they were both smiling.

The picture was charming, even Miss Campbell could not deny it a few words of grudging appreciation. 'That's quite good, Joseph. Don't spoil it with the colouring.' Then she opened the card to see what Joseph had written inside, and her face turned purple. Poor Joseph – for once he hadn't meant to be cheeky. He had forgotten that Miss Campbell would see what he put; he had just written from his heart: 'Dear Mrs Lloyd we miss you so much we don't like miss cambel shes a spitful teacher. your faithful pupl Joseph.'

Miss Campbell went berserk. 'What a cheek! Who do you think you are? Stay in next playtime, and the one after that, and write out five hundred times *I must not be rude*. Don't let me have to say that to anyone else,' she added, glaring round at the class. 'Yes, Gillian, what is it?'

'Please, Miss Campbell, Mrs White wants Joseph.'
'She's more than welcome,' said Miss Campbell.

It doesn't never end, does it, thought Gillian, despairingly. As soon as he's out of one trouble, he's into another. So what's it going to be next? What's my silly, awful, terrible, *nuisance*, RESPONSIBILITY brother going to do next?

3

Dippy Dora

They were late again going home, because Gillian had to go to Mrs White's room to collect a letter for her mother, explaining about the plaster on her cheek and the blood on her clothes. And Grace waited for Gillian, and Joseph waited for Grace. In the street, empty of children now, Joseph offered sweets to his lady.

'No,' said Grace, 'I don't want your sweets. You do too much wrong things.' The time had come for plain speaking.

'Don't you love me, then?'

'No.'

'Well I love you, I really love you, you know. I do, Grace, I do.'

His gifts having been spurned, Joseph proceeded to demonstrate his devotion to Grace by tormenting her. He ran round her in circles, sometimes managing to tread on her toes, sometimes grabbing at the top-knot of springy hair bulging through the woolly cap she wore. It was a pretty cap, in a mixture of colours – red, purple, blue and green. Grace loved pretty things and she thought, quite rightly, that she looked particularly fetching in this one.

'Go away,' said Grace, linking arms with Gillian. 'Me and Gillian don't want you this evening.'

'That's right, we don't,' said Gillian, whose shoulder still ached, and whose cheek still throbbed from the accident.

'Only playing,' said Joseph.

'There's a time and place for all things,' said Gillian, severely.

'Yeah,' said Grace, rubbing it in, 'when you're good.' She put her nose in the air to show she meant it, and both girls marched ahead. Slightly crestfallen, Joseph watched their retreating backs for a moment, then darted forward and snatched the woolly cap from Grace's head.

'You're horrible, Joseph! Give it back!'

'Come and get it, then.'

Tantalizingly, Joseph waved the cap at Grace. He stood still while she lunged at him – then dodged neatly, whisking the hat out of her reach.

'Give it to her, Joseph,' scolded Gillian.

'Catch me, catch me,' Joseph teased, skipping backwards in the raw November air, through the brown leaves on the pavement, waving the woolly cap always just beyond Grace's grasping hands. 'All right, I'll give it to you. I'll give it to you,' he promised. He stood stock still, and held the cap out invitingly. 'Come on then, no trick, no trick!'

Grace advanced, hands outstretched, almost trusting the innocent smile on Joseph's face. Then at the last moment he hurled the cap away from him and it went sailing – high, high, over the nearest garden wall to land on an upstairs window ledge.

'Look what you done!' said Gillian, furiously.

'My hat!' wailed Grace. 'That's my best hat in the world, Joseph Rundell.'

'Sorry,' said Joseph, penitent now, 'I'll get it for you, Grace, don't worry.'

'How?' said Grace. 'How you going to get it down from there?'

'I'll knock at the door, and ask.'

'But it's Dippy Dora's house!' said Gillian, horrified.

Indeed it was, and Joseph found that he was not quite brave enough, after all, to knock at the door and ask for Grace's hat. 'I'll climb up,' he offered.

'No,' said Gillian, firmly.

'No,' said Grace. 'She's going to turn you into a frog. And me and Gillian.'

'She don't *really* turn people into frogs though,' said Joseph. 'She says it but it don't happen. Who cares about silly old Dippy!' And he ran up the broken front path, beside the tangled wilderness that was Dippy Dora's tiny front garden, and scrambled on to the ledge of the bay window.

'You'll fall,' said Gillian, warningly.

'She's coming. She'll catch you,' screamed Grace, and she ran down the road to flatten herself against someone else's wall, hiding her eyes so as not to see what terrible fate was about to descend on Joseph.

But Dippy Dora was not coming; not just at that moment, anyway. And Joseph did not fall, because he was an excellent climber, and had climbed through the upstairs windows of his own house many times. Frequently in preference to using the front door. His fingers gripping any convenient protruberance, he now levered himself higher, dislodging ribbons of flaking paint as he went. Patches of bare and rotting wood appeared where Joseph's feet had been, but as the house was such a dilapidated mess already, the difference was hardly noticeable.

He was nearly there. Balancing on the tiny shelf above

37

the lower bay window, holding a pillar of the upstairs window with one hand, Joseph was not quite able to reach Grace's hat with the other. He stretched, failed, stretched again.

'Careful!' called Gillian.

Joseph held his breath and made one more mighty effort. The fingers of his left hand hurt horribly, where they gripped the pillar, and his right arm was about to snap off, or so it felt. But his task was one of honour, and he couldn't give up now. The tips of his fingers touched soft wool, he scrabbled to tease the hat towards him, then flicked it so that it fell to the ground, and Gillian picked it up.

The hat was retrieved, but the jerky movement caused Joseph's hold to slip. His fingers slid on the pillar, and he almost lost his footing. 'I'm falling!' he yelled – and Gillian screamed. And Grace, down the road, joined her screams to theirs, though she was by no means clear what she was screaming about.

With his free hand, Joseph regained his grip on the pillar, and his feet found their perch again.

'Come down now,' called Gillian.

But Joseph felt he had lost some prestige by slipping in the first place. His performance lacked style. He would improve it by lingering, just to show the girls how brave he was. Still balancing on his narrow ledge, Joseph pressed his nose against the upstairs window pane. Where the filthy old curtains met, there was a tiny gap. Joseph moved his head this way and that, trying to see inside.

'Look at that!' he exclaimed, suddenly.

'What? Come on down, Joseph, before you get caught!'

'But I can see! I can see what she got in there!'

'Can you really?' Gillian was interested, in spite of herself. Everyone wanted to know what Dippy Dora kept hidden behind those perpetually drawn curtains.

'All jewels,' said Joseph. 'All gold and silver and diamonds.'

'Do you mean it?' This was exciting news indeed. The mystery solved at last.

'Just joking,' said Joseph. 'I can't see nothing really. The space ain't big enough.'

'Come on down then,' said Gillian, annoyed and disappointed. 'And stop mucking about, Joseph. Come on, come on – oh, I can *hear* her! She's coming round the side, Joseph! She's coming round the side!'

There was a scuffling, and a shuffling, and a screeching voice. 'Get out of it, you dirty saucepans!' Then through the rickety side gate, almost falling off its hinges, Dippy Dora came. In split and gaping shoes, she shuffled and danced – toe-heel with the right foot, *down* with the left, shuffle, shuffle, then toe-heel, *down*, again. 'Get out, you dirty saucepans,' she screeched again. Her lips curled back in a fearsome grimace, and the one long tooth in her underhung jaw went up and down, up and down, over the yellowish gums, in a silent gnashing.

Gillian shuddered. 'Come down, Joseph,' she begged, getting ready to flee herself.

'Joseph, Joseph, where's Joseph?' The hoarse voice cackled, maliciously. 'Where's Joseph? Where's the dirty saucepan? Climbing on my house, is it? Hah – I got something for *you*, you cheeky climber!'

She had come out, in fact, armed with a broom, and she whacked at the pillars with it. She danced, and whacked, and the loose grey locks which straggled down her back danced too. The long tooth went up and down, and with it the wispy beard on her chin. 'Come on then, saucepan, come on down,' she jeered. 'Oh I'll make sausage and mash of *you*!'

'Let me down then,' said Joseph, frightened.

But she would not let him. Dippy Dora whacked at the

wall and the pillars with her broom, and every time Joseph cautiously lowered a foot, she whacked at that too.

'I'm sorry. I'm sorry. Forgive me!' Joseph implored. But the gaunt frame in its layers of soiled woollen garments continued to dance and whack. The actions were bizarre, but the eyes within their folds were shrewd and malevolent. 'I'll teach you to come climbing on my house! I'll turn you into a frog, you see if I don't! *Silas'll* turn you into a frog now, how about *that*?'

'Oh she's got Silas. She's got Silas!' screamed Gillian, in terror. Silas was round Dippy Dora's neck, and how could Gillian not have noticed before? He was only an old length of chamois leather, but Dippy Dora appeared to think he was alive. The things she could do with him, sometimes it seemed he really *was* alive. He was like a snake – lithe, and evil, and menacing. Dippy Dora, Silas and the broom, what hope did Joseph have, against that lot?

And Grace up the road, daring to peep through her fingers at last, thought the same. Now that the worst had actually happened, Grace was feeling quite ashamed of having run away. She sidled back and stood close to Gillian. The girls clung together, watching and waiting for a miracle.

'Please Dip – please, Miss Dipper, please let me get down,' begged Joseph. 'Please don't beat me. I'm sorry. I won't do it again.'

Whack, whack, whack.

'*Please*!' Joseph's cries were quite frantic now. '*Please* – I'm slipping, I'm going to fall!'

He would fall and hurt himself, and this monstrous old woman would set about him with her broom, and Silas would come alive, and there was no one to save poor Joseph. Why didn't someone come?

In her desperation, an idea struck Gillian. Unthinkable for her in the normal way, but she'd seen Sean doing it, and some other bolder ones. She'd wondered at the time how they dared, and she'd hurried on, lest frightful unknown consequences fall on her too. And now look what she'd come to! *Bother* Joseph, to need so much looking after.

Pushing Grace aside, Gillian began to shout, and gesticulate. 'Oooh-yah – ooh-ooh – ooh, ooh, ooh!' She stretched her mouth into a manic grin with her fingers, she thumbed her nose, she danced and jeered and cat-called. Timidly, Grace joined in a bit, and they mocked and taunted together. 'Dippy, Dippy, Dippy Dippy Dora! Come and get us then!'

It worked.

'You cheeky little brats!' The gums and the tooth advanced on the girls. Grace fled across the road, but Gillian backed only a little way. Toe-heel, *down*, shuffle, shuffle, shuffle. There were food stains all down Dippy's front, and a sour smell of unwashed body came from her as well. Gillian was disgusted as well as frightened, but she stood her ground. 'Yah, come and get me!' And she made faces, the ugliest she could think of, pulling down her lower lids and rolling her eyes so that only the whites showed. 'Dip, Dip, Dip, Dippy Dippy Dora!'

Dippy Dora dropped the broom. She whipped Silas from round her neck and cracked him in the air. Crack, Crack, his head darted at Gillian and back again, back to touch the lumpy fingers of his mistress, and the mess of unravelling sleeves around her wrist. 'He'll get you, you dirty saucepan. He'll turn you into a frog. He will, he will.'

She was on the pavement by now. Gillian ran across the road, and Joseph landed neatly on his feet. 'I don't believe you,' screamed Gillian, triumphantly, from the safe distance of the opposite pavement. Joseph dodged round Dippy, and joined the girls.

Dippy Dora gazed around her, bewildered now and disappointed. The eyes, sharply aware a moment ago, glazed over, and the grimace disappeared. She cracked Silas once or twice, half-heartedly in the air, then began a disconsolate little dance back into her house. Toe-heel *down*, shuffle, shuffle, shuffle; toe-heel *down*.

'Shall we go home now?' said Joseph, cheerfully.

They started to go. Unfortunately, however, although Castle Street was empty since the other children had all gone home, and such teachers as were still in school were not looking out of the windows at the time, there had been one witness to the episode outside Dippy Dora's house. Part of the incident, that is. Mrs Jones the caretaker's wife, whose house was directly opposite, had been so filled with righteous indignation at the sight of Grace and Gillian taunting Dippy Dora, that she had failed to notice Joseph at all. She came out now and began scolding.

'Ought to be ashamed of yourselves; ought to be really ashamed of yourselves. I'm surprised at you an'all, Gillian – thought you was a nice little girl.'

'What did I do?' said Gillian. She thought she had been brave, not naughty.

'Making fun of that poor old thing! Anybody can see she ain't right in the head. You didn't ought to make fun of her.'

'She was going to hit us, though,' said Grace.

'And you! You was just as bad. I saw you. It's not right, you know, making fun of the poor dotty old thing. It's not funny, neither.'

'I know,' said Grace.

'What you smiling about then? You think it's just a great big joke, don't you? Just a good giggle, that's what you think. I know. No feelings – that's what's the matter with you kids. I'd tan the lot of you if I was the headmistress. Go on, you cheeky little cow, smiling away! You'll smile the other side of your face time I've finished with you. I'm telling the headmistress, I'm telling her tomorrow. So you can have a good smile about that, the pair of you.' She went indoors, still snorting, and the children trudged homewards.

'It's a pity you always laugh, Grace, when it ain't funny.' Gillian was worried, anticipating more trouble.

'I know, I can't help it though.'

'Well you ought to try. There's a time and place for all things . . . . What do you think she's really hiding – you know, Dippy Dora, in her house?'

'Jewels,' said Joseph, without hesitation. 'And money.'

'You always say that, Joseph, but she's poor. Her house is all peeling. I don't think she got any jewels in there.'

'Might be a miser,' said Joseph. 'Might be saving up all her money. Piles and piles of it. All on the tables, up to the ceiling. And all over the floor. Might have chests, full of gold and silver . . . . That's how misers live, you know. Didn't you know, Gillian? They save up all their money, and they go about in rags so everybody thinks they're poor but they ain't really.'

'I know. Why do they do that though?'

'They just do. Because they're misers.'

'I think she's a witch,' said Grace.

'Nah!' said Joseph. 'She ain't a witch. There's no such thing as witches.'

'Yes there is, in Jamaica there is. And ghosts. And magic.'

'That's in Jamaica though.'

'*And* here,' said Grace, firmly. 'I think there's all spells in her house, and books about magic and . . . well you know, spells . . . .

Gillian shook her head. 'She ain't a witch. She's creepy, but she ain't a witch.'

'How do you know though?'

'She just pretends to be a witch. She just says that about making people into frogs. She can't make people into frogs.'

'What about Silas then?'

'Silas can't make people into frogs neither,' said Gillian. Silas was a safe way away, so it was possible to be brave about him. 'Actually, I think she's something worse than a witch.'

'What could that be though?' said Grace.

'I dunno.' Gillian's fears about Dippy Dora were foggy and unclear, but all concerned with dark and evil deeds; kidnap and murder and torture – a jumble of half understood news items from the telly, and stories from the Sunday papers. She struggled to give her thoughts form, and words. 'I think her house is full of little babies,' she said, at last. 'That she stole away from their mums.'

'Nah!' said Joseph, scornfully. 'She ain't got no babies! I bet it's jewels. I bet you a thousand pounds it's jewels. I bet you a million trillion pounds she's a miser, like I said.'

'She's just a potty old woman,' said Mum, dishing chips and sausages out of the pan. Mum's no-particular-coloured hair was in her eyes as usual, escaping in untidy strands from the clip that was supposed to hold it in place. Her big face was red and sweaty from the frying, and the tiredness of the day hung round her, clinging to the folds of her no-particular-coloured dress like the cooking smells, and creasing the corners of her eyes. 'That's all she is, just a potty old woman. And she drinks too much sometimes. Have you seen her when she been at the booze?'

'Yeah – she gets worse then, don't she? What does she always pull the curtains for though?' said Joseph. 'She must be hiding something. What do you think she's hiding, Mum?'

44

'How should I know? She's potty, ain't she? Potty people don't have reasons for things. Not like ordinary people. Go easy on that tomato sauce, Joe, that's half the bottle you got on your plate. Leave some for your dad when he comes home.' The words were reproachful, but the tone was warm and indulgent, and the smile that was like glowing coals hardly flickered.

'I think it's a load of money,' Joseph insisted. 'And she hides it so the burglars won't see.'

'Pity she don't pay her electricity bill then,' said his mum. 'If she got all that money, why's the electricity cut off?'

'Who says it's cut off?'

'Must be. She buys a load of candles from up Patel's, she's always doing it.'

'Perhaps she does make spells,' said Gillian. 'Perhaps the candles are for the spells.'

'Hah, hah!' Joseph jeered, 'Dippy don't do spells. You're a silly, stupid baby if you think that.'

'You didn't say Grace was a silly, stupid baby.'

'No well, that's Grace, innit!'

'Just because you love her!'

'Come on,' said Mum, 'eat up. You're too young to love anybody, Joe, except your mum and dad.'

After the meal, Gillian unpacked her school bag to tidy it. There was no homework again tonight, no one had bothered to give any to Class 4L. Inside her homework book Gillian found the letter she had written yesterday, to Mrs Lloyd. What with one thing and another, she had quite forgotten to ask the secretary for an envelope, and the address. She read the letter through again, and added on the bottom:

P.S. Joseph drawn a nasty picture. Mrs White laffed but I think she dident ought to laff really. Joseph did more bad things coming home and I think me and Grace are

45

going to get in trouble from Mrs Jones and Mrs White. How is your baby getting along? Me and Grace wish you would come back to our class. We wish it a million times.
From Gillian. X X X X X X X

4

The teacher who didn't quite make it

'Don't you have no more feelings about Joseph's going to do something bad! Don't you dare, Grace Johnson!'

'Why not?' said Grace.

'Because they come true,' said Gillian. 'You know, that card, and Dippy Dora. So don't you dare have no more!'

'All right,' said Grace.

The girls were sitting huddled together under the shed in the playground, and Grace was trying to concentrate on her knitting. The knitting required a great deal of concentration because Grace was not very skilled, and she kept dropping stitches. There were little ladders all the way down the finished bit, where the stitches had come off the needle. Also the wool was looking decidedly grey, from having rolled so often across the dirty ground, and passed so many times through Grace's sticky fingers.

'Anyway,' said Grace, 'we haven't got in trouble yet, have we – from Mrs Jones? Perhaps she forgot.'

'*She* won't forget,' said Gillian, gloomily. 'Do you like our new teacher, Grace?'

'She's all right, only she doesn't give us no proper work. Sean likes her, doesn't he?'

'Yeah – and all the boys.'

Sean was, in fact, deeply smitten with Miss Croft, who had replaced Mr er-er as supply teacher for Class 4L. He had stopped being in love with Michelle from 4D, and started to be in love with Miss Croft instead. Miss Croft was very young; well, she looked about fifteen, but she must actually have been a *bit* older than that. She was small and slender and very pretty, with blue eyes, and shiny blonde hair falling in waves around a delicately chiselled face. Sean thought she was terrific, and he hung around, waiting to carry things for her, and even open doors for her. *She* thought he was charming, as indeed he could be, when he liked.

Miss Croft had not had much practice at being a teacher. It was bad luck, getting a class like 4L, when she was so new to teaching but she had certainly brought some interesting ideas into the classroom. They were not going to do ordinary lessons, she said, they were going to do a Project. The class had been doing a Project with Mrs Lloyd; it was about the Middle Ages, and there was already a half completed display of written work about it on the Project table, and a model of a mediaeval castle in one corner of the room. With Mrs Lloyd, though, they mostly only did the Project in the afternoons, and not every afternoon at that. Miss Croft's Project was about Homes round the World, and it took up all the time.

Miss Croft had brought in piles of books and magazines about Homes round the World, and each group in the class had to choose one country. They were supposed to read about it, and study the pictures. Then each group had to build a model of the kind of house the people in their chosen country lived in. That was all they did. For three days now, the class had done nothing but draw, and cut, and paint, and stick. The children had enjoyed it very much, at first. It was a welcome change from English Exercises with Mr er-er, or struggling with maths on their own, under the supervision of Miss Campbell. But one or two were beginning to get a bit uneasy.

'Aren't we going to do no work, miss?' Gillian enquired anxiously, on the third day.

'This *is* work, Gillian,' said Miss Croft, with a sunny smile.

'Course it's work,' said Sean, defending Miss Croft. 'Shut up asking silly questions, Gillian. We're learning about houses, ain't we, Miss Croft. All the different ones. In the other countries.' His group was building a splendid Thai house on stilts; it was a beautiful piece of work, and Sean was justly proud of it.

'I mean *real* work,' Gillian persisted. 'I mean maths, and writing.'

'When we've finished the models we can write about them,' Miss Croft explained. 'And the maths will be – er – well, anyway, we'll fit the maths in, you'll see.'

'That's right,' said Sean. 'We got to make the models first, haven't we, Miss Croft?' He did not like maths, and he intended that his model should take a long, long time to complete. Every imaginable detail was going to be included – inside and outside the house. And when that was finished, the group could make others like it. A whole village, perhaps. With luck, and ingenuity, there need be no more maths this side of Christmas.

Gillian was still not happy. 'I don't want to get behind with my maths,' she said.

'I think it's rather a pity to chop learning up into sections,' said Miss Croft with a tinkly little laugh. 'This bit goes here, and that bit goes there, each in its little box. It's all one thing, really.'

'Yeah,' said Sean. 'We don't want to put it all in boxes, do we, Miss Croft? It's all one thing, innit? It's all learning.'

Some of the models were coming along splendidly, but as Miss Croft was not very good at making the children clear up at the end of the day, the classroom was getting very messy. Pots of paint with dirty brushes in them stood around everywhere – on the floor, on the desks, on the window ledges. Sometimes the pots got knocked over by accident, and Miss Croft was not really strict enough about making the children mop up the spills. Also, bits of card, and masking tape, and other discarded materials lay just where they had fallen, since everyone was too enthusiastic about the work to bother about tidiness. Gillian and Grace were finding it increasingly difficult, after school each day, to cope with the debris.

Mrs White thought the classroom was a tip – you could see it in her expression when she came in, on the morning of the fourth day. 'Are they going to clear up when they've finished?' she asked. She spoke quite sweetly, because supply teachers were not easy to come by these days, and she didn't want to upset Miss Croft.

'Oh yes, Mrs White,' said Miss Croft, as though they did that every time anyway.

'Good,' said Mrs White, 'I'll come back at home time, and see how neat everything is . . . . Now, I want every-one's attention for a minute. All stop what you're doing. Eyes this way . . . . Did you hear me, Sean? Leave that for now, Stephen. Right. I've just been listening to a story that gave me no pleasure whatever to hear. It concerns chil-dren in this class, and I believe a number of you have been involved, at some time or another, besides those whose names have been given to me.'

Pause . . . . Involved in *what*? Consciences were searched, and quite a few people began to feel uneasy.

'I am talking about a neighbour of this school's,' Mrs White went on – and quite a few people breathed again. Their particular sin had not been found out *this* time. 'An elderly lady,' said Mrs White, 'who is not – er – very well – and yet I'm sorry to say, it seems that some children in this class have actually been unkind to that poor lady. I was *deeply* ashamed when I heard about it – *deeply* . . . . Grace Johnson and Gillian Rundell, stand up . . . . Did you call names at Miss Dipper? Yes? Then I can't tell you how disappointed I am in you. Gillian, and Grace . . . . Is there something funny, Grace? I have said something amusing, perhaps? Is there something humorous about unkindness? Is there? Does anyone think there is something humorous about the cowardly teasing of a poor unwell lady who . . . .'

But she's not a poor lady, thought Gillian, indignant in the midst of her shame. She's a wicked old monster. She does wicked things, I know, and she might have *killed* Joseph, if Grace and me didn't stop her. Joseph ought to own up why we done it, but he won't. If she asks him he'll make up some silly story that nobody will believe, and that will just make it worse. I wonder why she *doesn't* ask him? Anybody can see by his face he was in it.

But Mrs White was after bigger quarry. 'Now stand up anyone else who has been teasing Miss Dipper. At any time this term.'

No one moved.

'No one?'

Silence, except for a few coughs.

'Stand up, Sean Adams.'

Reluctantly, Sean dragged to his feet.

'What about you, Sean?'

'No, Mrs White, I never.'

'But Mrs Jones distinctly says she saw you. She knows you very well, and she saw you doing it, just before half term.'

'Not only me.'

'That isn't what I asked you. All right, where's Stephen

51

Arnold? . . . and Harjit Thakor? . . . Stand up, both of you. Why were you not standing already? You know you were involved, just as much as Sean.'

There was resentment at being named, if not shame for what had been done. But Sean was the angriest because he was being humiliated in front of the class, his subjects – and in front of Miss Croft, his beloved.

'I am ashamed of all those standing,' said Mrs White, 'and of all those who ought to be standing, but who have not the courage or sense of personal honour to own up. These are the children who are spoiling this happy school. I hope that all those who have been involved in unkindness to Miss Dipper will think very carefully about their behaviour and decide to act differently in future. I know Miss Dipper seems a little strange, but has it occurred to any of you she might be lonely? What about a smile, next time you pass her? A smile costs nothing, does it, Gillian?'

'No, Mrs White.'

'Grace? . . . A real smile I mean, not that silly smirk. A *friendly* smile.'

'Yes, Mrs White.'

'Sean?'

'I suppose so.'

'Try it. All right, now get on with your – er – work.'

She left, and the sticking and cutting and sloshing around of paint recommenced. But the mood was not as before, there was too much bad feeling around. Besides, the class had done nothing but cut and stick and slosh paint about for three and a half days now, and the fact was they were all getting just a little bit tired of it. Not to mention the discomfort of working in chaos, wading through mountains of shredded paper and pools of spilled paint, whenever any of them needed to cross the room. They began to bicker amongst themselves.

The bell for dinner-time came before any serious trouble

52

could develop, and Miss Croft, who was keen and optimistic as well as young, thought everything would be back to normal after the break.

It wasn't. If anything, it was worse. There had been an argument in the playground between Sean and Stephen. Five minutes after it started, neither boy could remember what the original dispute was about, but by then it had degenerated into a bitter exchange of insults, and by the time the bell for afternoon school went, it was threatening to develop into a full-scale fight. The white boy and the black boy were glaring hatred at one another as they went to their places, and since they were working in the same group, prospects for a peaceful afternoon were not good.

The boys in Sean's group got on with their work, after a fashion, but without the usual matey chit-chat. Paul and Joseph were backing Sean, since Sean was the more powerful of the two, but Harjit had decided to throw in his lot with Stephen. He had been thinking recently that it would be good if *he* could be best friends with Stephen. Less crafty than Sean, but almost as mean, and even tougher in appearance, Stephen was naturally much admired by the rather sneaky Harjit.

So there was whispering now as they worked, and jeering, and unkind laughter – and presently, inevitably, the situation exploded. Stephen had been making the curly decorative bits for the Thai house, and being in a bad temper he had made them clumsily. When he tried to attach them to the main roof they didn't fit. He tried to force them, and the whole roof caved inwards. There was no damage that could not be easily repaired, but Sean was very angry.

'You stupid wally, look what you done!'

'Good.'

'You mend it, or I'll do you!'

'All right, all right.' Stephen put out his hand, but Sean pushed him away.

'You ain't touching it, you'll spoil it.'

'You said mend it,' said Stephen.

'You ain't touching it. You ain't in our group no more.'

'Yes I am. You're not the boss of the world.'

'I'm the boss of this group,' said Sean.

'Prove it,' said Stephen, squaring up.

Sean landed him one, and Stephen hit him back.

'Boys!' said Miss Croft, shocked.

'Sean started it,' said Harjit.

'I'll get you, Harjit,' said Sean, 'you little creep!' And he pummelled at Harjit's head as though they were in the playground, or the street, and not in the classroom at all.

'Stop it!' called Miss Croft, dismayed and not knowing quite what to do. Everyone had stopped work now, to watch the fight. 'Somebody stop them,' Miss Croft appealed.

'I'll stop them, miss,' offered Stephen. He seized Sean's arms from the back, and held them. Paul grabbed Harjit in a similar grip, and the combatants were pulled apart. They glared at one another, still snarling. Miss Croft tried to smooth things over.

'Whatever's the matter with you boys today? Come on now, that's not the way to settle differences, is it? And you were getting on so well with your model. I'd say yours is the best in the class, you know.'

The flattery was intended to create a better atmosphere, but it didn't work.

'No thanks to him,' said Sean, nastily.

'No thanks to who, Sean?'

'Him – that booby – Stephen.'

'I thought Stephen was your friend.'

'That dum-dum!'

'Oh come on, don't spoil the day. Shake hands and forget it, whatever it was. Won't you?' Miss Croft gave Sean her most winning smile, but it was wasted. Sean was not looking at Miss Croft. He was slumped in his seat, his chair pushed back, his long legs stretched in front of him, kicking sullenly at the desk leg, furious at being asked to shake hands with Stephen, when Stephen was in the wrong. 'It's not fair,' he muttered.

'I'll shake hands,' offered Stephen. He didn't say it to be nice, he said it to get one up on Sean.

'I will too,' said Harjit, to be the same as Stephen.

'Sean?'

Sean thought the anger, and sense of injustice, would choke him. He swung his chair round and sat rudely with his back to Miss Croft, refusing to speak to her or to anyone. His face was like thunder.

'I'm very disappointed in you, Sean,' said Miss Croft, pushing her luck. 'I really thought you were more grown-up.'

'Silly cow!' said Sean's lips, silently, to the back wall. He had gone right off Miss Croft.

The downward slide of Miss Croft's Project was rapid, and inevitable, after that. The class was sick of it by now, any-way. Some were still keen, and carried on regardless, but one by one they began to opt out. A few retired to the library corner to read; many just lounged in their seats, bored and peevish.

Sean was already stirring up trouble, to punish Miss Croft for putting him down. At first he contented himself with shuffling his seat right away from the group, and clat-tering it backwards and forwards, whistling and making other irritating noises at the same time. Miss Croft, her heart sinking with foreboding now, tried to ignore him, while she flitted round the class, making every effort to re-vive the flagging spirits of the rest. Then Sean got up and wandered round too. He was going to show everyone that he was still the king. He was going to entice them away from their silly models. He was going to spoil Miss Croft's rubbish Project.

In his pocket was a handful of conkers. Deliberately,

Sean took one out and rolled it along the floor. A boy called Sanjay left his group to join Sean rolling conkers along the floor. Then Richard came, and Paul, and Joseph. The conker players were fairly quiet at first, then rowdy, not caring how much disturbance they made. Sean organized the game into a mock battle, with a barricade of desks between the sides. They made a great deal of noise dragging the desks into position, treating poor Miss Croft as though she were not there. Miss Croft did not know what to do. She was losing control, and there was still the enormous task of clearing the classroom to be faced. She remembered that Mrs White was coming back at home time to see how well they had done it. Perhaps they had better make a start. After play – they would do the clearing up immediately after play. . . .

'Tidy up now,' she called, as they came in. 'Everyone help!'

But the class was noisy, and not many heard her. Miss Croft raised her voice. 'Come on, everyone, you know what Mrs White said.'

Grace and Gillian and Jennifer, together with Satibai and Minaxi, began to clear their own little space. No one else took the slightest notice.

'*I said "clear up"*'! Miss Croft screamed at them, suddenly losing her cool. A few looked up in surprise, most were indifferent. They had lost interest in Miss Croft and her Project.

'There's a prize for the best group,' called Miss Croft, desperately.

That was better. Hands suddenly became more willing. 'What's the prize going to be?' someone asked. Miss Croft had no idea, but she hoped she could find something when the time came. 'Something really good,' she promised them. 'But you won't know what it is until you've earned it.'

'Come on, boys,' said Sean, calling his supporters

round him again. 'We don't want no silly prize.'

Again, Miss Croft tried to ignore him. But there was worse to come. Since the fight before play, Sean had apparently ceased to care about the model he had so carefully laboured on all the week. But when Stephen and Harjit lifted it to put it on a side table, Miss Croft unwisely said, 'That's very good, Stephen,' and Sean was furious at hearing Stephen praised.

'Leave it alone; you'll break it,' Sean threatened from the other side of the room. 'Anyway, it's mine, not yours.'

'It's mine now,' said Stephen, 'and Harjit's.'

'You'll break it if you move it,' said Sean.

'They have to move it, Sean,' said Miss Croft. 'They can't clean the desks otherwise. I'm sure they'll be very careful.'

That was not the point. Sean wasn't really afraid the model would get broken, he just wanted to make it clear he was still the boss. But in her flustered and anxious state, Miss Croft failed to grasp the point. She was trying not to hate Sean for his mean and disruptive behaviour, and she was failing in that as well. 'Anyway,' she said, 'I don't see how it can be yours now, Sean, since you have chosen to leave the group.'

That did it.

'If it's not mine it's not going to be nobody's,' said Sean – and he crossed the room, and began smashing up the Thai house with his fists. Outraged, Stephen threw a full paint pot at Sean, which hit him and spilled all over his clothes. Dripping paint, Sean hurled himself at Stephen. This time there was a glorious fight which no one tried to stop. Flailing arms and legs knocked over one desk, three paint pots and a very full waste bin. Sharon's Swiss chalet also got knocked to the ground, and damaged, and the wails of Sharon and her friends added to the general confusion.

Miss Croft began to cry.

'Miss is crying!'

'Don't cry, Miss Croft,' said Grace, kindly. 'Me and Gillian will help you clear up the mess. Don't worry. We'll do it, won't we, Gillian?'

'Yeah,' said Gillian. She was looking a bit stern though, and disapproving. Teachers weren't supposed to cry, just because the children were naughty. You couldn't imagine Mrs Lloyd crying in front of the class, not in a thousand years!

Gillian thought, with an inward sigh, that it would take her and Grace *hours*, this time, to get the class straight. But she need not have concerned herself because Mrs White arrived just at that moment, took in the situation at a glance, and stayed to organize clearing operations. Under her directions, the classroom was respectable again within ten minutes, and there was hardly a whisper from anyone while it was being done. All the while Mrs White just stood there, looking grim, and ignoring poor Miss Croft. Miss Croft must have felt terrible, with Mrs White taking no notice of her at all. When she was satisfied, Mrs White just walked away, leaving Miss Croft to dismiss the class.

'Who's won the prize?' asked someone, hopefully, but Miss Croft was too sad to think about prizes. She was still crying quietly, her pretty face all blotched and puffy and spoiled. Perhaps in the morning, she said. In the morning they would see who had won.

But in the morning Miss Croft was not there. Class 4L trooped into their room, niggly and quarrelsome before the day had even begun. Disconsolately they regarded their Project, all the half-finished models ranged on tables and ledges round the outside of the room. No one had any heart for going on with it, but Sharon again began to lament the ruins of her Swiss chalet. In her grief, she forgot to be wary of Sean, and she accused him with great bitterness of having been the cause of the disaster.

'You done it, didn't you! You broke it, Sean Adams!'

'Hard luck.'

'You're a pig, Sean.'

'A-a-ah – it was a rubbish house anyway.'

'Better than your silly one!'

'A-a-ah – shut up!'

They glared at one another, with loathing.

Presently Mr Davis popped his head round the door to see what all the noise was about.

'Miss Croft ain't here yet, sir,' said someone, unnecessarily.

'So I see. Seats, everyone. I said *seats*. Come on, one two, one two, on the double. Are you deaf, Sean Adams? Joseph Rundell? Right – I'm leaving the door open, and anyone whose voice I recognize will come to me at playtime.'

They sprawled in their seats, muttering, waiting dejectedly. They did not have to wait long. Soon Miss Campbell arrived, very much put out at having been asked to take 4L's register and escort them down to Assembly.

'Isn't Miss Croft coming, miss?'

'No.'

'Are you going to be our teacher today?'

'No.'

After Assembly Miss Campbell divided them into groups of three or four, and sent them round the school to different classes. They had to take a maths book and an English book and a reading book, but no one actually set them any work. Grace and Gillian found themselves in one of the first year classes, where they ended up helping Miss Robinson hear the little ones read. This was pleasant enough, and useful no doubt, but Gillian felt they weren't learning anything.

At the end of the day, Class 4L had to go back to their room, because Mrs White had something important to tell them. There was a pile of sealed brown envelopes on Mrs Lloyd's table. Mrs White gave each child an envelope, and they had to address it to their own parents, but they still didn't know what it was all about.

'Pencils down, eyes this way,' said Mrs White. 'What I have to tell you is not very agreeable, but you have only yourselves to blame. . . . I said pencils down, Joseph, if you started when everyone else did, you might manage to finish on time. . . . These letters are to tell your parents that *there is no teacher for your class*, and you are *not to come to school on Monday*.'

Pause. Stunned and disbelieving silence.

'Can't Miss Croft come no more?' said Stephen.

'The Office do not send supply teachers for you to be unkind to them,' said Mrs White, coldly. She had been a *bit* unkind, herself, but she had conveniently forgotten about that.

'We wasn't unkind,' protested Sharon. 'It was just Sean and Stephen had a fight.'

'Is *that* all? I thought the whole room looked like a battle-field yesterday afternoon. And I might add, 4L, that you have caused me a great deal of trouble today. I have been constantly on the phone to the Office trying to get a teacher for you, and there are just none available at the moment. When there is one, your parents will be notified and you can come back. Take home an English book, a maths book, and a reading book – and I don't want to hear about anyone getting into trouble in the streets. Did you hear me Sean? Joseph? . . . Put your hand down Joseph, I haven't time to answer any more questions; I have an important meeting to go to. . . . Stand, make one line at the front. . . . Lead on.'

Dearest Mrs Lloyd (*wrote Gillian*)
I am very sad because we dont have a teacher for our

class but it isent Josephs fault this time thank goodness. Grace is making something for your baby I hope you will like it she is not a very good knitter but she is trying to do it good. How is your baby getting along? I expect you want it to be a girl because boys are horrid sometimes and they make so much truble. What are you going to call your baby? You could call it Melissa if its a girl and Sebastian if its a boy but lets hope it wont be. Please give my kind regards to your dear husband.

Love from

Gillian X X X X X X X X X X X X X X

5

A really bad thing

On Monday morning Sean, who was still bad friends with Stephen and Harjit, called for Joseph.

'He can't come,' said Gillian, who answered the door. 'He got to do his homework.'

'Nobody give us no homework,' said Sean, with truth.

'*I* give him some,' said Gillian, 'and our mum says he got to do it.'

'Is your mum there?'

'No, she's gone to work.'

Sean's mum had gone to work too, so he was gloriously free to do as he liked. In any case Sean came and went much as he pleased, since he had no dad, and a gentle mum he could wrap round his little finger. He pushed Gillian out of the way now, and called into the passage, 'Joseph, Joe, you there?'

Joseph appeared in his dressing gown, having only just managed to get out of bed. His hair stuck up in spikes all over his head, and his round cheeks were flushed with pleasure. He was amazed that Sean had called at his house. Amazed that Sean knew where he lived, even.

'Coming out?' said Sean.

'Don't mind,' said Joseph, trying to sound off-hand. He suspected he was only being asked because Paul couldn't come, but no matter. Sean was here, that was the main thing, and it was like a dream come true.

Joseph was well enough liked at school, but he never had a proper friend. No one took him seriously enough to think of having him for their friend. That hurt, in the inmost parts of him, so he covered the hurt with more clowning. Clowning was his best thing, it was what he did well, so he did it, and did it, and did it. And people laughed, and clapped, and appreciated him. He'd rather have had a real friend though. And now? A happy smile split Joseph's face from ear to ear.

'I'm telling,' Gillian threatened. 'I'm telling our mum!'

'Let's go,' said Joseph to Sean.

'Like that?' said Gillian, scornfully.

'Oh yeah, I ain't dressed, I forgot.'

'You're scatty, Joseph,' said Gillian, and she went back to the living room, and her self-imposed homework. 'Don't blame me if you get in trouble,' she called, banging the door to show she meant it.

'Women!' said Sean, with heavy contempt.

'Yeah,' said Joseph, disloyally.

'Get dressed then, hurry up!'

'Yeah – wait, wait, don't go!'

'You got one minute, I'm timing it.'

'Where we going then?' said Joseph, reappearing.

'Let's go down the High Street.'

'All right.'

'You got any money?' asked Sean.

'Nah.'

'Let's see what's cooking, anyway.'

'All right,' said Joseph. He didn't care where they went; he would go anywhere Sean wanted. He hoped lots of people would see him, going out with Sean.

The shops in the High Street were already decorated for Christmas. 'Let's go in Discount,' said Sean. 'There's good things in Discount.'

'All right, I ain't got no money though.'

'Don't matter.'

The boys wandered through the store called Discount, which sold all kinds of cheap merchandise, conveniently displayed on open counters. The smell from the sweet counter was enticing, and Joseph had had no breakfast. 'Wish I *did* have some money,' he said.

'What you want money for?'

'To buy some chocolate. Or something.'

'Just take it,' said Sean.

'What?'

'You heard.'

'You mean steal it?' asked Joseph.

'You scared then?'

'Nah – course not.'

'Prove it,' said Sean.

Joseph had done many naughty things in his life, but he didn't think he had ever actually taken something that didn't belong to him. He turned his head, and kicked at a group of plastic waste bins.

'You're chicken!' said Sean.

'No I ain't.'

'You are – you're windy,' Sean jeered.

'So are you.'

'Me? Not me. Who's afraid to do a little thing like that. I done it millions of times. All the boys done it.'

Joseph did not want to be left out of what all the other boys had done. He did not want to be a thief either. It was all a bit confusing.

'Go on,' said Sean. 'I'll watch – now!'

Joseph put out his hand, took the chocolate bar, and

slipped it into his anorak pocket. It was like doing something in a dream, not something really happening. It was very easy. Joseph walked on, feeling quite excited.

'Nothing to it, is there?' said Sean, coming up behind him.

'Easy peasy,' said Joseph. 'Easiest thing in the whole world. Easiest thing I ever done. Easiest—'

'Now get one for me,' said Sean.

'Why not you get it?'

'You still scared then?'

'Nah!'

They walked round again, and Joseph took another chocolate bar. They sauntered towards the entrance, and Joseph could not help feeling a bit frightened, in case someone had seen them after all. But no one challenged them, no one took the slightest notice of two small boys pushing through the big glass doors into the windy street. They had got away with it.

It was cold outside. The boys put up their anorak hoods and mooched down the High Street, munching chocolate bars. They stopped outside a toy shop and stood, noses pressed against the window.

'Look at that!' said Sean.

'Yeah – them cars!'

'They got some like that in Discount,' said Sean. 'Better ones.'

'Oh yeah.'

'Shall we go back then?'

'Nah. Perhaps. A bit later.' Joseph's excitement had begun to ebb away. He was still pleased to have impressed Sean, but not really happy about the stealing part.

'You're windy again,' Sean jeered.

'No I ain't,' said Joseph, uncomfortably.

'You want one of them cars, don't you?'

'Yeah.'

'Come on then.'

'Why not you, this time?'

'But you're good at it,' said Sean, craftily. 'You're really good at it, guy. I didn't think you was going to be good like that. You're better than Paul, you're better than Harjit even.'

'Am I better than Stephen?'

At the mention of that name, Sean spat. 'Oh you're better than *Stephen*. You're millions better than *Stephen*.'

Joseph preened himself. He was enormously flattered by all this praise. The two boys retraced their steps up the High Street, and once more pushed their way through the big glass doors at the entrance to Discount. There were the toy cars on display, new and shiny and tempting.

'They're too big to put in my pocket though,' said Joseph, uneasily.

'Put them inside your coat.'

'It'll show the bulge.'

'Nah. Put it under your arm and keep your arm down.'

'I can't.'

'Yes you can. Why can't you?'

'I'm scared,' Joseph admitted.

'Might as well go home then,' said Sean, coldly.

'All right, I'll do it, I'll do it.'

'Hurry up then, before somebody comes.'

Joseph leaned over the counter, fingering the toys, pretending to choose one to buy. On Monday morning there were few people in the store, and none at all in the toy section. Suddenly Joseph snatched at the car nearest him and thrust it inside his anorak, nervously now, and with clumsy movements. The card and plastic cover caught against his zip the first time, and it required two thrusts to get the toy car safely into his armpit.

Joseph trembled, terrified that his bungling had been seen. He wanted to run, knowing that he mustn't. But nothing happened, and Joseph breathed again. 'That's enough,' he said. 'I ain't taking no more.'

'That's my one then,' said Sean.

In his deepest heart, Joseph knew he was being used, but that was a truth too painful to face. 'All right,' he said, a bit sulky now.

'If you want one for yourself you know what to do,' said Sean.

Joseph looked at the cars still on the counter, hesitated, looked again. The car he had already taken was prickly and bulgy under his left arm. He pulled down the zip of his anorak and let his right hand hover over the counter once more.

'Go on,' Sean encouraged him.

Joseph grabbed, and thrust the second car into his arm-pit. It went in smoothly this time; it was a very neat manoeuvre indeed. Joseph's heart was thumping though – he couldn't wait to get out of the store. Anxiously, he looked all around. 'She seen me!' he whispered, in sudden panic.

'Who?'

'That lady over there. That lady with the push-chair. She's looking right at me!'

Cool and confident, Sean shook his head. 'Nah,' he said. 'She ain't looking at you. She's looking over the end – at the kids' clothes and stuff. She's looking to see where they are. She's going there now, look. Told you!'

It was true. No one had seen Joseph take the toy cars, no one at all. He wasn't quite happy until the two of them were safely in the street, but once there, triumph and excitement surged through him, driving away misgivings. 'I done it, I done it,' he crowed. 'I done it, didn't I, Sean?'

'Give us mine then.'

'Yeah.'

There was a little patch of waste ground at the end of the

High Street, and the boys went there to gloat over their haul. 'Look at that, man!'

'Yeah – good, innit?'

'Let's go again tomorrow,' said Sean.

'All right.' Joseph was feeling on top of the world – powerful, successful. What glittering prizes might not tomorrow bring? The possibilities seemed endless.

The wind whipped over the scrubby grass, carrying with it a few drops of icy rain. 'It's raining,' said Joseph.

'Clever boy to notice!' mocked Sean.

'Better go home, hadn't we?'

'You 'fraid of a drop of rain then?'

'Nah – course not. My mum'll be home soon though, she only works mornings.'

'Go on then – little baby go home to his mum! See you!'

Sean walked off, arrogant, whistling. Joseph felt disappointment in the midst of his happiness. It wouldn't hurt Sean to be a bit *nicer*, he thought. Never mind, he was Sean's friend now, wasn't he? He'd been out with Sean, nothing could alter that, and tomorrow they were going to do it again.

Joseph slipped into the house and ran quickly up the stairs, past the open kitchen door, where Gillian was peeling potatoes for their lunch. She heard him, and called out. 'That you, Joseph?'

'Yeah.' He pushed the toy car under his mattress, and came downstairs trying to look innocent.

Gillian's eyes were big and anxious. 'Have you been doing wrong things?'

'No.'

'You can't hide it, you know. You can't hide that look on your face.'

'What look?'

Gillian sighed. 'All right, leave it. What about your maths?'

'I can't do them, Gilly, they're hard.'

'Suppose I'll have to help you then. As usual.'

'Yeah, you help me, you help me.'

'How about we make you really good at maths, and give them all the shock of their life at school?'

Joseph grinned. He knew she was joking. He knew that idea could never be more than a very funny joke. 'You won't *really* tell our mum I been out, will you?'

Gillian sighed, again. 'Course I won't, Joseph. You know I won't do that *really*!'

Next morning, when Sean arrived, Joseph was up and ready. Gillian was amazed to see him appear at a respectable hour for breakfast, but, answering the doorbell, she understood. 'It's Sean and Paul,' she said disgustedly, coming back into the kitchen, where Joseph was still cramming milk and cornflakes into his mouth.

'Coming!' shouted Joseph, spitting cornflakes. 'I'm coming, I'm coming. Wait for me! I'm coming!'

He was sorry that Paul had come this morning. Just Sean and him, that would have been much better. Besides, he really didn't like Paul at all. Not even Paul's mother liked Paul. Black like Sean, but without any of Sean's undoubted charm, and not very bright either, Paul was accepted in the gang because of his fearlessness. Apart from that, his main claim to distinction was being the most moody and bad-tempered boy in the neighbourhood. He was not often allowed out, which might partly have explained his surliness; but occasionally his mother got so sick of him she said he could go with his friends this once and good riddance.

'Let's go Discount again,' said Sean.

It was taken for granted what the boys were going to do. It also seemed to be taken for granted that Joseph was going to do all the actual stealing. Paul was quite willing to do his share, but Sean insisted. 'Joseph's better'n you,' he told Paul. 'He's quicker.'

Paul sulked, and glowered jealously at Joseph. 'He's silly,' Paul complained.

'I know,' said Sean. 'But he is quicker.'

Joseph did not much mind being called names, as long as he could be Sean's friend. Even if he had to share him with Paul. It occurred to Joseph that he was one of the gang now. *Really* one of the gang. 'What we going to take today, then?' he enquired, cheerfully.

'Let's walk round first, and see what they got,' said Sean.

One one counter were some flashy digital watches, which took all the boys' fancy. 'We can't wear them though,' said Paul. 'Everybody going to ask where we got them from.'

'We can wear them when nobody's looking,' said Joseph. It was the same with his car, from yesterday; he could only play with it when there was no one around to see. Never mind, the important thing was to have it. He had quite dismissed the idea that it was wrong to steal. The important things were to be Sean's friend, to be accepted in Sean's gang, and to have secret treasures under the mattress at home.

Joseph was feeling excited again, but he wasn't at all nervous today. Everything had gone so well yesterday, he couldn't wait to begin. The boys walked around the store, and Joseph put three watches into his pocket – one after the other, with casual ease, as though he had been shoplifting all his life. The boys went to the waste ground, put on their watches, and played with the knobs.

'We better take them off now,' said Sean, 'before we forget.'

'Where shall we go next?' said Paul.

'Back to Discount, eh?' said Joseph.

'Let's go Cash and Carry for a change,' said Sean.

'What about Woollies?' said Paul.

'That's no good, they got cameras,' said Sean.

'I rather go back to Discount,' said Joseph.

'Nah,' said Paul. 'Cash and Carry's more better.'

'I want to go to Discount though,' said Joseph.

'Let him go to Discount if he wants to,' said Sean, in generous mood.

'Well I ain't coming to no stupid Discount,' said Paul, sulkily. He didn't really mind where they went, but he minded very much that Joseph's wishes were getting preference over his.

'Stay here then,' said Sean.

Paul began to kick at the scrubby turf. 'I'm going home,' he threatened. 'Discount is rubbish. Cash and Carry is more better.'

'Go home then,' said Sean, to taunt him. He knew Paul would do no such thing. He knew his power.

The boys trailed back to Discount, Paul lagging sullenly behind.

'I'll go in by myself if you like,' Joseph offered. He was suddenly shy, not wanting the others to see what he was going to take. It was the fashion to be in love with someone just now, but they still might tease him.

Sean was quite happy to have all the gain and none of the risk. 'Get something good then,' he said.

Joseph entered the store. He was so confident now, he hardly bothered to make sure he was not being watched. He took three ball-point pens, then hovered near the thing he really wanted. A shiny brooch, in the shape of a butterfly, studded with sparkling pieces of brilliantly coloured glass. Joseph glanced around quickly. No one looking. Not as far as he could see. He grabbed the brooch, and

71

thrust it deep into his anorak pocket.

'I saw you! I saw you take that!'

Who? Where? Where was the voice coming from? Joseph spun round, flustered and dismayed. The voice belonged to another customer, a large, red-faced man, whose out-stretched arm was rapidly advancing towards the scruff of Joseph's neck. Panic for a moment, then Joseph's spidery legs began to move. Lightly built and agile, he dodged round the aisles, making for the door. 'There he goes!' 'Catch him!' 'Little thief – I'll get you!' Joseph heard the cries, and they seemed to be coming from all directions – but miraculously, he was out of the shop and sprinting down the road before shop assistants and customers could organize a capture.

Out of the corner of his eye, Joseph saw Sean and Paul sprinting off in the opposite direction.

Joseph ran until his knees buckled, and the stitch in his side was unbearable. He sat down on the kerb, all alone in the wintry street. A cold gust of wind brought dirty brown leaves swirling round him and flapping into his face. Tears prickled his eyes, because the others had left him, and every-thing had gone wrong. Then he felt the brooch, hard with sharp corners, jabbing into his leg as he sat. He still had the brooch, didn't he? He still had the brooch for Grace.

Home, then. Joseph let himself in, and ran up the stairs. Gillian was in the sitting-room, doing her homework, and didn't even hear him. In his bedroom, Joseph put the pens under his mattress, then remembered to put the digital watch there too. He took the brooch off its card, so it would take up less room, and put it into the pocket of his trousers.

Downstairs, Gillian greeted him with surprise and sus-picion. 'Why you back so early?'

'No reason.'

'I worry about you, you know.'

'Worry about *me*? What you worry about me for?'

'*You* know. Going with Sean and them.'

Joseph turned his head.

'Are you getting in trouble?'

'No. Course not.'

'I think you are though. I think you are by your face. Is that why you come back early?'

'No.'

'Why, then?'

'I got chased by a stranger, didn't I? Like in the police film. A great big Kojak man with a scar down his face.'

'You made that up,' said Gillian.

'All right, don't believe me.'

'Come on then, let's do your homework. Suppose I'll have to help you again. I don't want a dunce for a brother, do I?'

He *did* try to concentrate, but it was hard to think of English exercises when there was a knobbly brooch in his pocket. clamouring to be offered to his love. He kept thinking how pleased Grace was going to be, and wondering when he was going to get the chance to give it to her.

As it happened, the chance came that afternoon. Grace came in to say she had to go on an errand for her mum, and ask Gillian to go with her. 'I'm helping Joseph with his work though,' said Gillian.

'It's all right, I don't mind,' said Joseph.

'You're just trying to get out of it,' said Gillian.

'You go along with Grace,' called Mrs Rundell from the kitchen. 'I'll see Joe finishes his writing.'

Gillian ran upstairs to fetch her coat, and Joseph whipped the brooch out of his pocket. He held it out to Grace, and she just stood gazing, eyes bright with aston-ishment and desire. 'For me?' she whispered.

'Don't tell Gillian.'

'Where you get that from?'

'I saved a baby from being run over, and his mother gave it to me for a reward.'

Grace knew there was something wrong with that story, but she wanted to believe Joseph because she wanted the brooch. She thought it was the most beautiful thing she had ever seen. 'Thank you,' she said in a small choky voice, and she took it from Joseph's outstretched hand.

'It's a secret, mind,' said Joseph.

'Oh yes.'

'They'll tease me.'

'Yes.'

Grace undid her coat, pulled up her jersey, and pinned the brooch to her vest. Nobody could see it, but *she* knew it was there, and that was the main thing. She gave Joseph a warm little smile, and changed it into a sneeze because Gillian was coming back.

'Shall we go round Castle Street first?' said Gillian, wistfully. 'Just have a look at school?'

'Perhaps it's playtime. Perhaps they'll all be in the playground.'

'Nah – they had their play already.'

'Lucky things, being in school!'

The girls went to the big gates all the same, and pushed their faces against the railings, gazing into the empty front playground. The classroom windows were too high to look into properly, but you could just see some of the pictures on the walls, and you could hear the cheerful buzz of activity coming from the rooms.

'Lucky things!' said Grace, again. She turned her head. 'Oh look Gillian, look, there's Dippy Dora!'

Miss Dipper had just come out of her house. Toe-heel *down*, shuffle, shuffle. Toe-heel *down*, shuffle, shuffle. The grotesque dance continued the length of the broken path, and through the wilderness of the front garden. The girls watched, in fascinated horror.

'Ugh!' said Gillian, with a shudder. 'She gives me the creeps.'

'Yeah,' said Grace, thoughtfully. 'Shall we do it though?'

'Do what?'

'You know – what Mrs White said. Smile at Dippy Dora. In case she's lonely.'

'I don't want to,' said Gillian.

'Nor I don't want to neither. . . . But shall we?'

'All right. If you like. A smile costs nothing.'

Dippy Dora was passing them now, on the other side of the road. Over the straggling hair she wore a flowery brimmed hat which had once been smart. Silas was in her hand and she was cracking him. She had soaked him in water so he would make a more fearsome noise. She waved him in the air, round and round her head, and *crack* went Silas down to her side and up again, circling the air to begin all over again.

The girls ran to get in front of the old woman. They smiled their best but Dippy Dora was talking over her shoulder to someone who wasn't there, and didn't notice them. Every now and again she spoke to Silas too, bringing the end of him close to her face, and rubbing him against her cheek. The three of them – Silas, Dippy Dora, and the person who wasn't there – danced and shuffled and gabbled their way down the road.

'She didn't see us smiling,' said Grace.

'Shall we try again?' said Gillian.

'I will if you will.'

Once more the girls ran in front of Dippy Dora, and smiled earnestly into her face. They were quite close to her. They could see all the lines and furrows on the leathery skin; they could smell the sour odour. They were not in her world though; she didn't want them in her world. She saw them hovering on the edge of it, and tried to brush them away.

'What do you want, saucepans? Dirty saucepans? What

do you want then?' Her eyes focussed suddenly, sharply aware again.

'We're smiling,' Gillian explained.

'Don't you smile at *me*! What they smiling for, Silas? What for?' She cracked him smartly a couple of times, and the girls stepped back. 'That made you jump! That made the saucepans jump, didn't it, Silas? Go on home! Go on now, go on, I'll turn you into frogs, mind. We'll turn 'em into frogs, won't we, Silas?' The gums leered, the tooth and the beard went up and down, up and down.

The girls retreated across the road. 'She don't want us to smile at her,' said Gillian.

'Anyway, we tried. What's she doing now, though?'

'She's looking in that house.'

'She *is* potty, ain't she, Gillian? What's she looking at?'

'It's a broke-up oil stove somebody thrown out for the Old Iron Man.'

'Oh look, she's going in the gate!' said Grace.

'I wouldn't want her to come in *my* gate!'

'Look, she's picking up the old oil stove. What's she doing that for, Gillian?'

'I dunno. She's a nutter, ain't she? Come on, let's go to the shops for your mum.'

At the corner of the road, the girls turned once more. There was a squealing noise, the sort that set your teeth on edge, like chalk on a board, or dustbins being scraped over the pavement. It wasn't dustbins though, it was Dippy Dora, dragging her oil stove home.

'Did we ought to help her?' said Grace.

'Nah – she'll only shout at us.'

Silas was round her head now, they noticed, on top of the filthy old hat with the flowers.

At home, Gillian asked her mum what she thought about Dippy Dora and the oil stove.

'I think it's downright dangerous,' said Mum. 'Those old stoves are really dangerous, you know, they can tip over and set the house on fire.'

'Is Dippy Dora going to catch her house on fire?' asked Joseph, with interest.

'I should think it's more than likely,' said Mum. 'What with the candles an' all, and she don't know what she's doing half the time. It's a disgrace. They should do something about it.'

'What do you mean "They"?' said Gillian. 'Who's "They"?' 'You know, *Them*. The Social. They should take her away, put her in a Home.'

'Is she really going to catch her house on fire though?' said Joseph. 'That'd be good.'

'Don't be wicked,' said Gillian.

'It'd be good though. All the fire engines coming. I hope we're in school when she does it. Then we can see out the window.'

'Don't look like we're ever going to *be* in school again though,' said Gillian, with a sigh.

'Yes you are then,' said Mum. 'You're going back tomorrow. Mrs White rung up while you was out. They got a teacher for you.'

'A nice one?'

'I dunno, do I? You'll find out, soon enough.'

6

Worse and worse

Dear darling beloved Mrs Lloyd
I hope you are in good health and your husband Winston. Thank you for your wonderful letters. Me and Grace are glad your baby is going along all right. Graces knitting is getting longer she is trying very hard I hope you will like Graces knitting. I think Helen is all right for a girls name but I rather Melissa and James if its a boy but lets hope it wont be. We got a new teacher and she is very old and strict and she got a lot of wrinkles and nobody in the class likes her. I think she is about eighty but I dont know for certain and she keeps telling us about schools in the olden days and she keeps picking on Joseph and I think schools in the olden days were horribul. They use to get the cane and Miss Beale says Joseph would get the cane every day if it was in the olden days and I wish you would come back but we cannot always have what we want and I am longing to see your baby when it is born.

Love from Gillian X X X X X X X X X X X X X X

Miss Beale had come out of retirement to be supply teacher for Class 4L. She had done it as a favour to Mrs White, because the staff situation at Castle Street was getting so desperate. She had actually been a colleague of Mrs White's many years ago, and although during her working life she had kept up with some of the changes in teaching methods, since she retired she had forgotten most of them. In any case, she much preferred the old ways.

When Miss Beale was a young teacher, children stayed in their seats, and did writing and arithmetic most of the day, and reading round the class. The desks were arranged neatly in rows, all facing the front. Miss Beale made Class 4L move their desks so that theirs were in rows too. That way Miss Beale could see them all properly, and they could see the board. They did a lot of work from the board with Miss Beale, and of course they were not allowed to talk.

It wasn't all writing and maths and reading round the class, though. They had a painting lesson once, and handwork twice. For painting they had to do a vase of flowers, and for handwork they were making calendars for Christmas. They had to rule them very carefully and accurately. They did one step at a time, all together, then they had to put their pencils and rulers down, while Miss Beale came round to see who had done it right. If the line was a tiny bit wrong, you had to rub it out and do it again. Joseph had rubbed his out more times than he could count, and his calendar was a terrible mess, but Miss Beale wouldn't let him have another piece of card to start again.

They were also learning a play for Christmas. It was a nativity play, and Miss Beale had written it herself. A long time ago, it would seem, for the pages of script were all dog-eared, as though they had already been used by generations of children. Some pages even had ink blots on them, from the days when children in school used dip pens for their writing.

In the play, Sharon was Mary, and Stephen was Joseph. Joseph thought he should have been Joseph, since that was his name already, but Miss Beale said his voice wasn't loud enough, and it was too high-pitched, and anyway he was too silly to be Joseph. Really, he was too silly to be in it at all, but the play required a large chorus of angels, so Joseph had to be an angel. All those who had no speaking parts were either angels or shepherds. Harjit was an angel, and so was Paul. Sean was a wise man, because he was handsome, and because he had a good loud voice.

You had to have a really loud voice to be in Miss Beale's nativity play. Never mind saying the words with any sort of feeling; the important thing was if you could be heard at the back of the hall. Never mind if your voice was pleasant to listen to, either. Actually, Sharon had a voice like a fog-horn, but she still had to be Mary because she could shout, and because she was willing to pronounce each word slowly and separately, not gabble like so many of them.

Strict, as she was, Miss Beale was quite fair on the whole, but she did have one hate in the class, and that was Joseph. He just could not seem to do anything right. In return, Joseph disliked Miss Beale more than any teacher he had ever known, more than Miss Campbell, even. He wished Miss Beale would have a heart attack, or walk under a bus one day, and he was surprised to find himself thinking like that, because he hardly ever wished ill to anyone, even if they *were* not very nice to him.

The class practised the play every afternoon. Joseph began to dread the afternoons. It was so boring, waiting to be an angel, while Sharon and Stephen went over and over their parts. One day Joseph even found himself wishing there was no such thing as Christmas.

'*No*, Stephen, *not* like that,' Miss Beale was saying.

'Loudly and clearly, COME . . . MARY . . . LEAN . . . ON . . . ME. Come along now, deep breath!' Waiting for Stephen to take his deep breath, Joseph tried it himself: '*Come . . . Mary . . . lean . . . on . . . me.*' Unfortunately, the words that were meant to be only mouthed, came out quite loudly, and Miss Beale thought he was mocking.

'Lose your play, Joseph Rundell. And go and stand over there by yourself. That's right, by the window. Where I can see you.'

In fact, standing by the window was not too bad a punishment. At least there was the street to look at, and the front playground. It was a sunny day for once, and Class 1R were having playground games with their teacher. Joseph wished he could be a first year again, and have Miss Robinson for his teacher, instead of nasty old Miss Beale. Or that Mrs Lloyd would come back, of course, that would be the best of all.

His eyes wandered across the road, and up the road, and on to Dippy Dora's house, blind and secretive as ever. What *was* she hiding, behind those tattered curtains? Joseph still thought it was jewels. He'd bet anything it was jewels. He wished *he* had some of the jewels in Dippy Dora's house. All flashing and sparkling and different colours, he wished *he* could get hold of some. He wouldn't keep them for himself, though, he'd give them all to Grace. He wondered if Grace still wore his brooch on her vest. He thought she probably did, she had been giving him some very kind looks just lately. He wished he had some of Dippy Dora's jewels to give Grace for Christmas.

Another thought struck Joseph; what about Dippy Dora was going to set fire to her house? What about that then? Perhaps she was going to do it today. Perhaps she was doing it right this minute! Joseph looked eagerly, hoping to see smoke, and flames. If she did it today, he could be a hero. He'd climb out of the window and down to the playground in no time. He wouldn't care about Miss Beale – she could give him lines, or make him lose his play, or *expel* him, he wouldn't care! He'd run across the playground, and run into Dippy Dora's house, and save Dippy Dora, and she would give him handfuls and handfuls of jewels to thank him for saving her, and the fire-engines would come. . . . Joseph began to imitate the noise of the fire-engines – 'Woo-ooo-ooooo.'

'Joseph Rundell – have you gone *quite* daft?' Miss Beale was very cross; the loose fold of skin under her chin was positively quivering. 'Really, I don't know what's the matter with you. You behave more like a six-year-old than a fourth year boy. Are you playing at being a police car, by any chance?'

'Oh no, Miss Beale, it's my throat, Miss Beale, I can't help it. It makes me make funny noises all the time. The doctor says it's very rare, and I got to have special medicine for it.'

'I never heard such rubbish,' said Miss Beale, angrily. 'Go to Mrs White this minute, and tell her that Miss Beale can't tolerate your ridiculous behaviour any longer.'

Joseph was quite dismayed. He had been sent to Mrs White twice the previous week, and she had hinted at dire unspecified consequences if such a thing were to happen again. But there must be some misunderstanding. Most teachers only laughed, when he told his silly stories. 'Please, Miss Beale, forgive me, Miss Beale,' he tried. 'Oh forgive me, dear Miss Beale, kind Miss Beale, you're so kind you will let me off this time, won't you?'

There was a deathly hush now, while the class waited to see what Miss Beale's response to this outburst would be. Everyone knew Joseph meant no harm, but Miss Beale would be sure to take it the wrong way. Alarmed, Gillian watched Miss Beale's face turn purple.

'You impertinent boy – how dare you speak to me like that!'

Joseph was puzzled. *Now* what had he done to upset her? She ought to like it if he said she was kind.

She thinks he's making fun of her, thought Gillian. *She* knows she's not kind, anyway she's never kind to him. She thinks he's mocking at her – oh Joseph, do shut up now! But Joseph blundered on, thinking he hadn't made himself clear. 'I'll do anything, Miss Beale, only don't send me to Mrs White. . . . I'll kneel down to you – look—'

'There's a mouse!' shouted Gillian, suddenly. There was no mouse, of course, but Gillian thought Miss Beale was going to do something terrible to Joseph, if something were not done to distract attention from his antics. Some of the girls screamed about the mouse, but Gillian was quite unprepared for the reaction of Miss Beale. Strong-minded as she was, Miss Beale had one secret terror, and that was mice. Spiders she did not mind, snakes and frogs left her unmoved – but *mice*. Mice gave Miss Beale the shuddering heebie-jeebies. In true story book tradition, Miss Beale scrambled on to her chair and began to shriek.

Everyone was very surprised to see Miss Beale on her chair, screaming about a little mouse, and they began to laugh. Even those who had been screaming themselves laughed at Miss Beale doing it. Miss Beale began to suspect she was making a fool of herself. 'Hands on heads,' said Miss Beale, and the class, who had recently learned to obey this strange command, did so. 'All right, what mouse? How could there be a mouse?'

'Mr Davis got mice in his classroom,' faltered Gillian. 'One of them must have escaped.'

'No he ain't,' said Sharon, in her fog-horn voice. 'There's no mice in Mr Davis's room. There's no mice in any of the classrooms.'

'Yes there is.' 'There ain't.' 'Miss Robinson used to have some.' And so on. Opinion was divided as to whether currently there were, or were not, pet mice in any of the other classes, but the majority seemed to feel that there were not. Miss Beale, with as much dignity as she could muster, climbed down from the chair. Being old, her legs were stiff and awkward, and she almost slipped coming down. Gillian would have been sorry for her, if she were not so alarmed about what she had done. Miss Beale transfixed her now, with sharp accusing eyes.

'Come here, Gillian Rundell.'

The class was very happy to have this diversion from Miss Beale's tedious old nativity play. They watched with interest as Gillian pushed her way to the front, and stood there, looking frightened and guilty.

'You said something about a mouse, I believe.'

'Yes, Miss Beale.'

'*Was* there a mouse? No look at me, look at me . . . *was there a mouse?*' It might have been Mrs White speaking. Probably Mrs White copied from Miss Beale, in the olden days. '*There was no mouse, was there, Gillian?*' said Miss Beale finally, in a deeply accusing voice.

'No, Miss Beale.' What would happen to her now? Her mum called up to school? Suspended? Expelled? Clearly she had done something very bad.

'Was it an intelligent thing, would you say, Gillian, to say there was a mouse when there was not?'

'No, Miss Beale.'

'Whatever made you do it then?' In case Gillian should answer, and make her look foolish again, Miss Beale answered her own question. 'You did it because you are a silly, naughty little girl. What are you?'

'I'm a silly, naughty little girl,' said Gillian, obediently.

'What are you in the play?'

'An angel,' said Gillian.

'Right,' said Miss Beale, 'no more being in the play for you. Go and sit at the back, you can be in disgrace from now until Christmas. If anyone asks you why you are not in the play, you will have to tell them that it is because you are a silly, naughty little girl. Won't you, Gillian? There will be no need to mention the mouse, that will just make you look sillier. Won't it?'

'Yes, Miss Beale.' Gillian slunk to the back of the class, her face burning with shame. She felt very grateful that Miss Beale had not sent her to Mrs White, and at least Joseph's performance seemed to have been forgotten. What Gillian did not realize was that the last thing Miss Beale wanted was for the story to get out, perhaps as far as the staff room, where the teachers would all have a good laugh at her expense. Miss Beale was very sensitive about being laughed at.

Next day, Miss Beale was stricter than ever. She also had a new hate now, and that was Gillian. Gillian was so miserable, sitting at the back of the class and feeling Miss Beale hating her, that she did not know how she was going to bear it quite, all the long time till Mrs Lloyd came back. If she ever did.

No one was particularly sorry when, on the Wednesday, Miss Beale didn't turn up. Miss Beale had some family problems, Mrs White told them, and wouldn't be coming to school that day. They would have to be split up round the classes again, and Mrs White was sure Class 4L would be glad when Miss Beale's family problems were sorted out, as they had been doing such neat work in their books since Miss Beale was their teacher, and getting on so well with their Christmas play.

On Thursday morning Mrs White told the class that she had some very unfortunate news for them indeed. Miss Beale's sister, on the other side of London, had fallen ill and needed nursing. There was no one else to look after her, so Miss Beale had to go and do it. It was not likely that she would be able to come back. Mrs White knew how sorry Class 4L would be, that Miss Beale was not coming back, and this morning they could all write thank you letters to Miss Beale, for helping them as much as she had.

Tomorrow, Mrs White said, they would have to stay at home again, as there was no teacher for their class.

On Friday afternoon Sean and Stephen and Harjit and Paul all called for Joseph. Gillian looked disapproving, but Mum thought it was nice for Joseph to be going to the park with his friends, seeing how well (for him) he had done his homework that morning. Joseph was exultant that they had come. Now Sean and Stephen were friends again, they hadn't seemed to want him much any more, and Joseph had found himself once more excluded from the inner circle – tolerated, but only hovering on the edge of the group.

And now they had *come* for him! All of them! Great! They had even forgiven him for his bungling in Discount that time. Of course he was willing to have another go! Of course he was! Long as they'd watch for him, inside the shop, so he wouldn't get caught again.

The shops were bursting with goodies. There was a silent agreement to avoid Discount – plenty of opportunity elsewhere. Walker's, for instance, a large newsagent's, which featured all kinds of sweets and toys, and novelties as well. Joseph helped himself to a variety of stuff from Walker's. He didn't feel a bit guilty about the stealing now. What was there to feel guilty about? Everybody did it, it was quite an ordinary thing to do. And stealing from Walker's was so easy it was almost boring. Joseph came out only when his pockets and armpits would hold no more, and they all went to the waste ground, to share out the spoils. There were three chocolate bars, a doll with 'real' hair, a card of plastic soldiers, five packets of sweets, two water-pistols, and a very splendid tree decoration.

'Let's go Pearce's now,' said Sean. Pearce's mostly sold china and fancy goods; at this time of year it was crammed with things that would make good presents for people's mums.

'You go in this time,' said Joseph. 'I done my share.'

'You're better at it, though,' said Sean.

'What about Stephen, then?'

'Nah!' said Stephen. 'You're better'n me. Boys, innit Joe's the best out of all of us?'

'Yeah – good old Joe!'

Joseph glowed with pride.

At Pearce's they collected two little snowstorms, a china rabbit, a set of coasters, and a small brass windmill. And at Warren's, the other big newsagent at the very end of the High Street, they got four packets of Smarties, a roll of Sellotape, a set of felt-tip pens, a box of water colours, and a rude poster. The anoraks of all five bulged.

'Let's go outside school now,' said Stephen. 'Watch them having play. Have a good laugh 'cause we got a holiday and they haven't.' He was a large boy, heavily built, and his red face and little piggy eyes were puffy with unpleasant excitement.

'In a minute,' said Sean.

'Why not now?'

'In a minute.' There was no reason for waiting except that Sean wanted to assert his authority over the group. They were not to move until he said so. 'All right – now we'll go.'

They stood along the railings in Bridge Street, round the block from Castle Street, and watched the classes being released into the back playground, used by the third and fourth years. 'Ha-ha-ha!' they jeered at 4D. 'Who's got to work and we haven't?' 'Being good little girls and boys, then?' 'Mind you get all your sums right.'

Some of those still in captivity cast looks of envy at the free ones; most ignored the jibes. School was, on the whole, more interesting than holidays, especially when it was nearly Christmas, and especially with a good teacher like Mr Davis. 'Fourth years got films this afternoon, and you're missing it,' someone pointed out.

Slightly put out, the five moved off round the block. Outside Dippy Dora's house they paused. 'Do you think Dippy's in there?' said Stephen.

'My mum says she's going to set the house on fire,' said Joseph.

'You dum-dum – she ain't going to set the house on fire,' said Sean, scornfully. 'She ain't that mad. . . . All right, how is she then? How does your mum know that?'

'She got a oil stove. A old one that don't work properly, and you can tip it over.'

'Oh well yeah,' said Sean, 'she might then. If she got a oil stove. I didn't know about the oil stove. Yeah, she will then, she most probably will.'

'She might get burned to death,' said Stephen, with relish.

'Yeah,' said Sean. 'Horrible old thing.'

'Hope she does it soon,' said Stephen, 'then that'll be the end of her.'

'We don't really want *her* to be burned though,' said Joseph, 'only the house.'

'Yes we do,' said Paul. 'Dirty old drunk. Disgusting old mad lady.'

'What you think she really got in there?' said Harjit, for perhaps the fiftieth time in his life.

'Bottles of booze,' said Paul.

'Yeah but – besides that?'

'Secret documents,' said Sean. 'She's probably a spy for the government. . . . Perhaps she's a spy for Russia.'

'Do they have mad people for spies?' said Stephen, doubtfully.

'She's probably just pretending to be mad,' said Sean. 'She ain't mad really.'

'She must be mad though,' said Stephen. 'She goes in people's dustbins. My mum see her do it.'

'That's just pretending,' said Sean.

'I see her pick up rubbish,' said Harjit. 'She put it in her bag, all dirty from the street.'

'How do you know it was rubbish?' said Sean.

'Well, it *looked* like rubbish. It was just a old paper book somebody dropped, all wet and tramped on.'

'Might have been a secret message, in code.'

'Yeah, it might.'

'If she ain't really mad, she won't set the house on fire,' said Joseph, disappointed.

'That's right,' said Sean.

'But you said she will.'

'I changed my mind.'

'*I* think she's a miser, not a spy,' said Joseph. 'I think she's got all money and jewels in there.'

'She ain't a miser. She's a spy,' said Paul, to be the same as Sean.

'I think she's a spy too,' said Stephen. 'What you think, Harjit?'

'I think she's a spy.'

But the idea of the jewels was attractive too. 'She could be a miser as well,' said Sean. 'The jewels could be her payment for being a spy. I bet she *has* got jewels in there, you know.' He glanced speculatively at Joseph. 'I bet you could get in there easy, Joe.'

Joseph shifted, uncomfortably, from one foot to the other. 'Nah.'

'I bet you could.'

'Nah – Grace thinks Dippy Dora's a witch.'

Hoots of derision. 'She ain't a witch! Who's baby

enough to believe that?'

'I didn't say I *believe* it,' said Joseph.

'Well then—' said Sean.

'She could be something else bad.'

'You're just too chicken to climb in.'

'All right then, you.'

'*I* ain't scared,' said Sean. 'And Paul ain't scared, are you, Paul? And Stephen. We just want to see if you are.'

'Well I am,' said Joseph, honestly.

By Monday, another supply teacher had been found for Class 4L. Miss Kennedy was a visitor from Australia. She travelled all round the countries of Europe, and when she ran out of money she did supply teaching to earn some more. She had been a teacher back in Brisbane, and she missed her own school very much. She was actually quite homesick, but Class 4L did not understand this. They did not know why they were having so many lessons about Australia, and kangaroos, and koala bears. These lessons were interesting at first, but Class 4L got tired of them. They also got tired of hearing Miss Kennedy moaning all the time, about the cold weather in London, and about how much she missed the lovely Australian sunshine.

Miss Kennedy was preferable to Mr er-er, and Miss Beale – at least she tried to give the class good things to do. And she might have got away with the moans had she been pretty like Miss Croft, but unfortunately for her she was not. She had spots and stringy hair, and her brightly coloured jumpers did not suit her muddy skin. The children did not take to her, but they accepted her at first, because it was good to be making Christmas decorations and writing stories with Miss Kennedy (when they weren't having lessons about kangaroos and koala bears), instead of writing a composition entitled 'My Pet', or practising the nativity play with Miss Beale.

The trouble began with the maths, on the third day.

Miss Kennedy's maths were different from Mrs Lloyd's, or Mr er-er's. Miss Beale's maths had been different too, but no one had dared to challenge her. Class 4L did not understand Miss Kennedy's maths because she taught them a different way than they were used to, and when she became impatient with them, they suddenly rebelled.

'Come on, come on,' said Miss Kennedy, to Stephen. 'What's this? A fourth year boy can't do long division?'

'I'm getting muddled, miss.'

'Well it's about time you were unmuddled, then. How old are you?'

'Eleven, miss.'

'I don't know any boy of eleven in Australia who can't do long division.'

'We do it a different way,' said Stephen.

'Well, show me how you do it, then.'

But Stephen could not. He had been shown at least three different ways since the beginning of term, and now he was totally confused. 'I forget,' he said, lamely.

'You'd better do it my way then,' said Miss Kennedy, not unreasonably.

'It's wrong though,' said Stephen.

'Yeah,' said Sean, 'our real teacher does it different.'

'Different*ly*,' said Miss Kennedy.

Sean glared at her. 'Different,' he repeated, with deliberate insolence.

This was real defiance, real nastiness, and Miss Kennedy was not quite up to dealing with it. 'Don't be rude, Sean,' she said. But Sean sensed the uncertainty in her voice, and took advantage, as usual.

'Our real teacher's better'n you,' he said, with a sneer.

'Yeah, our teacher's a lot better'n you,' said Stephen.

Miss Kennedy flinched, and swallowed. 'Tough,' she said, trying to pass it off. 'You'll have to make the best of it, won't you?' But the words came out too weakly, and the listening class was not fooled.

'We want Mrs Lloyd,' Sharon began to chant, and a few others joined in.

'Silence!' Miss Kennedy screamed at them. 'Stop your nonsense this minute, all of you!'

'Silly old Kangaroo Kennedy,' said Sean, loud enough for most people to hear. There was quiet for a while though, after that, but soon a muttering growl which spread along the rows, swelling and subsiding and swelling again, threatening rebellion, striking fear into the heart of Miss Kennedy from Brisbane, who had heard about this sort of thing but never actually encountered it. She had had difficult classes before, but never one like this.

From then on, the authority of Miss Kennedy crumbled quite rapidly. For two days, the noise from Class 4L grew hourly louder, the rows of 4L members banished from the class grew longer. They stood outside the door, or outside Mrs White's room, until the other teachers were sick of seeing them. Mr Davis complained he could no longer teach properly because of the din, and Miss Kennedy worried, and wept in her bedsit at night, because the class was going to pieces, and such a thing had never happened to her before, and she was afraid she would have to admit she had failed.

Anyway, there was only a week to go now before the Christmas holidays. If she could just hold out till then, perhaps the children would have calmed down by the beginning of the new term. Meanwhile, it was anything to keep them happy. So Miss Kennedy let Class 4L do whatever they asked to do. They had the lessons they chose and 'free choice' for much of the day. The trouble was, the more they got their own way, the more discontented they became. There was mess in the classroom, there were fights in the playground, and the line of wrongdoers outside Mrs White's room grew longer still.

Mrs White decided to take action.

This time, when Mrs White entered the room, there was

92

no immediate silence. Mrs White had to clap her hands to get their attention, and even then some were not listening. 'I'm waiting, Joseph Rundell, Sean, Sharon. . . . Did you hear me, Joseph? Put that paintbrush down. *Down*, I said. . . . Right, eyes this way. . . . Put that away, Paul, whatever it is.'

'It's my star,' said Paul, resentfully, 'for the decorations.'

'I daresay, but you don't do decorations when I'm speaking to you. There's a time and place for all things. And that brings me on to what I've come to say. . . *Joseph*, I shan't tell you again. . . . Right, the Christmas concert. All the classes are putting on an item. How are you people getting on with your nativity play?'

'We ain't doing it no more,' said someone.

'Not *doing* it?' Mrs White's surprise was pretended; she knew very well that the nativity play had been abandoned, but she judged it would help pull the class together, and help Miss Kennedy get a grip on the class if the play were resurrected.

'Miss Beale isn't here no more.'

'Oh but surely,' said Mrs White, 'surely she left the play behind. Have you looked for the play, Miss Kennedy? Let me help you.'

Miss Kennedy had, in fact, found the play on her first day with Class 4L. She thought it was a terrible play, and she had put it into the table drawer.

'Shall we look in the drawer?' suggested Mrs White, in a syrupy voice, having a very good idea that was where the play would be hidden. 'Ah yes, here it is. Now let's see . . . who is in the play? Hands up all those who are in it. Everyone? What about you, Gillian, haven't you got a part?'

'No, Mrs White.'

'*No*? Why not?'

'Because I'm a silly, naughty little girl,' said Gillian, in a low voice.

'Because you are *what*? Is there something funny, Grace

Johnson? Because you are *what*, Gillian? Oh yes, that's right, you have been rather naughty lately, haven't you? . . . AND A GREAT MANY OTHER PEOPLE! . . . A great many people in this class seem to have forgotten that there are rules in this school. We do *not* fight in the playground, we do *not* shout in the classroom, or throw litter about, we do *not* answer our teachers back. If everyone obeys the rules we can have a happy school. We all need rules. Is there anyone who doesn't understand what I'm saying? . . . Very well – I shall come back on Monday to see how you're getting on with the play. You can take your parts home and learn them over the weekend. You all have your parts still, I imagine? . . . Good, good. . . . They will all have to work very hard, won't they, Miss Kennedy, as there are only a few days left. Perhaps you will very kindly let me watch a rehearsal, Miss Kennedy, on Monday afternoon.'

Since Miss Kennedy could hardly say no to the head-mistress, Mrs White took it that she was to be kindly allowed to watch the rehearsal.

'Now, what about costumes?' Mrs White went on. 'Did Miss Beale organize costumes for the play before she left? No? . . . We had better look in the dressing-up cupboard then. I know there are some angels' wings from last year, and I'm sure some of you can bring things from home. Gillian Rundell, as you are not in the play, would you like to be in charge of the costumes? Grace Johnson, you can help her. There – that's a nice little job for the two of you. . . . All right, if Miss Kennedy will excuse you, you can both come with me now, and see what we can find together.'

Without enthusiasm, Gillian and Grace followed Mrs White to the dressing-up cupboard.

Back in the classroom, the bickering and complaints began.

'Don't want to do that silly old play.'

94

'Wish Miss Beale took the play home with her.'

'I'm Mary, Miss Kennedy. Miss Beale said I got to be Mary.'

'I'm Inn-keeper.'

'No you aren't, you was only Inn-keeper because Richard was away.'

'Miss Beale said I'm a better Inn-keeper than Richard.'

'I'm Mary.'

'I don't want to be a angel, I want to be a shepherd.'

'Miss Kennedy, don't forget I'm Mary.'

Miss Kennedy, with dread in her heart, foresaw that the run-up to Christmas was going to involve even more misery than she had thought.

Dearest Mrs Lloyd (*wrote Gillian*)
How is your baby getting along? Our class did a play and it was terribul and me and Grace was not in it thank goodness. Sharon was Mary and she wanted to be Mary but on the day she got fritend and she forgot all what she was supposed to say and Miss Kennedy had to say it behind the curten instead of Sharon and it sounded funny and Sharons face was red and she was nearly crying. And that was not the worst the worst was when the curten went back at the second scene and the angels were supposed to be standing with there hands up and they were not standing with there hands up they were fighting. Mrs White was very angry because the angels were fighting and everybody saw them fighting and some of the parents as well. And Mrs White said our class is a disgrace to the school and I wish you would come back to be our teacher again. And I hope you have a happy Christmas and your dear husband Winston and your baby will be born soon.

    Love from
     Gillian X X X X X X X X X

7

The unmerry Christmas

On Christmas morning, Joseph gave Gillian a very attractive doll. Gillian had been thinking she was getting a bit old now to play with dolls, but she was delighted with this one. For instance, it had realistic hair that you could comb, and set into different styles. Joseph gave his mother an ornamental brass windmill, and his father a cigarette lighter.

'Your dad don't smoke no more though, Joe,' laughed Mum. 'Never mind, it'll come in handy for something. I like my one, it's really pretty.' She put the brass windmill on the mantelpiece, right in the centre, in front of all the Christmas cards. 'Fancy Joseph saving all his money to give us such good presents!'

Gillian was silent, as a terrible thought presented itself. She herself had given her parents a salt-and-pepper set between them, and it had taken her weeks to save the money. She knew how much Joseph's pocket money was, because it was the same as hers, and she knew how much he liked sweets, and how he had not been seen to deny himself in the run-up to Christmas. A faint suspicion, condensing into a cold fear, began to clutch at her.

'He's good-hearted, he really is good-hearted, our Joseph,' Mum was saying in a pleased voice.

Gillian stopped combing her doll's hair – suddenly she didn't like it so much. 'Where's Joseph now?' she asked.

'Where do you think? Gone next door to give his girlfriend her present. It's a real joke that, innit!'

Gillian had a present for Grace also; it was a set of felt-tip pens from Warren's. She wondered what Joseph had given her, and suddenly she wanted very much to know. She took her own brightly coloured packet, so lovingly and carefully wrapped, from its place under the Christmas tree. 'I'm going too,' she said.

Grace and her sisters, four big, noisy, good-natured girls, were all celebrating Christmas in the front room of their house. There was a lot of laughing and loud music; Joseph was there too, trying to enjoy the glass of wine they had given him for fun. Grace was looking radiant and very pretty in the red dress which was a present from her mum. She had red bows in her hair to match the dress, and round her neck a smart white necklace. She was wearing a white bracelet, as well. Her eyes were shining with rather troubled joy. 'Look what Joseph gave me,' said Grace, proud and evasive at the same time. The butterfly brooch was still pinned to her vest, but this new present did not have to be concealed. All the same, Grace wouldn't meet Gillian's eyes.

'This is from me,' said Gillian, in a small choky voice, and she looked the other way as well. Grace knew very well there was something wrong about that necklace, didn't she? She probably had a 'feeling' about it and no wonder. Of course Joseph could never have afforded to buy a lovely present like that, not with all the other stuff he had produced this year. Why, last year he had given her only a pencil, Gillian remembered, with a rubber on the end of it. Not because he was mean, but because he hadn't remembered to save. And Mum and Dad had received a bar of chocolate each. Grace had had no present at all from Joseph last year, because he was not in love with her then.

There was no way round it, the truth had to be faced – *Joseph had been stealing*. And now Grace couldn't look at her, and she couldn't look at Grace, and Gillian thought she was probably going to die of shame. She ran back to her own house, and curled up on the couch pretending to read. Her dad was watching a programme on television. It was a cartoon film, and meant for children really, but Dad seemed to be enjoying it enormously. His great laugh boomed out every other minute and Gillian thought bitterly that her dad wouldn't be laughing like that, would he, if he knew what Joseph did.

'Look, Gilly, that's good – that's funny, that is.' Dad had a big red face, just like Mum. He had a big beaming smile like Mum too. 'Come on, love, what's the matter? Cheer up now, it's Christmas. Don't you like your presents? Don't you like the watch me and your mum give you? It's a good one, mind.'

'It's lovely,' said Gillian. 'It's a lovely present, I love my present from you. Thank you very much for my lovely watch.'

'Well *smile* then.'

Gillian tried, very hard, to smile.

'Don't you feel well? Is that it?'

'That's right,' said Gillian, gratefully. 'I don't feel very well. I feel sick.'

'I know what it is – you been stuffing your face with chocolate! Breath of fresh air do you good. What about you and me go up the park for half an hour, while your mum's cooking?'

'I rather stay here. Actually, I think I'll go upstairs for a bit. Have a lay down.'

'What? On Christmas day?'

'Just for a little bit.'

98

'Go on then, have a little sleep. Feel better by dinner-time I expect.' It didn't seem right, a ten-year-old girl going to her room to sleep in the middle of Christmas morning! *Something* was wrong. Oh well – back to the telly.

Gillian did not really want to sleep; she only wanted to be by herself. She didn't want anyone guessing her thoughts from the look on her face. It was so obvious to her now – what Joseph must have been up to – and she just couldn't think why her mum and dad hadn't thought of it too. They're too trusting, she decided, that's their trouble. Just because *they're* good, they think everybody else is, too. And what about when they find out?

Find out what, though? After all, Gillian reminded herself, she didn't really *know* anything. Perhaps she was just jumping to conclusions. Perhaps Joseph had a job he didn't tell anyone about. Perhaps he did a paper round, and nobody knew. No – of course he didn't do a paper round. The whole house would know if Joseph was going out early in the morning, and anyway he always had to be dragged out of bed for school.

Saturdays, then. Perhaps he had a Saturday job in a shop, or washing people's cars. Gillian tried to remember what happened on Saturdays, but all she could think of was Joseph hurtling up and down Tower Street on his roller skates. Then she thought again about the days they didn't have a teacher, when Joseph was with Sean and that lot. And after school as well just lately; he was always late home these days, and vague about where he had been. It had to be that, didn't it? It had to be Sean Adams made Joseph a thief.

On the way to her bedroom Gillian passed the open door of Joseph's room. It was always untidy, but this morning it looked like a disaster area. The bed was still unmade, of course, and the whole place littered with clothes, toys, sweets and crumpled pieces of Christmas

99

wrapping. Gillian averted her eyes from the mess, and went into her own room, where she lay on the neatly made bed. She lay still, and stiff. Visions of the chaos in Joseph's room swam persistently before her, and suddenly she had a thought. Probably Joseph stole things for himself, as well as to give away. Probably he had things hidden in his room – evidence, to prove what he did.

She sat up slowly, trying to decide what to do. It wasn't nice, searching someone's room, and besides, Joseph might come upstairs and catch her at it. But she had to know, she had to! Gillian went to the landing, and peered over the bannisters. There was no one in the hall. The telly was still on in the sitting room; she could hear sounds of 'Once in Royal David's City' coming through the closed door. There was the warm smell of roasting turkey wafting up the stairs, and clattering sounds in the kitchen.

Gillian thought Joseph was probably still at the Johnsons' next door, drinking wine and getting giggly. Anyway, she decided to risk it. She waded through the muddle, and stood beside Joseph's bed, wondering where to look first.

Where would Joseph hide a secret if he had one? At the bottom of a drawer, perhaps, under his clothes. Mum didn't often go into Joseph's room. Once a week to dust and Hoover, and that was all, except for the spring cleaning; the twins were supposed to make their own beds. Sometimes Mum went in, took one look at Joseph's mess, and came out again. Just occasionally she lost patience and had a blitz on the drawers. She would pull them right out, tip their jumbled contents on to the floor, and stand over Joseph, scolding indulgently while he tidied them. If Joseph had any sense, he wouldn't hide a secret in the drawers, in case Mum decided to have a blitz. But then, Joseph didn't have much sense, did he? Gillian scrabbled about in the drawers, and found nothing.

Where else? Behind the wardrobe? Gillian peered and

poked, but there were only two dusty comics, fallen down by accident.

Under the floorboards? Were there any loose floorboards in Joseph's room? Gillian had no idea if there were, and no idea where to start looking. Paddling through the litter, she went round the bed to the window side, and crouched down to try pulling up the carpet. But it was wall to wall carpet, securely fastened down, and there was no sign at all that it had been recently disturbed. Gillian did not think anything could be hidden underneath it. Neither could she think of anywhere else to look.

At that point, the front door banged and Joseph, singing 'Away in a Manger', all out of tune, could be heard bounding up the stairs on his spidery legs. Gillian was mortified. He would come in now and find her spying – and there had been nothing to spy on after all. She found space to hide under the bed. 'Away in a Manger' was right above her now. Joseph was sitting on his bed, bouncing up and down, eating a chocolate bar and singing between bites.

It sounded awful, but it sounded happy. Joseph hadn't noticed anything funny about Grace, then. Perhaps there *wasn't* anything funny. Perhaps the whole thing was in her own imagination. In fact, the more she thought about it, the more foolish Gillian felt.

Among Joseph's presents was a toy police car, and he began playing with this now, pushing it backwards and forwards, and doing the siren with his voice. He *is* a baby, thought Gillian, and then she was really frightened because the car ran under the bed and stopped there. Gillian was sure Joseph was going to look for it, and find her hiding. She stretched out her hand, gave the car a little shove so that it ran out the other side of the bed, and then waited without breathing to see if Joseph would notice the car had stopped in the middle.

But Joseph was too happy to notice any such thing. He

101

dived across the bed, picked up the car, and went out with it. Gillian heard him go into the bathroom and click the lock, singing 'Away in a Manger' again, still excruciatingly out of tune. She crawled out from under his bed, and escaped back to her own room, feeling really guilty and ashamed. She had done a terrible thing, after all; she had suspected her own brother of stealing, when really he had saved his money to buy good Christmas presents for his family, like Mum said. Probably he had been saving all the year, and she hadn't noticed. He was generous and kind, and *she* was the mean one, to think bad things that weren't true.

After a bit, Gillian decided to go downstairs, and say she felt better. She would forget all about it, and help Mum with the Christmas dinner, as she ought to have been doing anyway.

The day after Boxing Day, Grace came in to spend the afternoon with Gillian. The girls went up to Gillian's bedroom and showed each other their Christmas presents. Gillian was suddenly aware of something missing. 'Where's that necklace Joseph give you?'

Grace looked uncomfortable. 'I left it home – look at my new cardigan I got!'

'Don't you like it?' Gillian persisted, her misgivings flooding back. 'The necklace Joseph give you. And the bracelet. Don't you like them?'

Grace turned her head away. 'Oh yes, they're lovely, they're beautiful, but—'

'You got a "feeling", haven't you!'

Grace nodded, miserably.

'You think Joseph thiefed those things, don't you! You can say, I don't mind if you say.'

Grace pulled up her dress, and showed the butterfly brooch, pinned to her vest. 'He gave me this too, a long

102

time ago. And I think he told a lie how he got it.'

Gillian felt as though all the joy in the world had turned to gloom. Responsibility settled like a dead weight on her shoulders. 'Grace,' she said, 'if you was hiding something in the house, where would you put it?'

Grace considered. 'Under the bed,' she said, at last.

'There's nothing under Joseph's bed,' said Gillian.

'I mean under the mattress, not on the floor.'

'I didn't think of that.'

There was a long pause.

'He's out the street,' said Grace. 'I saw him on his roller skates.'

Another pause.

'Shall we go and look then?' said Gillian in a low voice.

'All right.'

They went together. They lifted the mattress on Joseph's bed, and underneath they found a digital watch (*not* his Christmas present from Mum and Dad), a toy car, three ball-point pens, and a very beautiful Christmas tree decoration.

'That's it then,' said Gillian. Her small pointed face was white with strain.

'He wouldn't hide them, would he?' said Grace, sadly.

'Only if he stole them.'

The girls collected Joseph's hoard and took it back to Gillian's room. 'We'll make him give them back,' said Gillian.

'Supposing he won't?'

'He will if I say so,' said Gillian. 'You call him, Grace, he'll come for you.'

Joseph came, all unsuspecting. 'Did you say a surprise, Grace? What surprise? A nice surprise?'

'That surprise!' said Gillian, indicating the spoils spread out along Gillian's bed. Joseph turned to run, but the girls had their backs firmly pressed against the closed door.

103

'Well?' Gillian accused him, her eyes hard and unforgiving.

'Well what?' he blustered.

'You pinched them things, didn't you!'

'No, I never.'

'Don't lie, Joseph.'

'It was a long time ago.'

'Like last week.'

'It wasn't only me.'

'Oh we know *that*,' said Gillian, bitterly. 'We know who you went stealing with.'

'Sean Adams, Stephen Arnold, Harjit Thakor and Paul Guthrie,' said Grace. 'Your friends and good luck! *I'm* not going to be your friend no more.'

'Oh, Grace, no, that's not fair! Do you want to break my heart then? Oh, Grace!'

'You can have all the things back you give me, and I'm not speaking to you no more because you're a thief.'

'Oh, Grace!'

'*And* you got to take them back,' said Gillian fiercely.

'What?'

'You heard.'

'I can't, I'll get caught.'

'That's your problem,' said Gillian.

'Well, I'm not going to.'

'All right,' said Gillian, '*we'll* take them back. Me and Grace will take them.'

'You can't, you don't know where they come from.'

'We'll ask in all the shops, till we find the right ones.'

'You're mad! Grace, ain't Gillian mad?'

'That's what we're going to do, though,' said Grace, loyally.

'All right,' said Joseph. 'I'll take them.'

'That's better,' said Gillian.

'You'll have to come as well. . . . Grace, will you speak to me again if I take the things back?'

104

'Why do *we* have to come?' asked Grace.

'To be look-out. Will you, Grace? Will you speak to me?'

'I don't know,' said Grace. 'I haven't made up my mind.'

'We'll go now,' said Gillian, 'and we'll do my doll first.' She hated it now; she couldn't get rid of it fast enough.

'Wish *we* didn't have to go,' said Grace, apprehensively.

'It'll soon be over,' said Gillian.

'That's right,' said Joseph cheerfully. 'It'll soon be over, Grace.'

'It's serious, Joseph. It's nothing to laugh about,' said Gillian.

Joseph tried hard to feel how serious it was, but really he thought the girls were making a big fuss about very little.

'Where was it you got the doll from?'

'Discount, I think – no, Warren's.' He had been in so many shops, and taken so many things, it was hard to re-member what came from where. He couldn't be sure now, but it didn't really matter. As long as the doll was put back somewhere, the girls would be happy.

They went to Warren's, and Joseph told the girls what to do. 'Look all round and tell me if anybody's watching, then I put it back and we go.' It didn't seem difficult. 'Don't run when we go,' said Joseph. 'Don't act funny whatever you do. Make out you're looking at things.'

Being the slack time after Christmas, there were only two other customers in the shop: one was choosing a birthday card, and the other was thumbing through the magazines near the door,. The children went to the shelf where the toys were, and the deed was done. Then Grace and Joseph walked out together, staging a conversation about the weather, and Gillian dawdled behind, as she had been told.

At the door, the stout figure of Mrs Warren blocked her way. 'Just a minute, love.'

'Yes?' Gillian felt a stab of fear.

'You were with those other kids, weren't you?'

Gillian panicked. 'What other kids?'

'*You* know what other kids. Don't pretend. A white boy and a black girl – went out just now. That boy took something.'

'No he didn't. I mean – I don't think he did, I didn't see him.'

'*I* saw him. You didn't think I was watching, did you? But I was. There's not much happens in this shop *I* don't see. I didn't see what he took, but I know when kids are up to no good. It was standing out a mile.'

'It ain't nothing to do with me,' said Gillian.

'You came in with him.'

'No I didn't, I didn't. It's nothing to do with me. Anyway, he didn't take nothing, he put something back.'

'Pull the other one,' said Mrs Warren.

'It's true, it's true, I'll show you. . . . That one,' she said, pointing to the doll with the real hair.

'You put it *back*?'

'Yeah – no, not me, my brother.'

'Oh, it's your *brother* now. Does your brother play with dolls?'

'No. Anyway, he only borrowed it.'

'Stole it, you mean.'

'He put it back, didn't he?' said Gillian.

'A blooming funny story if you ask me. I'm getting my husband. Ron? Ron, come here a minute. . . . No, my lady, you stay *here*.'

Gillian had thought to make a run for it, while Mrs Warren was calling into the back of the shop, but Mrs Warren's arm was too quick for her. It shot out, and a hand like a vice closed round Gillian's wrist. Gillian waited in helpless fear to see what would happen next.

Mr Warren was a burly man, and he was not pleased to

have been called from his ten-minute break and his cup of tea. His angry face loomed down at Gillian. 'You been pinching then?'

'No,' said Gillian, beginning to cry.

'Now then, stop that. No use turning on the water-works when you get caught.'

'I haven't done nothing. We put it back.'

'Shall we get the police?' said Mrs Warren. She had no intention of doing any such thing, but thought it would do no harm to frighten Gillian some more.

'Is this what you're on about?' said Mr Warren to Mrs Warren, picking up the doll with the real hair.

'She's trying to say they borrowed it.'

'It's not one of ours.'

'It's not?'

'Nah – we never stocked this make.'

'They got it from somewhere else then.'

'Must have.'

'So what do you reckon we ought to do?'

Gillian waited, in something like terror, while Mr Warren made up his mind. He rubbed his sparsely thatched head, and considered. Oh – it was all too much trouble, he really couldn't be bothered. 'Take it away,' he said to Gillian, thrusting the doll into her hands.

'What shall I do with it?' said Gillian.

'Why ask me? Take it and don't come back. And I *mean* don't come back,' he added, threateningly. 'I don't want to see your face in this shop again.'

'Nor your brother, nor that other one,' added his wife.

Gillian fled. Her heart was racing and she felt quite sick. She had never been banned from a shop before. The shame of it! And what now?

Grace and Joseph were waiting on the corner. Grace's store of courage, very small at the best of times, was now totally used up. She was weeping copiously, and pushing

107

Joseph away as he tried to comfort her. 'It's all your fault; it's all your fault. You made my best friend in trouble.'

'She's coming,' said Joseph, suddenly. 'You can stop crying now, Grace.'

Grace ran to Gillian, and flung her arms round her.

'You brought the doll back,' said Joseph, puzzled.

Gillian was so upset she could hardly speak. 'It – n-n-never come from – W-w-warren's. Why did you s-s-say it come from Warren's, Joseph?'

'I must have forgot. It must be Discount after all.'

'You mixed them all up, didn't you? You forgot all of them! What we going to do now?'

Joseph shrugged. He looked at the ground and scuffled his feet. He dribbled a small stone neatly in a circle, while he waited to be told what to do next. He was not over-worried. Gillian was in charge now. He would let Gillian be in charge – she would sort it out.

'Let's just throw them all away,' said Grace. She wanted to be finished with the whole business. She wanted to get back to safe and cosy things, like the knitting she was doing for Mrs Lloyd.

Gillian shook her head. 'I don't think it would be right to throw them away. I don't think it would be *right*. They're not our things. I don't think it would be *right*.'

'We better hide them then,' said Grace.

'Yeah, we better do that,' said Gillian. 'For now. Till I think.'

'We'll hide them in a secret place that Joseph doesn't know.'

'Could I just keep the car?' said Joseph, hopefully.

'Certainly not,' said Gillian.

'Any way I tried. I tried, didn't I, Grace? Grace, didn't I try to put the things back, like you said? Are you going to speak to me now?'

'I'll *speak* to you, because you're my best friend's brother,'

108

said Grace, with dignity. 'But you haven't got to be in love with me any more.'

'Oh Grace – do you mean it's over?'

'For ever and ever,' said Grace, firmly.

Joseph was sad. The sadness did not go very deep, but any sort of sadness was unusual for him, and this lasted a full three days.

8

The Good Club

Dearest, dearest Mrs Lloyd (*wrote Gillian*)
Thank you for your lovely Xmas card and I have it by
my bed and I shall keep it for ever and ever and ever
and ever. How is your baby getting along is it going to
be born soon? Miss Kennedy is still our teacher and
they call her Kangaroo Kennedy and the class is very
naughty and me and Grace are getting worried because
we arent learning nothing. The boys are all shouting at
Miss Kennedy when she tries to teach us and they wont
listen and some of the girls shout too. There was a
nother fight yesterday between Sean and Stephen. All
the class was cheering and throwing things about. Mrs
White had to come in to stop the noise and she said our
class is a disgrace to the school and she doesent know
what she is going to do with us. and your lovely model
of the castle got broke and the houses we done with
Miss Croft but most of them was broke already. When is
your baby going to be born? I know you cannot come
back to school until your baby is born but please please
please please can you come back after. Can somebody

else look after your baby and you come back to be our teacher? PLEASE.

Love from

Gillian X X X X X X X X X X X X X

She wrote nothing about Joseph, nothing about the worry that nagged at her night and day, whenever she thought of the secret hidden in the flower-pots, the unresolved problem of what to do with Joseph's loot.

Gillian and Grace had conferred long and earnestly, in the first place, about where to hide it. The hiding place should not be in Gillian's bedroom, they decided, because that was the first place Joseph might look. And it should not be anywhere else in the house because Gillian's mum might find it when she was doing the housework. That really only left the tiny back garden, and at first they thought of digging a hole, and burying the stuff, and covering the hole over, so no one knew they had been digging. Grace still thought it would be better to burn the things, or throw them in the canal, but Gillian could not bring herself to do anything so wicked. She had no idea what she was going to do with them in the end, but destroying them was too final.

The girls chose a morning when Mum and Dad were at work, and Joseph was at the park. They found a spade and fork in the shed, and looked for somewhere to dig. But now January held London in an icy grip, and everywhere they tried, the ground was hard as rock. This was no good, they would have to think of something else.

The empty flower-pots were piled ten deep beside the shed. The doll and the necklace went in the fourth from the bottom, the other things in the one above. No one would disturb them until the spring. Or so the girls hoped. Gillian worried about them most of the time, but there were other problems too.

111

Class 4L was at the top of the school. They were fourth years, and in September they would be going to their secondary schools. 'We shall all be dunces,' worried Gillian. 'We shan't know nothing, Grace. We shall have shame when we go to our new schools because we're all behind in our maths.'

'I wish we had a proper teacher,' said Grace on the way home. The girls had been tidying the classroom, as usual, after school.

'Miss Kennedy would be a proper teacher, only the boys won't listen to her.'

'I quite like Kangaroo Kennedy,' said Grace. 'It's a pity the bad ones won't let her teach us anything, isn't it, Gillian?'

'Why have we got to be ruled by the bad ones though?'

'They make all the noise, that's why,' said Grace.

'And they make the good ones bad.' The classroom always seemed to be a terrible mess.

'I wonder if it could be the other way round,' said Grace, thoughtfully.

'What do you mean?' said Gillian.

'Supposing the good ones could make the bad ones good?' said Grace.

'How, though?'

'I dunno. Suppose the good ones was all together, and they didn't let the bad ones be the boss?'

'There's lots of good ones really,' said Gillian.

'Lots,' said Grace. 'There's Jennifer and Satibai, and Minaxi.'

'And Chandra and Richard, and Sanjay,' said Gillian.

'I know,' said Grace, glowing with the excitement of her sudden idea, 'I know, I know, I know! We could have a club for being good!'

'Brilliant!' said Gillian. 'You are clever, Grace. We could

112

call it the Good Club.' (It was a pity about the things in the flower-pots.)

'We could have badges.'

'Oh *yes*. And you have to be really good to belong. You have to do a page of sums every day.'

'And not talk out loud while you're working.'

'How will that make the bad ones good though?' said Gillian, descending into gloom again. '*They* won't care, they'll just go on being bad.' (And sooner or later, someone was bound to find the things in the flower-pots.)

'They can't join if they aren't good,' said Grace, triumphantly. 'They can't have a badge.'

'I don't think they're going to *want* a badge though,' said Gillian. 'I don't think Sean's going to want a badge.'

'Well course *he* won't. He's one of the bad ones, isn't he? He's one of the ones the club's against! And Paul . . . and Joseph. But there's plenty others, there is, you know, Gillian,' said Grace, who could see her wonderful idea beginning to drown in the sea of Gillian's pessimism. 'Shall we try it then? To have a Good Club?'

'All right, we'll *try*. Where shall we get the badges from?'

'We could make them.'

'Oh yeah – I know, that gold card in the Art room. That'd be good. Shall we ask Miss Robinson?' It was Miss Robinson who held the keys.

'Miss Robinson's away,' said Grace.

'Oh yeah, I forgot. Miss Campbell got the keys now.'

'We can't ask Miss *Campbell*,' said Grace.

'I'll do it,' said Gillian. 'You don't have to say nothing.'

'Have I got to come?'

'Well, you could just come *with* me. It's for the class, Grace. It's for *Mrs Lloyd*.'

'All right, then.'

It was dinner-time, so the teachers were all in the staff

113

room, drinking cups of tea, and eating their sandwiches, and marking books. The dinner hour was precious, and the teachers did not like to be interrupted. Miss Campbell in particular was far from pleased to be told by a colleague that two of 4L were asking to speak to her. 'That shower!' she exclaimed. 'Can't we have any peace? Who is it, do you know?'

'It's Gillian Rundell,' said the colleague. 'And that friend of hers, Grace something. The one who's always smiling when you tell her off.'

'Oh *those* little twits!' said Miss Campbell, not troubling to lower her voice. Gillian, standing at the staff room door, heard what Miss Campbell said, and wished she had not come.

'Well?' said Miss Campbell, discouragingly.

'It don't matter,' said Gillian. 'We don't want nothing. . . I mean, we'll ask another time.'

'Have you dragged me out of my chair, in my lunch hour, just to tell me it doesn't matter? Who do you think you are, Gillian?'

'We just wanted some card for our club,' Gillian blurted out.

'What club? What are you talking about?'

'Me and Grace's club,' said Gillian, faintly. 'I'm sorry we come at dinner-time. It's the Good Club. For doing good things. It's to stop them all being bad to Miss Kennedy.'

'No doubt I'm very thick,' said Miss Campbell, acidly, 'But I don't see how a piece of card is going to turn the horrors in your class into reasonable human beings, let alone saints.'

'It's for the badges,' said Grace, bravely doing her bit even though Gillian had said she needn't.

The penny dropped. 'Oh I *see*,' said Miss Campbell. She thought Kangaroo Kennedy was probably quite a good teacher, if a little wet, and with any other class she'd have

114

been fine. It was just her bad luck to have fallen into the clutches of a foul mob like Class 4L. She might have been all right with Class 4L even, if she'd had them earlier; before they had been made too unsettled, by too many changes. Miss Campbell was rather taken with the idea of the Good Club. She did not think it had much chance of succeeding, but it took her fancy to help. 'All right,' she said, unexpectedly, 'come and show me what you want – I'll give you five minutes.'

'Oh *thank* you, Miss Campbell.' They couldn't believe it, they just couldn't believe it.

'Come on then, hurry up. I haven't got all day.'

Miss Campbell gave them some gold card and some silver card, and half a packet of coloured paper squares as well. 'Do you need some glue?' she suggested, and she gave them a whole tube. 'What about safety pins to fasten the badges with?' Miss Campbell was getting quite interested, and she raided the sewing cupboard to find the safety pins. 'Don't tell Mrs Singh I gave them to you.'

'Thank you, Miss Campbell, oh *thank* you, Miss Campbell. Thank you very much, Miss Campbell.' They thought if they didn't keep saying it, she might change her mind and take the things back.

'All right, all right, that'll do,' said Miss Campbell, suddenly tiring of the whole matter. 'Good luck with your club though.'

The girls spent the whole evening in Gillian's bedroom, making badges. It was good to have something to do. No one gave them homework any more, and they had given up trying to set their own, since there was no one to mark what they had done. That left only telly in the evenings, and it was boring watching telly *all* the time. Making badges was much more fun.

They cut large circles of the silver card, and smaller circles of the gold card, which they stuck on top so that each badge was a gold disc with a silver rim. Then they cut G's and C's out of the coloured paper, and stuck those on the gold discs. It was too difficult to cut whole words out of the coloured paper, and anyway Gillian said it was better to have just initials. That way they had a real secret society, and people would wonder what the initials stood for, and get interested.

'What are you doing in there?' Joseph called, through the keyhole.

'None of your business,' they called back.

Joseph called several times to be let into the secret, and then several more times that he didn't care about their silly old secret, and he wouldn't bother to come in even if they invited him. He wouldn't come and look at their old rubbish for a million pounds, and anyway he was going down to watch telly, so there!

That night, for the first time since the Christmas holidays, Gillian went to sleep without thinking about the guilty secret in the flower-pots. And next day, instead of dragging to school depressed and apprehensive, she skipped with a light step, carrying the badges carefully in a plastic bag, eager to be there, and hopeful.

Grace skipped by her side, and Joseph trailed behind, still loudly not caring about their boring old secret. In the playground he joined some other boys who were kicking a football around, and blowing on their fingers at the same time, the little puffs of breath steaming in the freezing air. Most of the children were stamping their feet on the frosty ground, or shivering under the shed. A few girls skipped, to keep warm. Only Grace and Gillian were warm enough anyway, too excited to feel the cold.

They approached Jennifer first. 'We're having a club,' said Gillian. 'Do you want to join?'

'I don't mind,' said Jennifer, jumping up and down.

116

'Don't you want to know what the club is for?'

'Br-r-r-r,' said Jennifer, 'it's *cold*. . . . All right, what's it for?'

'It's for being good,' said Grace. 'And you have to not shout at Miss Kennedy.'

'I don't shout at her anyway.'

'You have a badge though – look!'

'Oh yeah – they're nice. Can I have mine now?'

'I suppose so.'

The badges were very large, and very grand. 'What are those badges?' asked Richard.

'It's our club,' said Gillian. 'It's called the Good Club. Do you want to join?'

The badges looked fine, but Richard suspected it might be sissy to want one. 'What's it *for* though?'

Gillian opened her mouth to explain, but Sarah from the third year shouted her down. 'Can I join?'

Gillian tried to say, 'No, it's only for our class,' but then a lot more children from the third year and Class 4D started clamouring for badges, and even trying to snatch them out of the plastic bag. Gillian turned her back on the mob, and clutched the plastic bag to her stomach. 'Go away, go away, leave me!' The mob lost interest, and drifted away.

'We'll have a meeting at playtime,' said Gillian. 'Just our class.'

'Do you think that'll work?' said Grace, who was beginning to have her doubts.

'We'll have a meeting anyway,' said Gillian, firmly. She perceived now that the two of them had given a great deal of attention to making the badges, and none at all to organizing the club. Never mind, a meeting would put all that right. She had only the vaguest idea what she would *say* at the meeting, but the important thing was to have one.

In school, Gillian wrote a note about the meeting for playtime. On the outside of the note it said, 'Pass this along but not the back row.' The desks were still arranged in rows, from the time Miss Beale had been their teacher. Along the back row sat the gang – Sean, Paul and the rest. They mustn't know about the Good Club, not yet. If they knew they could spoil it perhaps, before it was even begun.

The note went round. Because it was about a secret, there was a fair amount of interest. Even Sean, contemptuous of secrets not his own, thought the note might be about something rude, and thus worth looking at. 'Give it here,' he said, poking Chandra in the back.

'It ain't for you,' said Chandra.

'Get on with your work,' said Miss Kennedy, with little hope that anyone would take the slightest notice. She had written up a board full of maths, but only a few children were making any serious attempt to do them. The rest were breaking off every now and again to gossip or play, or shout to friends or enemies across the class, or occasionally to scuffle with their neighbours.

'I am working,' said Chandra, rudely. His mother would have been appalled to hear him. Only weeks ago, Chandra had been an exceptionally well-mannered boy – now he was getting to be as loud-mouthed as the rest.

'Quietly though,' pleaded poor Miss Kennedy.

Chandra ignored her. 'This note ain't for you,' he said to Sean. 'It says it on the front.'

Sean leaned over the desk, and snatched the well-thumbed paper. 'A meeting!' he jeered. 'About a Good Club. What's a Good Club? What's a Good Club, Paul, do you know what a Good Club is? Do you know, Joseph?'

'Must be good if it's a Good Club,' said Harjit, and the whole row exploded in mirth at Harjit's wit.

'Can't we come?' Sean called, mockingly.

'No!' said Gillian, fiercely. 'No you can't, you can't! It's

118

not for none of you boys at the back, it's only for us.'

'Oh who cares?' said Sean.

'Get on with your work,' said Miss Kennedy.

At playtime, about half of Class 4L went into a huddle under the shed. Most of the huddle were girls; the boys had decided they were more interested in football. Gillian regarded the football players warily, out of the corner of her eye.

'So what's it a Good Club for?' said Chandra, who did not care much for football.

'It's for being good so our class isn't a disgrace to the school no more,' said Gillian.

'And so we can learn,' said Grace, 'and not have shame when we go to our new schools.'

'Who's going to be captain?' said Sharon, who had come because of the badges, not because she wanted to be good.

'We haven't thought,' said Gillian, wishing she had remembered about that.

'Can I be captain?' said Sharon.

'I think Grace ought to be captain,' said Gillian. 'Because it was her idea.'

'*I* want to be captain,' said Sharon.

'Well you can't,' said Gillian. 'Grace is it. Go on, Grace, you stand on the seat and be captain.'

Grace climbed on the bench which ran the length of the wall under the shed. Once there, however, and seeing so many faces looking up at her, she was overcome with bashfulness. 'I think I rather not,' she whispered.

'*I'll* be captain,' said Sharon, climbing on to the bench, and pushing Grace down.

'But it's *our* club,' said Gillian. 'If Grace don't want to be captain, I ought to be it. I helped make the badges, not Sharon.'

119

'We ought to vote,' said Richard. 'Hands up who wants Gillian.'

Most of the assembled company thought it was only right that Gillian should be captain. Sharon went into a sulk. 'If I can't be captain I'm not going to join,' she said.

'Don't then,' said Chandra. 'We don't need you anyway.'

'Don't need you, neither.'

'So! Fatty!'

'Rather fatty than skinny like you!'

'You eat too much sweets.'

'Don't matter.'

The senseless exchange of insults threatened to take over the meeting. 'Stop it!' said Gillian, stamping her foot with frustration. 'It's going to be the end of play in a minute, and we haven't even said about the rules.'

'What rules?'

'There's got to be rules for the club. We all need rules.'

'What are they then?'

'Cheek Miss Kennedy every day,' said a new voice. Gillian turned her head and saw that Sean had joined the outskirts of the group. The other members of the gang were still playing football, but they were glancing this way. Any minute now and they would be coming too. Gillian's heart sank. 'Go away,' she said fiercely, to Sean.

'Temper, temper,' teased Sean.

'Leave off spoiling it then,' said Gillian, nearly in tears.

'What's it all about?' said Paul, coming up.

'It's the Good Club,' said Sean. 'The goody-goody club. All the good little girls and boys. Are you a good little boy, Paul?'

'Don't think so,' said Paul. He was chewing gum, with which he blew a revolting grey-ish balloon. The balloon collapsed, and Paul sucked the mess back into his mouth. All the gang was there now, grinning, and mocking. Looking at that row of malicious faces, Gillian saw all her bright hopes of the morning crumbling. 'I *hate* you, Sean,' she said, bitterly.

Sean laughed. He didn't care if Gillian hated him – it was power he was interested in, not popularity.

'It's a sissy club, innit?' said Paul.

'Yeah,' said Joseph, disloyally. 'Who cares about the little sissies in the sissy club?'

'It's a sissy club. It's a stupid club,' said Sharon. 'It's a baby club for stupid babies.'

'Yeah, it is a bit babyish,' said Richard. 'We look silly, with those silly baby badges.'

'That's right,' said Chandra, changing sides. 'Come on, Richard, let's go.'

Several children drifted away, and Sean's jibes followed them. 'Don't you want to be good no more then?'

Gillian made one last, desperate attempt. 'Let's have a different meeting. After school,' she suggested.

'Well I ain't coming,' said Sharon.

'Don't then. You'll come, won't you, Jennifer? And Satibai, and Minaxi.'

'Don't you have nothing to do with their silly club, Jennifer,' said Sharon, spitefully. 'You just make yourself look like a baby, being in a silly club like that.' Jennifer hesitated, then took off her badge and twisted it in her fingers, not sure which way the wind was going to blow.

'You wanted to be captain just now, Sharon,' Gillian accused her. 'You didn't think it was silly then.'

'Well I do now. And I'm going to tell everybody it's silly. *It's silly, everybody*!' Sharon's fog-horn voice boomed across the playground. 'Yeah, it is silly,' most people seemed to agree. 'It's no good.' 'It's a rubbish idea.' 'I don't want to be good, anyway. It's more fun being bad.'

'You didn't give it a chance, you didn't *listen*,' sobbed Grace, quite broken hearted.

'We spent all last evening, you know,' said Gillian, 'working to make those badges.'

'Good,' said Sharon. 'You wasted your time.'

Gillian flew at her. Sharon was taller and heavier, but Gillian had the advantage of surprise. She grabbed a handful of Sharon's hair and tugged so hard that Sharon roared with pain. Sharon's arms flailed uselessly – with her head held down by her hair, she could see nothing of Gillian but her feet. Sharon stamped on Gillian's feet and Gillian yelled too. She let go of Sharon's hair, and as Sharon's head came up, Gillian's nails scratched her cheek. Sharon's nails on Gillian's face were equally sharp. Grace, to her everlasting shame, abandoned her best friend, and fled from the horrid spectacle to hide in the toilets.

Most of the other children stayed to cheer. Indeed, more were arriving every moment. A fight in the playground was always good entertainment. 'Come on, Gillian,' 'Come on, Sharon!' Gillian heard Joseph's high-pitched voice, rising above the rest of the clamour – and shouting for Sharon. That hurt. More than Sharon's kicks and scratches, Joseph being on Sharon's side hurt.

The chanting attracted the attention of Mrs Singh, who was on playground duty that morning. A fight under the shed, clearly. Mrs Singh approached the mob with fear in her heart. Now she would have to separate the combatants, and they would be fourth years of course, much stronger than her. Mrs Singh was only a little bit of a thing, and she was often quite scared of the fourth years when they got angry.

The crowd opened willingly for Mrs Singh to come through; this was part of the fun of a fight – seeing the teachers break it up. Mrs Singh seized Gillian by the shoulders, and valiantly tried to drag her away from Sharon. But by this time, Gillian was in a frenzy. She was gripping Sharon's hair again, and buffeting Sharon with her knees.

Gillian's knees were hard and bony, and Sharon was getting hurt. She was quite ready to let the fight be stopped, but Gillian was beside herself with rage and disappointment, and past being aware of anything, really, except wanting to hurt Sharon.

'Stop it!' Mrs Singh begged – but Gillian would not let go. 'Somebody get Mr King, or Mr Davis! Go to the staff room! Go on!'

Two or three willing pairs of legs scuttled off across the playground, happy to be playing a part in the drama. In fact Mr Davis, who was in the hall at the time and had seen the fight through the window, was already on his way to the battleground. He separated the girls, holding them at arm's length from each other. They stood under his grip, both trembling and sobbing and wounded. The gang were still grinning – they had really enjoyed that! Mr Davis rounded on them. 'All right, Sean Adams, you can take that nasty smirk off your face for a start. And you, Paul! Useless great lumps! Why couldn't *you* help Mrs Singh? What do you think you're in the world for?'

Mr Davis marched the girls into school, and dumped them outside the open door of Mrs White's room. 'Fighting, Mrs White,' he announced, and went back to his cup of tea.

Mrs White was short on patience that morning. She had two teachers missing, and the Office were being difficult, as usual, about sending a supply teacher. Miss Campbell, whose bark was worse than her bite, had agreed to look after Miss Robinson's little ones for a few more days; but now Miss Sullivan was away as well, and Mrs White did not think the other teachers would accept any extra children in their classes after today. That meant Miss Sullivan's class would have to be sent home. And it was touch and go how much longer poor Miss Kennedy was going to last with that dreadful 4L. Though, it had to be said, she *was* bravely sticking it out. And behold, here were two of the said 4L, weeping and bleeding on her threshold, having clearly been tearing each other's hair out in the playground.

'Gillian Rundell, really!' the exasperated Mrs White exclaimed. 'I'm getting sick and tired of seeing you in trouble. What on earth is it this time?' Mrs White wasn't being fair, blaming Gillian without even hearing the story. But Mrs White wasn't feeling fair today, she was feeling too harrassed and worried to make the effort.

'She started it,' blubbered Sharon.

'Is that right, Gillian?' said Mrs White.

'Yes but—'

'*Did you start the fight, Gillian?*'

'Yes,' said Gillian, in a small shamed voice.

'Then I'm ashamed of you,' said Mrs White, severely. 'And your mother would be ashamed of you. And Mrs Lloyd, I *know*, would be ashamed of you.'

Gillian began to cry again. 'But she spoiled our c-c-club!'

'What club is this?'

'Our c-club for being g-good.'

'And is this what you call being good? Fighting like little vixens?'

'N-no.'

'*No, Mrs White.*'

'No, Mrs White.'

'You must learn to practise what you preach, Gillian. Now go and wash your faces, both of you. And get some Dettol on those scratches. Really – as though I haven't enough to do!'

(And there was *still* the guilty secret in the flower-pots.)

9

A nasty turn of events

Gillian curled into a tight little ball, her mouth down-turned, her eyes tragic. She was hiding her poor scratched face against a cushion, and refusing to speak to Joseph.

'Come on, Gillian,' he wheedled. 'I didn't mean it, I didn't mean it, I was only joking.'

Gillian sniffed, woefully, and buried her head deeper into the cushion.

'I didn't *really* want Sharon to win,' said Joseph. 'Come on, Gilly, I did want you to win *really*.'

'What's the matter with you two?' said Mum, coming in to lay the table.

'Gillian won't talk to me,' said Joseph.

'What you do to upset her?'

'Nothing.'

'Well say you're sorry for nothing, and make up.'

'I did.'

'Leave her then. You got your mates now. What about that good-looking black boy come here one time? Why don't you ask him to come over for tea?'

Joseph shuffled, and turned his head. 'I don't think I like to.'

'What you mean you don't like to?' said his mum.

'I don't think Sean would want to come to tea with *me*.'

'Why not? Is he royalty or something?'

'He *is* the king of the class,' said Joseph.

'Well, I daresay we can find something for His Majesty to eat. Go on – you ask him. You want to push yourself a bit more, Joe.'

'If Sean comes here to tea I'm going to run away,' said Gillian's voice against the cushion.

'You have got the hump, haven't you?' said her mum. 'Go on, Joseph, you ask that Sean to come. We'll get out the gold and silver plates, how about that? And we'll put the red carpet down. . . . Come on now, the pair of you, your tea's ready. Come on Gillian, put that cushion down. . . . My heavens, what's happened to your face?'

'She's been fighting, hasn't she,' said Joseph, treacherously.

'*Gillian?* I don't believe it. . . . Yes I do though, seeing's believing! I'm *ashamed* of you, Gillian. What's your dad going to say?'

What indeed? Sobbing now, Gillian fled to the sanctuary of her room. 'Come on, silly, your tea's getting cold,' her mother's voice floated up the stairs – but Gillian was beyond hearing. Alone, disgraced, clearly deserving to be shunned by the world, how would she ever live it down?

Even Grace would have nothing to do with her. All the rest of that miserable day Grace had turned her head and wouldn't look, and stood at the other end of the yard when it was playtime. And suppose Mrs Lloyd should get to hear? Suppose Mrs White told her in a letter? She had better come clean about it herself. The paper got wetter and wetter as Gillian struggled through her tears to write.

Dear Mrs Lloyd

Thank you for your kind and lovely letter its all right if

you dont anser all my letters I like to write to you anyway. But I don't think you will want to write to me any
more because I had a fight and I am ashamed and I
wish I was dead.
From your broken harted friend
        Gillian.

She was not sure if she really meant to send the letter,
but she felt better for having written it.

Since Christmas Sean had lost interest in Joseph. He was
not called for any more, or included in the gang's exploits.
Joseph was quite embarrassed about asking Sean to tea. A
refusal would hurt. But Mum said he should push himself
– all right, he *would* push himself. He took a deep breath,
and blurted out the invitation. 'All right,' said Sean
unexpectedly. He had accepted, he had accepted! Sean
had accepted, and Joseph was much too happy to ask himself why.

When Sean came to the Rundells' house, Gillian would
not speak to him, which her mother thought very rude.
'What's got into you, Gillian?' she scolded, after the boys
had disappeared into Joseph's bedroom. 'I think he's a
really nice boy – lovely manners! Wish you and Joe was
polite like that.'

'You don't know him,' said Gillian, darkly – and if Mrs
Rundell could have been a fly on the wall of Joseph's bedroom at that moment, she might well have changed her
own opinion.

'You got a bike?' said Sean, carefully preparing the
ground.

'You *know* I haven't,' said Joseph. 'My dad says they cost
too much.'

'You can get one second hand. You can get one twenty
pounds down the Portobello.'

'Yeah, but my dad ain't got twenty pounds.'

'Me and you could share a bike,' said Sean.

'Where we get the money though?'

'Yeah, well, I got an idea about that.'

'I don't want to do any more stealing,' said Joseph, uncomfortably.

'No not that, not that. Not *that*,' said Sean.

'What then?'

'There's lots of little kids at school got money. You know, from their mums and their uncles and that.'

'So?'

'Well – they could give some of it to us, couldn't they?' said Sean. 'You know, if we asked them nicely.'

'I don't get it though – why would the little kids give us their money?'

'Well – they wouldn't want to get hurt, would they?' Sean was playing with a little puzzle game of Joseph's, the sort you have to tip this way and that, trying to get all the metal balls into the holes in the picture. Sean manoeuvred the little metal balls, and watched Joseph slyly out of the corner of his eye.

Joseph looked as though he had been struck. 'Oh no! No, I don't want to do that.'

'Why not?' said Sean.

'It's bullying, innit?'

'No it ain't. Not really. I don't mean really *hurt* them. I don't mean *that*. Just make out.'

'You mean scare them?' said Joseph.

'Yeah.'

'That's bullying an' all.'

'Well – don't matter. They soon get over it. And you and me could have a bike. We soon collect twenty pounds, I reckon. What do you think?'

Joseph turned his head away. 'Nah – I don't want to.'

'All right – forget it – I'll ask Stephen.' Sean omitted to

mention the fact that he had already asked Stephen, and Paul, and Harjit – and all had declined. Bad they all were, and quite proud of it, but you had to draw the line somewhere. Besides, anything like that, you could easy get caught.

'I could think about it,' said Joseph.

'No, it's all right,' said Sean. 'You don't want to. It's all right, Stephen'll come in with me, or Paul.'

'No, don't ask them.'

'Well,' Sean shrugged. 'Make up your mind.'

'I don't see how we could really have a bike, anyway. Where we going to keep it?'

'We'll find somewhere,' said Sean.

'Where, though?'

'I know somewhere. There's a old hut, down by the canal. I see it in the summer one time. I was going to have it for my secret place.'

Long pause.

'Well, what about it?' said Sean.

'If we really don't hurt them—'

'Cross my heart.'

'All right then,' said Joseph – and immediately felt a nasty queasy qualm, as though he had crossed over an important bridge, and wasn't at all sure he liked being on the other side.

Next morning Sean moved his books from the double desk he shared with Stephen, into the empty space next to Joseph. Stephen pretended not to care; it would be great to have the desk all to himself for a change, he said. But his eyes spat jealous hatred at Joseph, before he turned his back on both of them, scowling and sulking.

At playtime, Sean and Joseph lagged behind, and hung around the downstairs toilets to see if any likely quarry would appear. The downstairs toilets were better hunting

ground than the playground. The boys would be conspic-
uous in the front playground, where the younger ones
played, but the teachers hardly ever went into the children's toilets. They were not likely to get caught there.

Barry from 1R was the first to come along, and they let
him go; Barry's family were as poor as church mice, and
couldn't afford to pay for his school dinners, let alone give
him any pocket money. Peter, from the same class, was a
different proposition. 'Get him,' said Sean, not troubling
to lower his voice since there was no one to hear. 'Hold his
arms.'

Joseph stepped behind the small boy and grabbed him.
'What you want? Let me go!' Peter struggled; he was clearly
terrified, being held by these two big boys. 'No, Sean, no
please don't hurt me! Don't hurt me, please. I'll do what
you want.'

Sean held a hand over the small boy's mouth, to stop
him calling out any more, and Joseph thought – Sean's
really cruel, I think he's going to do something really cruel.
Joseph felt the queasy qualms again, and half of him
wanted to back out, but the other half didn't, and since it
was easier just to carry on, that was what he did. Sean, with
one hand still clamped over Peter's mouth, searched
Peter's pockets with the other. A packet of chewing gum in
one, two 10p pieces in the other.

'We'll look after this for you,' he said. 'You going to
shout, if I let go your mouth?' Peter shook his head;
Joseph, still behind him holding his arms, could feel the
small body quivering all over.

'Can I go now?' said Peter.

'Not yet. . . . You got a money box at home?'

'No.'

Sean hit him. Not very hard, but hard enough to show
he meant business. 'That's for telling lies. It's naughty to
tell lies. How much you got in your money box?'

'Nothing – I don't know.'

'How much you got, I said?'

'I think it's four pounds.'

'Bring it tomorrow.'

'I'm telling my dad,' said Peter, with sudden spirit.

'*What* did you say?'

'I'm telling my dad,' said Peter, faintly.

'You want me to show you what's going to happen if you tell *anyone*? Anyone at all?'

'No! No, Sean, don't show me!'

'I think I'll show you anyway. Hold his mouth, Joe.'

Swallowing down the queasy qualms, Joseph held Peter's mouth, and Sean gave Peter's arm a twisting wrench. 'Now you going to tell? Let him speak, Joe.'

Doubled up with pain, but too frightened to cry, Peter stood between the two bigger boys, looking desperately from one to the other.

'*Are you?*'

'No.'

'If you do, there's going to be a hundred times what you just had. And if you don't bring the money there's going to be two hundred times. Go on now, and don't forget.'

Peter fled. 'Told you,' said Sean, 'it's easy.'

'You hurt him though,' said Joseph, in a troubled voice. 'You said you wasn't going to hurt them.'

'Well we got to hurt them a *bit*. Naturally, we got to show them who's boss.'

'You don't have to enjoy it though.'

'Who says I enjoyed it. Who says that?'

'Nobody,' said Joseph, miserably.

Next morning Peter arrived at school with one pound coin and two 50p pieces. 'You said four pounds,' said Sean, sternly.

'What's my mum going to say if my box is empty?' pleaded the wretched child.

'That's your problem,' said Sean. 'All right, bring the rest next week – no later, mind.'

'We can't get a bike with four pounds,' said Joseph.

'We've only just started,' said Sean.

Next day Sean and Joseph loitered again in the downstairs toilets but Mr Davis found them, and sent them out to play. 'We'll try after school,' said Sean.

They hung around, outside the gates, waiting for the mobs to disperse, hoping to catch some late home-goer. Regretfully, they had to let Prakesh Patel go. Prakesh's father kept a shop, in which all the family helped. Prakesh could have been a splendid source of income, but unfortunately he was with his two sisters, and also Nilesh from the same class. It was just too risky to take on that lot.

In the end they had to settle for Tracey, who had been helping Miss Robinson to tidy the classroom. They followed her round the corner, out of sight of school, then swooped. Tracey sensed them coming and began to run, but they caught her easily, and pinned her against a wall. Joseph felt the little heart beating wildly against him, as he held her arms with one hand and covered her mouth with the other. He tried to be tough about it, but there was no way he could make himself like what he was doing.

Tracey had just 10p in her pocket. 'How much you get Saturday?' said Sean.

'50p,' said the child, shrinking in terror from this great menacing fourth year boy.

'Bring it Monday.'

'All right.'

'Give us her arm,' said Sean to Joseph.

'She'll bring the money,' said Joseph. 'She will.' But he released the thin little arm, nevertheless.

'Just making sure,' said Sean, giving the arm a painful

twist. 'Now, now, that didn't hurt *much*. Shut up crying, Tracey. I mean it. There's a lot worse than that coming if you don't bring the money, *and* if you tell. Go on home now.'

The boys watched her go.

'Let's not get a bike, eh?' said Joseph. 'Let's get something else. Something for four pounds fifty. Eh?'

'You don't want to collect no more, do you?' said Sean, contemptuously.

'Not really.'

'You ain't got no guts!'

'Yes I have, I got plenty guts.'

'Well then.'

'Well then.' Joseph wanted to say that bullying small children for money didn't seem much like having guts, it seemed more like *not* having guts, but he most desperately didn't want to offend Sean, so he just turned his head away, and scuffled at the ground.

'Let's go home now,' said Sean. They retraced their steps to pass the school once more. 'We'll try some more tomorrow, eh? Eh, Joseph?'

'All right.' Joseph didn't want to, but he didn't want to refuse. It was all very confusing.

The distraction of Dippy Dora, coming round the corner, was a welcome relief from tension. Toe-heel, *down*, shuffle shuffle. Toe-heel, *down*, shuffle shuffle. There was something wrong with the dance today though. On the toe-heel bit she wobbled perilously, on the *down* bit she lurched, and twice almost toppled into the road. 'They're all cheats,' she shouted at no one in particular. 'All cheats and robbers and dirty saucepans.'

'She been at the bottle again,' said Sean, gleefully.

Dippy Dora staggered up her garden path and, finally losing her balance altogether, crashed into the wilderness of weeds and dead bushes which flanked it. Interested, the boys stopped to watch. Dippy Dora's arms and legs thrashed around in the bushes as she tried to find her feet. The boys crossed the road, to get a better view.

Today she was not wearing the hat with the flowers; instead she had tied a duster, like a scarf, over her head. Her coat, which had only one button, gaped open to show the torn skirt, done up with a safety pin because the zip was missing. Much-laddered stockings, adrift from their fastenings, wrinkled over the waving ankles, and one of the leaking shoes was missing. Silas, wrapped over the holey stocking, was doing duty as a shoe today. Dippy Dora was looking right at the boys, but without seeming to see. She grimaced, and the tooth went up and down, up and down, in its rapid silent gnashing. Then she began to sing, in a cracked, defiant voice. She sang, *'Daisy, Daisy, give me your answer, do,'* and when she came to *'I'm half crazy,'* Sean said loudly, 'Yes, you are.'

She saw him then. She looked right at him, with eyes that were all bloodshot. 'Get away, you dirty saucepan,' she screamed, but Sean only laughed, because Dippy Dora was sitting in the bushes, and couldn't get at him. 'I'll turn you into a frog,' she threatened.

'You can't turn people into frogs,' said Sean. He hung back though, in case perhaps she could after all. Mumbling and swearing, Dippy Dora crawled out of the bushes and made it as far as the doorstep where she sat, blinking her red-rimmed eyes, and gnashing her one tooth. A twig from the bushes, caught in her beard, went up and down with the jaw.

'You can get away, you dirty saucepans, dirty thieves and robbers. Go on now, this is my house.'

'What you got in there then?' said Joseph.

'Mind your own business.'

'Come on, tell us,' said Sean, getting really bold.

'Is it treasure?' said Joseph.

134

'*My* treasure, you thieving little saucepans,' said Dippy Dora.

'I *thought* it was,' said Joseph in delight.

'*My* treasure. . . . they're all thieves,' she shouted again. 'All robbers, the lot of them!'

'Show us the treasure then,' said Sean.

'You dirty saucepans!' she screamed at them. 'You get away from my house! Go on, go on. I'll turn you into frogs. I'll set Silas on to you!' She started to untie him from her foot, and the boys backed away with the fear of habit. She hauled herself upright and began to crack Silas in the air and against the pillars of her front porch.

'You can't do nothing to us,' said Sean, from the safe distance of several metres.

'Yes I can, oh yes I can. You'll see. One of these days you'll see what I can do. You'll see, you'll see, never you fear.' As she spoke she jabbed at the keyhole with a key that refused to find its way. 'One of these days. All you dirty saucepans going to get what's coming to you. And bad luck to the lot of you!' She got the door open at last, and the boys peered eagerly, trying to see beyond her into the house. But it was no good because there was a thick curtain inside the door, cutting off the entrance to the passage. 'You go back to your mothers,' she screeched at them, as she disappeared into the mysterious depths. 'Go where you belong and leave me alone!'

Joseph began jumping with excitement. His cheeks were pink from the cold, and the spiky hair stood up, blond and stiff all over his head. 'I knew it. I knew it. It *is* treasure.'

Sean was not convinced. 'Perhaps she just *said* that. . . . Oh look, Joe – do you see what I see?'

'She didn't shut the door properly.'

'I *dare* you,' said Sean.

'Why not you?'

'I dare *you*,' said Sean.

Yes, well, all right, thought Joseph. Yes, well, he supposed it should be him so he could prove that thing about did he have guts. So, all right then, he *would* prove it. 'I'm going,' said Joseph.

'Go on then.'

'I'm going now,' said Joseph.

'I'll wait for you.'

Joseph charged up the dilapidated path, pushed at the door and slipped past the curtain into the dark hallway. He was terrified, and proud at the same time. No child, no adult as far as anyone knew, had ever before set foot in Dippy Dora's house.

There was a strange feeling. A feeling of fear, heavy in the passageway, and drifting down the stairs. There was also a smell. The smell was going to choke him, Joseph thought. It was like fifty overflowing rubbish bins on a hot summer's day, overladen with the sour fumes of cheap paraffin. Joseph held his nose, and swallowed, and tried to forget about feeling sick – but the stench was in his mouth now, and he retched.

He knew she must hear him, wherever she was in the caverns beyond the hall, so he turned to run. Stumbling and gagging, he plunged past the curtain and through the door into the lovely fresh air again. He heard the door being slammed behind him.

Sean was looking distinctly impressed. 'What happened, then? What you coughing for?'

'Going to be sick, innit!'

'Did you see a dead body or something?'

'There was a horrible smell.'

'Probably a body then,' said Sean, hopefully.

'Well I couldn't *see* a body.'

'What *could* you see?' said Sean.

'All boxes and plastic bags. They was piled up on top of

each other, you couldn't hardly move. I couldn't see properly though, it was all dark.'

'Look,' said Sean, with relish. 'There she is!'

Dippy Dora was at the window. She had stuck her head through the curtains, and was pressing her nose against the glass. You could see the bloodshot eyes and the gnashing tooth, but Dippy Dora had wrapped Silas round the middle part of her face, to hide it a bit perhaps.

'She's *weird*,' said Sean – but Joseph thought, uncomfortably, that if he didn't know better, if he didn't know for absolute certain fact that Dippy Dora was a wicked, evil old thing, and couldn't possibly have ordinary feelings like other people, if he didn't know those things, he might suspect that she was actually *frightened*.

'Come on,' said Joseph. 'Don't want to look at her no more.'

'What was in the boxes, then?' said Sean.

'The jewels I suppose, and the money.'

'You should have looked.'

'It's all right for you saying that, you didn't have to breathe that stink.'

'You could have held your nose. *I* would have looked,' said Sean.

'Yeah – well. . . .'

'You could have took a deep breath and looked. *I* would have.'

'All right, you don't have to keep on about it.'

Joseph was irritable, conscious of having missed an opportunity, but by the time he reached his house regrets had given way to jubilation. He had *done* it. *He had been inside Dippy Dora's house*. Nothing could take that glory away from him.

He was dying to tell someone. 'What you think?' he boasted excitedly to Gillian, forgetting that they were still not speaking. '*I been in Dippy Dora's.*'

'So what?' said Gillian, coldly. She was worrying a great deal, this evening, about the stolen goods in the flower-pots.

'All right, *be* like that,' said Joseph.

He considered going next door to tell Grace, but re-membered that she was being cool to him as well. Come to think of it, he rather thought Grace and Gillian were being cool to each other. And Stephen was huffy with Sean, for moving his seat. Everyone was being bad friends with every-one else just lately, it seemed – except for him and Sean.

Joseph went into the kitchen to tell Mum about Dippy Dora's house, but Mum had just caught the frying-pan on fire, and wasn't really listening. Joseph sighed – nobody seemed interested in his exciting news.

When the glow about Dippy Dora died down, Joseph dis-covered that he was profoundly unhappy. There was a tur-moil inside him which he didn't like at all, and which he didn't know how to deal with, because he wasn't used to turmoil. He wasn't used to being miserable, either.

It was all on account of the bicycle project and the bully-ing, of course. The thoughts churned round and round in Joseph's head, as he tried to find a way out of the muddle. At last he thought that perhaps if he gave Sean the slip at home time, he could get out of doing any more bullying that day. Perhaps he could do the same thing every day, and Sean would forget in the end, but they could still be Best Mates. Perhaps.

On Friday, Sean was clearly very much displeased. 'What happened to you last night?'

'Last night? Nothing. What you mean?'

'You know. Don't make out. You and me had things to attend to. Where did you disappear to?'

'Oh that. Oh yeah – wait a minute – oh *yeah*, I remember. I had to go somewhere for my mum.'

'No you never,' said Sean.

Joseph was silent.

'You got to make up your mind, haven't you,' said Sean. 'Are you with me or not?'

Joseph kicked at the playground wall. He made his decision, but it was like jumping into a nasty dark pit. '*With* you, of course.' The winter sunshine lost its brightness, and cheer, as he said the words.

'Right. Dinner time then.'

'Dinner time?'

'You heard. We'll get Prakesh. I got an idea.'

It was a well-known fact that Prakesh Patel was passionately interested in animals. At playtime, Joseph and Sean strolled into the front playground, as though they had legitimate business there, and Sean curled an arm round Prakesh's neck. 'Joe and me got a baby rabbit,' he whispered.

'What?'

'A baby rabbit. We found it in the road.'

'Did you *really*?' said Prakesh.

'Sh-sh-sh – don't tell everybody, they'll all want to see. Joseph just now took it by the bins.'

'Show me.'

'What a mug,' Sean thought, contemptuously, not to suspect a trap. He held Prakesh's arm, and guided him towards a walled-off annexe to the playground, where stood the huge cylindrical rubbish bins. Children were not allowed to go there, of course, but the dinner ladies on duty were playing a singing game with some of the first years, and no one else noticed.

Joseph was, indeed, lurking round the bins.

'Where's the rabbit, then?' said Prakesh.

'It's you. You're the rabbit,' said Joseph, grabbing his arms.

Prakesh struggled. He was surprisingly strong for such a little boy. 'Let me go!' Sean put a hand over his mouth, and held his arm too. Between the two of them, the eight-year-old was quite helpless.

'Do as you're told and you won't get hurt,' said Sean. 'Well only a little bit. We don't want much. Just two pounds a week from your dad's shop. Only two pounds – your dad won't miss that. Every week, though. . . . Right?'

Prakesh shook his head; the heavy fringe of straight black hair swung from side to side. 'No,' he spluttered, behind Sean's hand.

'*No?* Did I hear *no?*' Sean gave Prakesh's arm a vicious twist.

'Ah-ah-ah!'

'Two pounds a week, then?'

Again the shake of the head, and the muffled 'No!'

Sean punched Prakesh in the stomach. Joseph felt the blow almost as if it were *his* stomach that was being punched. He tried to think about the bicycle. Prakesh doubled forward, and Joseph with him.

Prakesh was clearly in a great deal of pain, but his mouth was a stubborn line. 'I'm not bringing you any money, I'm not! It's my dad's money, you're not getting it.'

Sean considered. 'What you had just now,' he said carefully, 'is nothing to what you're going to have if you don't do what I *say*.' He emphasised the last word with a blow to the side of Prakesh's head.

'I ain't afraid of you,' said Prakesh.

Sean was furious. He gripped Prakesh by the wrist. 'Hold his other arm, Joe. We'll see who's afraid of who!' Sean twisted Prakesh's arm backwards and up. There was a cracking sound and Joseph thought, with sick dismay, that Sean could have broken Prakesh's arm.

'*Now* are you going to bring the money?'

'No.' He wasn't even crying. This was beginning to be serious. If the threat of pain wouldn't make Prakesh bring the money, it wouldn't stop him from telling, either. Sean considered again, and found an idea straight from the news programmes, on telly.

'How about if your shop was to burn down?'

'What do you mean?'

'You know what I mean. There was a Indian shop burned down the other day, wasn't there? Suppose that happened to yours!'

Prakesh was silent, his determination wavering at last. The great brown eyes filled with tears.

'Well?' said Sean.

'I'll see,' said Prakesh.

'You won't *see*, you'll do it,' said Sean.

'All right then.'

'And if you tell, we'll burn your shop down anyway. With all your family in it.'

'Let me go now, please!'

'Don't forget, two pounds. On Monday. Otherwise – s-s-s-s-s!' Sean's gestures indicated Prakesh's grocery shop going up in flames.

'Don't burn my dad's shop!'

'Don't make us have to. And stop that crying. *Now*, before you go back in the playground. Else we going to burn it down *tonight*.'

The little boy ran off, nursing his hurt arm. 'We better not have broke it though,' said Joseph, in a troubled voice.

'He's all right – you're just soft!'

'No, but – I mean—'

'Ah, come on!'

Sean swaggered off and Joseph followed, kicking at the ground and silent, all the way to the back playground and

141

up the stairs to class. He sat at his desk, brooding and scowling, deeply upset, and casting around him for someone to take it out on.

Miss Kennedy had written three story titles on the board. There was *A Lucky Find, The Three Wishes*, and *A Narrow Escape*. Everybody had to choose one of these titles and write a story about it. They did something like this every week, and it was very boring, and also hard to think of a good story when you only had the title to go by, and nothing else to help you.

'Why don't we *talk* about the stories no more,' Sharon complained.

'Yeah,' said Paul, 'we ought to talk about them first, didn't we!' It wasn't just that his mind was a blank, and he couldn't think of anything to write: a good lengthy discussion would stretch out the time before he was expected actually to do some work.

'It's not fair,' said Sharon.

But Miss Kennedy never had discussions about anything in her class now. Discussions almost immediately would get out of hand, and there would be shouting, and everyone talking at once, and guffaws, and eventually fighting, even. These days Miss Kennedy played safe, and just put the work on the board, and hoped people would get on with it, more or less.

'I haven't got a pencil,' whined Harjit.

'I haven't got one, neither.'

'Where's my book?'

'What have we got to *do*?'

'Mrs Lloyd always let us talk about the stories first,' Stephen called out, disagreeably.

'Well I am not Mrs Lloyd, so just do as you're told, for once,' said Miss Kennedy, sick to death of being argued with. Apart from everything else, she had a streaming cold. She felt stuffy and unwell, as well as miserable.

'*I am not Mrs Lloyd*,' Sean mocked her, under his breath.

Joseph had an idea. He tore a page out of his English book and began to draw. He giggled as he drew, and Sean looked over his shoulder, and giggled too. All the boys wanted to see what Joseph was drawing, and they all seemed to find it hilarious, but Miss Kennedy did not ask to look. She had learned from bitter experience that it was best to let well enough alone. She did not interfere even when Joseph, quite openly, took felt-tip pens out of his desk to colour the drawing. He took some Sellotape out of his desk as well.

At last the fidgeting subsided and the class, most of them, appeared to be at least writing *something*. Jennifer came out to ask for a spelling, and immediately Joseph came out too. He stood behind Miss Kennedy, while she wrote Jennifer's spelling on a piece of paper, and then scuttled back to his seat because he had forgotten, he said, what it was he came out to ask.

'Scatterbrain!' said Miss Kennedy, trying to be jolly, but nobody laughed. Only popular teachers were supposed to joke with you, and call you teasing names.

They soon *were* laughing though, all of them. It happened when Satibai put up her hand, and Miss Kennedy went to see what she wanted. Miss Kennedy stood behind Satibai, and leaned over her shoulder, and everybody sniggered. Miss Kennedy thought she might have sat in something messy, and she glanced anxiously at the back of her skirt, but there was nothing wrong. She went back to her own seat, and looked along the rows of unfriendly faces. The children were all sniggering and nudging one another, but Miss Kennedy didn't know why.

'Do you like kangaroos, miss?' said Stephen.

'Get on with your work,' said Miss Kennedy, uneasily.

Sean began to sing 'Blow me kangaroo down,' and the

143

whole back row joined in. Joseph got out of his seat, and started leaping around the room, feet together, elbows bent, and hands curled forward. The class was in paroxysms of laughter by now. Children were sprawled across their desks, and falling into the aisles, hooting and cat-calling their mirth.

Miss Kennedy went very red. They were laughing at her, that much was clear, but what was the great joke? Helplessly, Miss Kennedy felt her cheeks growing hotter and hotter.

Grace took pity. Slipping out of her seat, she came to the front and whispered in Miss Kennedy's ear, 'You got something on your back, miss.'

'What? What? Take it off for me!' Miss Kennedy snapped, too flustered to be grateful to Grace for helping her. Grace pulled, and the little hinges of Sellotape gave way. Grace handed Miss Kennedy the drawing which had been on her back. The drawing they had all been laughing at. The drawing Joseph had done.

It was a picture of a kangaroo, of course, but a kangaroo with a remarkable likeness to Miss Kennedy. For one thing it had lank hair, which real kangaroos do not have. It had spots on its face, and its nose was running. Underneath were printed the words I AM NOT MISSIS LOYD.

It was an unkind thing for Joseph to have done, and to Miss Kennedy it was the final straw. Enough was enough.

'You're a horrible lot,' she told Class 4L. 'You're a nasty, mean, cruel lot of children, and I don't wonder your teacher is ill. You probably *made* her ill. But you're not going to make me ill, because I'm not going to be here for you to do it. I'm leaving this madhouse now, this minute. And Heaven help the next poor soul who gets sent here!'

She marched out of the room, sniffing and banging the door behind her. There was shocked silence for a moment, then the accusations began to fly.

'It's your fault, Joseph.'

'Yeah, you didn't ought to have done that drawing!'

'It wasn't only me,' said Joseph. 'You all laughed.'

Gillian was feeling terrible. Even *she* had laughed a little bit, when the others did. The drawing was so clever, and so funny, she couldn't help herself.

'We done it now,' she said, remorsefully. 'We haven't got a teacher now.'

'Ahh-h-h – *we* don't want a teacher!' said Sean, scornfully. 'What we want a teacher for? Just to make us do boring old work!'

'That's right,' said Paul. 'We don't want no teacher, do we?'

'Come on you guys, let's celebrate!' said Sean. 'Let's celebrate that we haven't got no teacher. We're the greatest! Nobody can't rule us!' He picked up his chair and began crashing it on his desk lid. 'Come on, everybody. . . . We're the greatest!'

Paul and Harjit copied Sean. Stephen, still sore with Sean, looked for something different to do. The remains of lovingly built models, at the side of the room, caught his eye, and he started throwing heavy books at them, to complete the demolition. Joseph climbed on his desk and began jumping up and down, wild with excitement, screaming at the top of his voice. 'We're the greatest! We're the kings of all the world! We're the greatest!'

The fever caught on. Everyone began to shout, or throw something, or bang something. Bodies milled around the room, kicking, smashing, bumping into one another. Pictures were torn from walls and ripped. One desk got knocked over by accident, and then a few more on purpose, their contents spilling across the floor. One or two fights broke out, and the mood turned ugly. Heavy books were flying everywhere. Someone was going to get hurt.

Gillian and Grace got under their desks to be safe. It was

quite frightening, really. Why didn't someone come?

The noise brought Mr Davis eventually, of course. He opened the door and stood there, and the class took no notice of him at all. It was as though they had all gone mad. Mr Davis stood there, and the class went right on fighting, and throwing things, and turning over desks.

'Hands on heads!' roared Mr Davis.

They knew what that meant, from when they did it for Miss Beale, and automatically most of them obeyed.

'*Heads*, Sean Adams! Don't you know where your head is, boy? Now – someone tell me what all this is about.'

'Miss Kennedy left,' said Richard, in a small tight voice, suddenly aghast at what he had just been doing.

'And she's not coming back,' said Joseph, still grinning.

'To this madhouse,' added Sharon.

'Good for her!' said Mr Davis. 'About time someone made you see what a rotten lot you are. Well now, what are you going to do without a teacher?'

'We don't want a teacher,' said Sean, sullenly.

'Yes we do though, we do really,' said Sharon, looking lost and pathetic all of a sudden, though she had been one of the naughtiest while Miss Kennedy was still with them.

'Of course you do, you nincompoops,' said Mr Davis. 'All right, Grace and Gillian, will you be good enough to clear up some of this shambles? I know I can trust *you*. The rest of you had better come into my room until home time. Mrs White is out of school this afternoon, she can sort you out on Monday. I wouldn't actually like to be in your shoes on Monday morning, Class 4L,' Mr Davis added, cheerfully.

10

Disaster

Mrs White was waiting for them in the classroom on Monday. Her eyes were hard and unsmiling. The yellow teeth were not showing at all. The horsy face on the end of the long neck regarded the children with cold dislike. She regarded them like this in silence, and for a very long time. For *hours*, it seemed to Gillian, who sat in the front row, feeling more and more uncomfortable, waiting for something to break the tension.

The silence continued, and the tension mounted. Why didn't she *say* something? A few people began to cough, and fidget. Mrs White rapped the desk in front of Jennifer, and poor Jennifer cowered in fear. Mrs White never hit anyone, of course, with a ruler or otherwise, but you never knew, did you?

'All eyes this way,' said Mrs White, at last. '*This* way, Sean. . . . Does anyone not know what I mean by "eyes this way"? Why aren't you doing it then, Joseph? You think perhaps that when I say "eyes this way" I mean "all except Joseph Rundell's".'

Another long, long pause.

'Now I must say, I am extremely bored with you, Class 4L. And the other teachers are extremely bored with you as well. We all think you are a very boring lot of children.' Pause, again. 'You have had four teachers in the last three months, and you have driven every one of them away. Except Miss Beale, of course. Your behaviour to those teachers was so abominable, so contrary to everything this school stands for, that those teachers said to themselves they wanted nothing to do with such nasty children, and I for one can't blame them. . . . Am I saying something funny, Grace Johnson? Something amusing? If there is a joke perhaps you would like to share it with us. No? Then kindly control yourself.

'Do you think after such behaviour you *deserve* to have a teacher? Hands up those who think they do. . . . No one? . . . You can stop crying, Jennifer. There's a time and place for all things, and the time to cry is not now. It's too late to cry, now the damage has been done. . . . Now, you will be surprised to know, and grateful, that the kind people at the Office have forgiven you! They are sending you a teacher, and she will be here very soon. *You will behave towards her as you are behaving towards me now*. Is there anyone who does not understand how they are to behave when Mrs Burnett arrives? . . . No one? . . . Everyone understands? Good, then we can have a happy day.

'You know, this has always been a good school, with a reputation for helpful and courteous behaviour. It has always been a *happy* school. If I have complaints from Mrs Burnett about the good manners of anyone in this class, I shall have to think *very carefully* about whether I want to keep that person *any longer* in my happy school!'

There was a suitable hush. Naturally, no one wanted to attract attention to themselves when Mrs White was in this mood.

'Take out *English for Juniors*. Find page – let me see, twenty-one. Do Exercise Ten. . . . No, Sanjay, I don't care if you have done it five hundred times already, you will do it again now. Neatly. And in silence.'

They were back, Gillian thought ruefully, where they had been the day Mr er-er left. They hadn't moved on at all since then, and they hadn't learned anything.

Mrs Burnett was clearly terrified. She was small and mouselike, and so nervous when she came into the room she could barely manage the shakiest of smiles. She had been in this school before, and she knew the reputation of this class. Mrs White welcomed her with a wide display of the yellow teeth, and tried to put her at ease.

'They're a good class, Mrs Burnett – some really good workers here. I'm sure they're all going to show you their best efforts, and their best manners . . . hands up those who are going to work hard for Mrs Burnett. . . . Good, you see they are all going to work hard this morning. You will find Jennifer especially helpful, Mrs Burnett, and Grace, and Satibai – and Gillian, I'm sure. . . . One or two lively people at the back, but they won't give you any trouble. Paul, Stephen, Sean, Joseph, Harjit – bring your work to me at playtime, so that I can see what you have done. All right, Mrs Burnett, they're all yours now. . . . We'll leave the door open, shall we? You know, I'm only along the corridor *if you should need anything.*'

The silence she had left in the class accompanied Mrs White back to her room. She crossed her fingers, and prayed that the appalling performance of yesterday was not going to be repeated today.

And for about five minutes, all was well. Mrs White's threatening speech was fresh in everyone's memory; no one wanted to be excluded from Mrs White's happy school. But the work was boring, and they had had their fill of boring work just lately. Besides which, they had done

Exercise Ten before. Some people began turning back in their books, now Mrs White was no longer there to restrain them, openly copying the work from when they did it with Mr er-er. The class was still reasonably calm, but the restlessness and bickering had started. People were accusing others of jogging them, and taking their rubbers, and copying, and so on. The morning limped along, until playtime.

Mrs Burnett was really an Infant teacher, and she had very little idea of what to do with big Junior children. At playtime, she cast her mind desperately back to her college days, trying to remember anything that might have been suggested then. *Poetry writing* – now *there* was an idea! Would this fiendish lot accept it? She could only try. She went to the library, and searched feverishly for a suitable book.

'I am going to read you three poems,' she announced – and her voice sounded quavery and uncertain in her own ears – 'all about the wind.'

'Get off my desk,' said Sean to Stephen.

'I ain't *on* your desk! I ain't *near* your desk!'

'Please settle down now,' said Mrs Burnett.

'What did you say, miss, about the wind?' said Harjit.

'Come on miss, we're waiting,' said Sharon.

'I'm waiting for *you* to be quiet.'

'We *are* quiet.'

'I'm quiet.'

'No you ain't, you're calling out!'

'Ha-ha-ha!'

'Come on, miss, about the wind.'

Mrs Burnett began, but the atmosphere was all wrong. You had to be in the right mood for poetry. Class 4L were more in the mood for punishing someone – her, for a start, because she was not their real teacher, and they missed their real teacher so much.

After the first poem, the boys at the back lost all pretence of paying attention. Stephen took some picture cards from his desk, and passed them along the row, not troubling to conceal what he was doing. An audible discussion about the picture cards followed. Mrs Burnett raised her voice, addressing herself to the front of the class only. By the end of the second poem she was almost having to shout, to make herself heard.

Mrs Burnett closed the book.

'What about the third one?'

'That's all I'm going to read,' said Mrs Burnett.

'You said we was going to have three.'

'I've changed my mind, two is enough,' said Mrs Burnett.

'But you *said*.'

'That will do,' said Mrs Burnett. 'Now what I want you to do next – WHAT I WANT YOU TO DO NEXT – is to tell me some good words that you can use in writing some poems of your own. Words for describing the wind. Who can tell me a good word for describing the wind, that I can write on the board?'

There was a lot of fidgeting, and fussing, but no offerings of words.

'Oh come along,' said Mrs Burnett, feeling desperate. '*Someone* can surely think of a word. . . . Yes, dear?'

'Cold,' said Satibai.

'Yes, *cold*. *Cold* is very good.' Mrs Burnett wrote *cold* on the board.

'Freezing.' 'Icy.' 'Bitter.' 'Warm.' 'Hot.' 'Boiling.'

'All right, all right, that's enough about the temperature of the wind. How about the sound of it?'

No one could think of any word to describe the sound of the wind. Not many people appeared to be trying very hard. Grace was trying very hard, and so was Gillian, but their minds were empty blanks because the noise from the back of the room was so distracting.

'All right, I'll start you off. *Whistling*. There – I'll write it on the board. Now what else?'

'*Howling*,' said Grace, triumphantly.

'Yes, *howling*, that's very good. That's very good, dear.' Mrs Burnett felt cheered that someone had thought of such a good word, but her happiness was short-lived.

'I know a word,' said Stephen, unexpectedly from the inattentive back row.

'Well?'

'Don't like to say miss, it's rude.'

'Ha, ha, ha!' The unspeakable back row began throwing itself about, in paroxysms of rowdy laughter.

'Come one, Steve, let's have it.' 'Don't be shy!' 'He's shy, miss.' 'I know a good word too.' 'Do you want my word, miss?'

'I think we've had enough words,' said Mrs Burnett, feeling quite cold, and sick. 'Now, I'm giving everyone a piece of paper, and you can write your own poems.'

'Oh *miss*.'

'Do we *have* to?'

'I don't know what to write, miss.'

'It's not fair.'

'Will you start us off?'

'Does it have to rhyme?'

'I haven't got a pencil.'

'I can't do it.'

'I can't find my pencil.'

'Can I have a new pencil, miss?'

'Can I?'

'But what have you *done* with your pencils?' pleaded poor Mrs Burnett. 'You all had pencils before play.'

'I got one, but it's broke,' said Sharon.

'Come and sharpen it, then.'

Sharon came out to sharpen her pencil at the waste bin, and was followed by two or three others. Within a minute, there was a queue of about ten children, all waiting to sharpen their pencils. The queue was neither patient nor quiet. Of the rest of the class, most were claiming to have no pencils anyway, and therefore to be excused from doing the work; it need hardly be said that they were not being particularly quiet either.

Only a few of the children in the front were actually trying to write a poem.

'What's a rhyme for *cold*?' said Gillian to Grace. She said it tentatively, because Grace had been so distant, ever since the fight, and Gillian was too proud to push herself where she wasn't wanted.

'What about *hold*?' said Grace – and then she said, all in a rush, '*I'm sorry I ran away from you when you was fighting with Sharon.*' She had wanted to say that for a week, but somehow the words wouldn't come. Now they had spilled out without any planning at all. 'I didn't ought to have run away, but I didn't like to see you hurt. I couldn't look, I couldn't look!'

'I thought you were 'shamed of me, for fighting!'

'Oh no,' said Grace, 'I was 'shamed of *me*, for running away.'

The girls beamed at one another, radiant with the joy of being best friends again. 'Let's write our poem together,' said Gillian.

'Yes, let's do that,' said Grace.

They put their heads close, and tried to shut out the sounds of mounting chaos, welling up around them. It was not long before the missiles started to fly. Mrs Burnett was crying, helplessly.

'Don't mind them, miss,' said Grace, kindly. 'They're always like that. Look – me and Gillian is writing a good poem for you.'

Just at that moment, however, a piece of crayon hit Grace on the neck, and it stung so much her eyes began to water. 'It was you, Joseph!' she accused him.

'Not me, not me!' but he threw another one, quite

153

openly, which upset Grace and made her cry.

'Look what you done!' said Gillian furiously.

Joseph's feelings were a riot of confusion, matching the state of the class. He had not wanted to hurt Grace; he had wanted, mainly, to make himself forget the guilt he already had – the sick disgust that clutched at his stomach whenever he remembered about Tracey and Peter, and Prakesh. Particularly Prakesh. He wanted to do something wild, to blot all that out of his thoughts. 'Let's have a party, everyone!' he yelled. 'Let's have some music!' He jumped on to his desk and began to sing the words of the newest chart entry from that week's *Top of the Pops*.

A few copy-cats joined Joseph in his antics and more sang, untunefully, from their seats. Paul improvised a drum with his fists. Joseph began to run up and down the rows of desks, the centre of attention, and loving it.

Mrs Burnett fled, sobbing, from the room.

The noise in the class died away. Only Joseph was left: running across the desks, grinning and bowing, and singing at the top of his voice. 'And what do you think *you're* doing?' said an icy voice. Miss Campbell had come from the library to see what all the racket was about. Caught red-handed, Joseph stopped in his tracks.

'Get off that desk, you clown,' said Miss Campbell. 'Who do you think you are?'

'Everything all right, Miss Campbell?' said Mrs White, who had come from her room also, to investigate the disturbance.

'I wouldn't say that, Mrs White,' said Miss Campbell, grimly. 'Mrs Burnett has done a bunk, I think. And Joseph Rundell has lost *all* his marbles.'

'So I see. Come here, Joseph.'

He came, looking very sheepish.

'What were you doing on the desk this time, Joseph? . . . Just a minute dear, I'll be with you in a moment. . . . Joseph?'

'It is actually urgent, Mrs White,' said the secretary, who was standing at the door. 'There's a parent to see you. He's waiting outside your room, and he seems – *very upset*.'

'Oh,' said Mrs White. 'Just hold the fort here, will you, Miss Campbell?'

'If I must,' said Miss Campbell, ungraciously.

Under Miss Campbell's stony gaze, the class settled sullenly to work. Presently the message came that Sean Adams and Joseph Rundell were wanted in Mrs White's room. Gillian wondered what they had been doing this time. Not the flower-pots, she thought, suddenly. Oh no, don't let it be the flower-pots!

Sean and Joseph did not return from Mrs White's room. As the minutes went by, and still they had not come back, Gillian's uneasiness grew. It *must* be the flower-pots – she couldn't really think of anything else.

At dinner-time Gillian peeped into the little passage which led to Mrs White's room. Sean and Joseph were both there, looking very frightened. Joseph's chirpiness, and Sean's arrogance, were all quite gone. They were not even talking to each other. 'Joseph!' Gillian hissed – but he wouldn't look at her. Something was badly wrong.

'He's really in trouble, I know,' said Gillian to Grace. 'Do you think somebody found those things in the flower-pots?'

'Probably about being wicked to Mrs Burnett,' said Grace.

'Oh yeah, must be,' said Gillian, relieved that it was only that. But then she thought again. 'Not all *this* time, though.'

The boys did not appear in the canteen, nor in the playground after dinner. Gillian was getting really worried. She couldn't play, or savour the pleasure of being friends with Grace again. When it was nearly time for the bell, Gillian saw her mother walking across the yard. Mrs Rundell had not combed her hair at all, and her coat was fastened to the wrong buttons. 'Mum, Mum,' called Gillian, running to greet her.

'Not now, Gillian, I got to see the headmistress,' said Gillian's mum. The easy-going smile was all gone from her face; the glowing coals were dead cinders today.

'Why you coming in this way?' Gillian faltered. 'Why not the front?'

'Because I'm ashamed for anyone to see me, aren't I?' said Gillian's mum. Dismayed, Gillian retreated to the seat under the shed, where she sat with Grace's comforting arm round her shoulders until the bell went.

When they reached the classroom they found that Sean and Joseph were still missing from their seats. Gillian plucked up the courage to ask Miss Campbell. 'Where's Joseph?'

'He's gone home.'

'Is he ill?'

'No.'

It *was* the things in the flower-pots, it had to be. The stealing had been found out, hadn't it, and Joseph had been suspended.

'Where's Joseph?' asked Gillian.

'Up in his room,' said Mum, grimly. 'Where I can't see his face.'

'But what's he done?' said Gillian.

'I'm not telling you. He's broke my heart, that's what he's done. And his dad's going to break him, I wouldn't wonder, when he comes home.'

'It was partly my fault, I put them there,' said Gillian.

'Put what where? How could it be your fault?'

'Well – he been stealing, hasn't he?'

'Stealing, no,' said Mum. 'A lot worse than that. He been bullying, that's what. He hurt a little boy real bad.

He done some really cruel, vicious things, that's what!'

'*Joseph*?'

'I know – I couldn't believe it, neither. It's true though, he's owned up. . . . He was always so soft-hearted, wouldn't hurt a fly. Bit of a tease sometimes, that's all. . . . I couldn't believe it when the headmistress said, I couldn't believe it.'

She began to cry, and Gillian cried too. Gillian and her mum sat on the couch and wept together, and comforted each other, until Dad came home.

Mr Rundell was an easy-going man, but his hands were like leather, and he used them to good effect that evening. Joseph's yells could plainly be heard, up and down the street, as Mr Rundell applied his leathery hands. But although Joseph made a great fuss about the punishment, in an odd sort of way he was glad it was happening. He *wanted* to be punished. Being punished was taking away the sickening things he had done. Well anyway, a bit.

He was never going to do anything like that, ever again in his life. He was going to start his life all over again now. He was going to start again.

Next day, Mrs Rundell said she would take the morning off work to be with Joseph, who was being suspended. She didn't trust him to be left on his own, she said, after the dreadful facts that had been coming to light. Joseph said she needn't bother, because he wasn't feeling like doing anything bad today, but his mum said she would stay all the same, just to make sure. Anyway, she could do with the time to wash the net curtains, and Joseph could make himself useful as well; he could clear out the garden shed. The garden shed was a disgrace, and with spring coming along, it would be nice to have it tidy for once. Also, it would be a pleasant surprise for Dad, when he came home, to find that job had been done.

Joseph did not want to clear out the garden shed. He, personally, did not mind if things were in a muddle. He rather *liked* muddle; the chaos of his bedroom, for instance, was comforting and familiar to him. But once he had started the mammoth task of restoring order to the garden shed he found he rather liked that too. He would make a good job of it, he decided. He would make the garden shed tidier than it had ever been before. His mum and dad would be pleased with him; they would praise him; they would exclaim in wonder at the marvellous way Joseph had organized the garden shed. They would put him in charge of the shed in future. When he was grown up he could make a living, tidying people's sheds. Joseph worked with a will, singing, until dinner time.

Just before dinner, his mum came into the garden to take the net curtains off the line. When she looked to see what Joseph had been doing in the shed, she was indeed pleasantly surprised. 'You *are* a good boy really,' she said. 'You done that really good.'

Joseph swelled with pride.

'There's room for them flower-pots now,' his mum went on. 'We'll put them inside, eh? Be tidier than a ugly great pile like now.'

Joseph knew of no reason why the flower-pots should not be moved. He lifted the top few, and the rest of the pile toppled over. Out of the pots, thus exposed, spilled a necklace, a doll, a digital watch, a toy car, three ball-point pens and a very beautiful Christmas tree decoration.

'Look at all them things!' said Joseph's mum, in amazement.

Joseph was aghast. He had genuinely forgotten about the things he had stolen. Well, that was last term, wasn't it! He couldn't be expected to remember things that happened *last term*. Oh, it wasn't fair, was it, that they should appear like this to accuse him, just when he was being good!

'Look,' said his mum, still in wonder. 'There's Gillian's doll you give her. And that pretty jewellery you give Grace. . . . What's these then? What's these things ain't never been took out of their cards? These pens, and this Christmas thing? Where they come from, Joseph?'

'I dunno.' But the look on his face said plainly that he did. The penny dropped. 'You pinched them, didn't you?'

'No I never.'

'Yes you did, and you hid them in them flower-pots. Oh, Joe!'

'I never hid them in the flower-pots, I never. Gillian done that!'

'Don't you try and put the blame on Gillian! Gillian's a good girl. It's you that's breaking my heart.'

'Forgive me,' said Joseph.

'I'll forgive you up your room,' said his mum, furiously. 'Your dad'll forgive you with another good thump, I shouldn't wonder.'

'It's not fair,' said Joseph. 'Gillian—'

'Shut your mouth,' said his mum.

11

Fettered

Dearest Mrs Lloyd

Thank you for your kind letter about we must forgive Joseph and Sean what they done and I expect I will forgive Joseph one day but I will never forgive Sean never never never. Because he is too wicked. Sean and Joseph was suspended for one day and serve them rite. Sean is not speaking to nobody now he has got the hump. Anyway me and Grace are not letting Joseph play with Sean or any of the horrible boys in the back row we are going to school with him and home with him and he does not like it but hard luck.

Mrs White is our teacher now because we havent got a nother teacher and nobody wants to be our teacher. I hope your baby will be born soon and I hope you are well and your husband Winston and all the children in his school.

Love from
Gillian.

X X X X X X X X X X X X X X X X X X X X X X X

Mrs White had made a speech in Assembly about something *very sad indeed*. Two boys in the fourth year, she told everybody, two boys whom she would not name, had been guilty of a crime so grievous that it had been necessary to suspend them from school for a whole day.

She went on and on about it. Prakesh Patel's arm had been damaged. No, not actually broken, fortunately, *very* fortunately, but his parents had had to take him to the doctor, and he would be away from school for the rest of the week. Prakesh Patel was a very brave little boy, Mrs White said. Although in great pain, he had kept quiet about his hurt arm, and it was only found out when he was discovered to be crying, in bed, in the night.

And why was Prakesh Patel keeping quiet about his hurt arm? Why didn't he just tell his parents, in the usual way? Because of the wicked threats made by two boys in the fourth year. The same two boys who had injured him in the first place. Prakesh Patel had kept quiet to protect his family. Mrs White was proud of Prakesh Patel, but she would not say, because she was sure the school had no wish to hear, *exactly* what she thought of the aforementioned fourth year boys.

Never, never, never, in all her years of teaching, had Mrs White heard such a disgraceful story. When Mr Patel came to school to tell her about it you could have knocked her down with a feather, she was so shocked! And, yes, disbelieving at first. There must be some mistake, she had thought. But no, Mrs White was deeply distressed to have to tell the school that there had been no mistake. Furthermore, it turned out that other small children had been threatened, and bullied, for money. And assaulted. Mrs White would not mince her words. The un-named boys had been guilty of assault, and they could consider themselves lucky that the police had not been brought in *this time*.

Castle Street had always been a happy school, with a good name. Now two un-named villains had spoiled the name of the said happy school, and never, never would Mrs White have expected the day would come when etc. etc. But the villains had been brought to justice, and their sins had found them out, as people's sins always found them out, and let no one in this hall think otherwise, for one moment. *'Be sure your sins will find you out'*, said Mrs White, her gaze sweeping searchingly up and down the lines of children – and since most people had a few secret sins tucked away, most people felt a bit uncomfortable when Mrs White said that.

Not as uncomfortable as Gillian, though. There she sat, her face scarlet with shame, staring at the floor, thinking everyone was looking at her. It was all very well for Mrs White to say that the guilty ones were not to be publicly named. Anyone could see who was missing from Assembly. Anyone could work out that Gillian Rundell's brother was one of the suspended ones. And in any case, even before Assembly, rumours had been buzzing around the school like bees in summer time.

At playtime, Gillian tried to retire unobtrusively into a corner with Grace, to nurse her humiliation in private. But surprisingly, the other girls wouldn't let her. 'It ain't your fault about Joseph,' said Sharon, of all people, grabbing Gillian's arm, and trapping it within her own.

'That's right, it ain't Gillian's fault,' said someone else.

'Good old Gillian.'

'Gillian's a lot better than Joseph!'

'Yeah!'

Gillian and Grace found themselves surrounded by quite a large crowd of supporters. Some of the boys as well, the nicer ones, added their words of encouragement. 'You haven't done nothing, Gillian,' said Richard, and

Chandra said the same. Gillian felt warmed, and comforted, but not satisfied.

Joseph's disgrace was still her disgrace. And what he had done now was so bad as to make all the other misdeeds of his life seem like nothing. He mustn't be allowed to do it again. He mustn't be allowed near Sean, or any of the other awful boys, in case he did it again. Or something else. Perhaps worse.

'We got to guard him all the time,' said Gillian to Grace. 'We've not got to let him out of our sight.'

'All right, then,' said Grace.

'Even if he makes a fuss.'

'All right.'

'Everybody says I'm better than Joseph, don't they, Grace!'

Joseph accepted the new regime meekly enough, at first. He did not miss his freedom, because what would he do with freedom if he had it? He had finished with being bad, for ever and ever. And anyway, the girls would get tired of guarding him, sooner or later.

He even refrained from making a fuss when Gillian asked Mrs White if Joseph could change his place in class and sit next to her. Grace could move across to be in the empty desk next to Jennifer, so that Joseph could be between her and Gillian. To begin with, Joseph even found certain advantages in this arrangement. For instance, now Mrs White was taking the class, you couldn't get away with doing no work, as you could with Miss Croft and Miss Kennedy. And since Gillian was much better at school work than he was, Joseph found it quite useful to have her to copy from, sometimes. Another advantage of sitting next to Gillian was not having, any longer, to sit next to Sean.

Even *thinking* about Sean made Joseph feel sick, still.

It was a pity the girls weren't being nicer to him, though. They escorted him to and from school, they stood over him in the playground, but they wouldn't *speak* to him at all, except to boss him about. Every time he tried to start a friendly conversation they cut him short, or just ignored him. Joseph persevered. 'It's *Star Trek* tonight,' he said, going home on the third day.

'That was a good story Mrs White read to us, wasn't it, Grace?' said Gillian, over Joseph's head.

'You going to watch it?' Joseph persisted. '*Star Trek*. Tonight. On telly. You going to watch it, you two?'

'I liked the bit about the prince got the magic ring out the bottom of the sea,' said Grace to Gillian.

'You going to watch *Star Trek*, Grace? I am,' said Joseph.

'I got better things to do,' said Grace, coldly.

'What better things?'

'Don't ask personal questions.'

Joseph sighed. It was not like Grace to be so snappy and unkind. He stopped to talk to a friendly dog, which wagged its tail, inviting play. Joseph picked up a twig from the pavement, and threw it for the dog to fetch. 'Leave that dog alone, Joseph,' Gillian called. 'You've got to go straight home, our mum said.'

'That's right,' said Grace. 'You got to go straight home Joseph, your mum said.'

He regarded, with envy, the groups of boys and girls spaced along the pavement, free to dawdle and play, if they wanted to, on their way home. How dreary his life had become!

At home, Gillian made Joseph do his homework, and he couldn't get out of it because Mum and Dad backed Gillian. 'You can't watch *Star Trek* till you've done your maths,' said Gillian. And when he thought he'd finished, Gillian scolded him and thumped him in the back because the work wasn't tidy enough, and wrong as well. He was getting to dislike Gillian, Joseph decided – really dislike her. He brooded, and plotted vaguely.

'Mrs White's going to be not pleased about your homework, Joseph,' said Gillian, self-righteously, on the way to school on Monday.

'Yeah,' said Grace, 'she's going to tell you off.'

Joseph wondered whether, in that case, it was such a good idea to go to school at all.

He was walking between Gillian and Grace. Like gaolers, they marched on either side of him. 'Look!' he said, pointing upwards.

'What?'

'Up there!'

'What about up there?'

'A flying saucer!'

'Where? I can't see. . . . Oh, he's gone. He's gone, Grace, we got to catch him!'

Joseph sped down the road. He leapt over the first low wall he came to, and crouched there. Running footsteps stopped by the wall. 'Come on, Joseph, we see you!'

Joseph went on crouching. Maybe they couldn't see him *really*.

'Come on out of there, you going to get told off, hiding in somebody's front garden.'

They *could* see him. Feeling silly, Joseph stood up, and allowed himself to be led schoolwards again.

At playtime, he sulked. 'Don't look so miserable,' Gillian scolded him.

'Let me play football then.'

'No.'

'It's all right. Sean ain't playing.'

In fact, Sean was sulking too, on the other side of the playground. He knew he was in serious disgrace about the bullying. The disgust and revulsion felt by the grown-ups had been made very clear to him. Even his mother, usually indulgent, had turned against him because of the bullying. Evidently it was a very bad thing he had done. Not in the same category as stealing, or baiting teachers – something much worse. Sean was not sure how acceptable he was now to the other boys. Safer to snub *them*, than have the humiliation of being snubbed first.

'Don't matter whether Sean's playing – *you* ain't playing,' said Gillian with total disregard for Joseph's feelings.

'You can't stop me,' said Joseph, trying to break past the girls. But they grabbed him, and some of the other girls helped, thinking it fun to make a prisoner of silly Joseph Rundell. They forced him on to the seat under the shed, and stood over him, and Joseph sulked some more.

After school, he thought, he would really get away. He began to put all his mind into thinking how he was going to do it.

'I forgot my homework,' said Joseph, when they were nearly down the stairs.

'You'd forget your head if it wasn't screwed on,' said Gillian sharply.

'I'll just go back for it.'

'Hurry up, then, Grace and me'll wait for you here.'

'You can go home if you like,' said Joseph.

'We'll wait for you, and you know it,' said Gillian.

They sat on the stairs, and waited for Joseph to come back. They waited, and waited. 'He's taking his time,' said Grace, doubtfully.

'We can't have missed him though.'

'He couldn't have climbed out the window, could he?' Grace suggested. 'At the back?'

Gillian shook her head. 'It's too high up, he's not that mad. . . . Oh Grace, Grace, I just thought.'

'What?'

'The little stairs.'

'You go and look,' said Grace. 'I'll stay here in case he comes.'

Gillian ran to the other entrance, but Joseph was not there. Fearfully, for the second time in her life, she climbed the little stairs, but Joseph was not on them. She looked right into the boys' toilets, which the girls were not supposed to do. No Joseph, nobody. She went to the class-room, and there was only Mrs Smith, the cleaning lady, sweeping the floor. 'It's a easier job cleaning your class now the headmistress is your teacher,' she said.

'Have you seen my brother?' asked Gillian, but Mrs Smith had not.

'He's tricked us,' said Gillian bitterly, to Grace, at the foot of the main stairs again. 'He's run off somewhere.'

Joseph was making for the canal. Running, skipping, leap-ing down the road, free as a bird and exultant, he passed Paul and Stephen and Harjit. 'Naughty boy!' they jeered. 'Where's nanny then?' 'I'll tell Gillian!' 'Who's a naughty boy, running away from his nanny?' 'Ha-ha-ha!'

'Get lost,' called Joseph, happily.

He passed Sean, mooching home all by himself. By mutual consent, the boys did not speak.

Joseph's first thought had been to go to the park, where there were swings, and slides and a roundabout. But then he thought the girls could find him easily there, so he de-cided to go to the canal instead. There was an old hut, wasn't there, the one Sean wanted to keep their bicycle in. He could hide in there till it got dark, if he wanted to, and nobody would bother him.

He found the hut, but it was locked up. He walked all round, but could find no way in. Some secret place! Some secret place, and you couldn't even get in. Anyway, on second thoughts Joseph didn't really want to hide in the hut. It would be boring in the hut, with nothing to do, and in any case there was no need. The canal was deserted, there was no one to see him. He could run, or shout, or throw stones in the water, and there was no one to see, and tell Gillian where he was.

For about ten minutes he did all those things by turns. Along the towpath, flanked by scrubby grass, Joseph ran. He circled his arms, and filled his lungs, and crowed and whooped with joy. On one side of the canal was the sheer face of tall buildings, rising out of the murky water; on the other side was a patch of wasteland, letting in light. Then the wasteland finished, and there were tall buildings on both sides of the canal. It was darker suddenly, and lonely. The oily water was black and full of rubbish. In fact, it was just a little bit creepy on the towpath, the fading winter light blocked out by high walls, the moored boats deserted, the straight ribbon of water stretching ahead and ahead and not a human being in sight.

Joseph began to feel uneasy. This was the sort of place where bad things happened. Strangers, for instance. Suppose a Stranger were to appear, the sort of Stranger you were warned not to talk to, or go with? If one of those Strangers came walking down the towpath now, and decided to capture him, there was not much he could do about it, was there?

Perhaps he had better turn back. If he hurried, there might still be time to go to the park, and play on the swings, with other kids around for safety. Joseph hesitated a moment, then began to trot back the way he had come. When he came to the wasteland bit again he felt less anxious, less trapped. True, there was a high, spiked railing, between the towpath and the wasteland, but he could climb that easily, and run, and escape from any Stranger that might be around.

Joseph's steps slowed. He didn't want to go home yet,

and he didn't really want to go to the park, either. The park was so ordinary. The canal was quite ordinary too, in summer, with people fishing, and the longboats creeping up and down. This was different – almost an adventure. He looked at the clusters of plastic bags, cardboard boxes and old shoes, moving sluggishly in the filthy water. Perhaps it wasn't all rubbish! Perhaps somebody dropped something valuable in there, for him to find, and get famous.

That white box, for instance; now there was something didn't look like anybody actually *threw* it in. It looked like a jewel box, with jewels in it. Some dark night a robber, perhaps, just robbed a house, and ran along the towpath to escape the police, and the jewel box fell out of his hand, and he couldn't stop to find it, in the water.

The longer Joseph regarded the little plastic box, the more he was convinced it was full of precious jewels, just waiting to be recovered. The box was floating quite near the edge. He could reach it, probably, if he lay on the bank and stretched.

The tufts of grass at the edge of the canal were soggy from recent rain, and oozing with mud. Joseph was vaguely aware that he was going to be told off for having a dirty coat, but hardly troubled, with this exciting prize almost within his grasp. He stretched with both arms, but his fingers could not quite reach. He wriggled further down the short bank, and felt himself sliding. That would not do! He dug the fingers of his left hand into the grass, holding on tight, while he stretched with his right.

He had it! The tips of his fingers touched the little floating box and curled to claw it in. But the fingers clawed in empty air. His touch had only pushed the box away, and now it was bobbing about, several centimetres further out than before, completely out of reach.

Joseph grunted with disappointment. He wriggled backwards up the bank and clambered to his feet. Something to hit it with! A stick! Joseph looked around the bank, and up and down the towpath. Nothing of any use. There was someone coming, though. A man and a dog it looked like, a long way away still, but coming towards him in the dark winter light.

A Stranger? Perhaps he ought to run, just in case. But he couldn't leave the jewel box now! The little box full of treasure, that was just waiting to be fished out of the water.

Joseph began threshing about in the bushes along the railings, still looking for a stick. The sleeve of his coat caught on a thorn, and tore. Joseph's coat was a very smart anorak, light grey with red, white and blue stripes down the sleeves and across the front, and Joseph was very proud of it. No one else at school had an anorak like that. It was a pity it had got torn, and that was something else he was going to get told off about, but never mind. Never mind, never mind, the box was the thing, and he could buy a new coat, probably, with the treasure.

Ah – that would do! A piece of broken railing, almost buried in the undergrowth, one end still embedded in the ground. Joseph wrenched and pulled at the rusty metal. It came up suddenly, and Joseph ran back to where the little white box still floated, jostling a mass of scummy debris, a metre or so from the bank.

Joseph was quite trembly with anticipation and excitement. He lifted the railing and tried to aim so that the end would hit the water *behind* the little box; then he could tap it, and coax it gently in to shore. But eagerness made him misjudge. The end of the railing came smartly down, right on top of the box. The weight of the railing coming down pulled him also, and he felt his feet beginning to slip. He dropped the railing, and sat heavily on the bank, to keep from falling into the water. The box ducked for a moment, bounced up, and settled down to float further along, parallel with the bank. Joseph scrambled to his feet and ran beside it, waiting for its pace to slow, so that he could have another go.

Then to his delight, he saw that the box was not moving *quite* parallel with the bank, it was actually coming in at an angle – slowly, slowly, drifting towards the grass and the mud at the edge. Joseph held his breath, willing it to come nearer. Its movement slowed, slowed, stopped. Half a metre from the edge, the box halted; surely he could reach it now!

Down into the mud again, reaching once more with both arms. Nearly, nearly! Joseph's knees dug painfully into the grass. One more stretch, just one! He took a deep breath and . . . *was suddenly completely submerged in filthy, icy water.*

He came up, for a moment, and began to thresh. He could swim a bit, but he'd never tried before like this, fully clothed for a winter's day. He opened his mouth to yell, and his mouth filled with water as the sodden quilted anorak dragged him down again. Threshing desperately with arms and legs, he somehow floundered to the edge, and grabbed at a tuft of grass. He held on, and his head was above water so he wouldn't drown, but he couldn't haul himself out. The water was colder than anything he had ever experienced. It was like holding a piece of ice in your fingers, and feeling like that all over. He shouted, and his voice sounded thin and far away in his own ears. He doubted very much if it was loud enough for anyone to hear.

Joseph's face was against the bank, and his hands were above the level of his head, clutching the tuft of grass. The first he knew about being rescued was the feel of a large, rough hand over his. The hand grasped, and pulled, and a warm voice said, 'Come on, son, it's a bad time of year for swimming.'

Joseph stood on the towpath once more, dripping, and shaking with cold and shock. His teeth chattered uncontrollably. 'Well, you're a dismal sight,' said the warm voice again, and Joseph found himself looking into twinkling blue eyes, set in a weatherbeaten face.

'I fell in,' said Joseph, unnecessarily.

'You better get home quick as you can, and out of them wet clothes.'

'My sister's going to nag me r-r-r-rotten.'

'Your sister! Blimey! But you'll catch your death if you stay like that. Where do you live?'

'Tower S-s-s-street.'

'Near Castle Street School?'

'Y-y-yeah.'

'Blimey, that's over a mile. You'll have double pneumonia by the time you get there. Best come to my place and dry off. It's only round the corner.'

'Could I dry off good enough so my sister won't know I been in the water?'

'Shouldn't like to get the wrong side of your sister, by the sound of her.'

The owner of the voice and the hand and the twinkling eyes pushed Joseph firmly along the towpath to make him go faster, while a concerned-looking small dog ran by his side, looking anxiously into his face from time to time. 'She's worried about you an' all. The most tender-hearted bitch in London I reckon she is, ain't you, girl! Ain't you, Bess!'

'My place' was the ground floor of a small terraced house, in a side street right by the canal. Its owner was called Alf Jennings, and he lived all by himself, he said, so it was nice to have visitors sometimes. He didn't even have workmates to keep him company these days as he was retired, and a pensioner. Bess was the only company he had, except when he was fortunate enough to come across people

172

who had fallen into the canal, and needed drying off.

There was a gas fire in Alf's sitting room, and it gave out a wonderful heat once it got going. Alf found a huge bath towel for Joseph to wrap himself in. 'I'll go and make us a cup of tea,' he said, 'while you get out of them wet things.' Joseph was still shivering, but not as much. Alf took the clothes into the kitchen, and put them in the spin drier. Then he arranged them on a drying horse in front of the gas fire where they steamed, and stank of canal water.

'Be all right when they're dry,' said Alf. 'Pity about this tear. Nice smart coat like that. Smartest coat I ever saw. . . . You feeling a bit better now? I'd give you a drop of brandy to warm you up, but you're a bit young, and your mum might not like it.'

They drank more hot, sweet tea, and Joseph watched his clothes getting drier and drier. Finally there was hardly any steam coming off them at all, and Joseph thought he should be dressing now.

'All right,' said Alf. 'I'll just go out and do the cups a minute, while you make yourself respectable.'

The clothes felt stiff and funny, but nice and warm from being by the fire. There were greenish stains on the light grey anorak, and the sleeves were still a bit damp, but no matter.

'I'll walk you home,' said Alf. 'Not too good for a youngster to be out on his own after dark. Some funny characters about, these days.'

On the way home, Joseph remembered about the box in the canal, the one with the jewels inside. He'd gone off the canal just now – but one of these days he might, he just might, go back and look for it again.

12

A daring climb

'Your dad's out looking for you!' said Mrs Rundell, torn between anger and relief. 'Where you been?'

'Nowhere,' said Joseph.

'All this time? Do you know me and your dad was going to the police if you didn't show? Why didn't you come straight home from school with Gillian?'

'I been late home other times.'

'Not so late as this – and it's pitch dark!' said his mum.

'I been out in the dark before,' said Joseph.

'Other times you was with your mates. Them wicked boys that got you into trouble, but still!'

'That's who I was with this time.'

'Don't lie, Joseph,' said Gillian. 'You coat's all tore,' she added, accusingly.

'You didn't have to say that,' said Joseph, turning on her.

'Yes she did,' said his mum. 'Look at the state of it! What you been up to?'

'It's wet, too,' said Gillian. 'The sleeves are wet.'

'It was raining,' said Joseph.

'Only on the sleeves? What's these funny green marks?'

'Nothing – they been there a long time.'

'You're not telling the truth. He's not telling the truth, Mum.'

'Come on, Joe, tell us where you been, there's a good boy.'

'All right, I'll tell you,' said Joseph. 'I got caught by a Stranger.'

'What you on about?' said his mum.

'Don't listen to him,' said Gillian.

'It's true. He took me to a house. I don't know where the house was. He kept me prisoner all this time – that's why I'm late.'

'Oh Joe,' said his mother, her face going white, 'what he do to you?'

'Nothing. I escaped.'

'I'm getting the police.'

'No, don't get the police,' said Joseph hastily. 'He didn't do nothing to me. I got away.'

'He's making it up,' said Gillian.

'No, I ain't, it's true. He locked me in a room, upstairs. And I climbed out the window and escaped. That's how my coat got tore.'

'How did you get home if you didn't know where the house was?' said Gillian.

'I just walked round and round till I found my way.'

'I'm getting the police,' said his mum. 'What did he look like, this fellow?'

'He was a great big Kojak man, with a scar down his face.'

'He's making it all up,' said Gillian, disgustedly. 'I heard that story before.'

'Yeah, I think you're right. But he's been up to *something*. You got to watch him, Gillian. More than you was before. You got to watch him all the time. Don't let him out of your sight, from now on.'

'Oh Mum!' said Joseph.

'Shut up, you,' said his mum, not smiling at all.

'I'll watch him,' said Gillian, grimly. 'I'll watch him so he can't *breathe* without I know he's doing it.'

They were being horrid to him. Just because he did one bad thing, once. Even Mum had turned against him. And now it looked like he wasn't going to have any more fun, ever.

The world was all grey, and sad. Gillian and Grace were like limpets, the way they clung to him. He couldn't stand it. They moaned at him if he dragged his steps coming home from school, they poked him to get on with his work if he daydreamed in class. They humiliated him in a hundred ways. They even stood outside the boys' toilet every time he went in, waiting to escort him again the minute he came out. Everyone was laughing at him, sniggering and whispering about him. Joseph was getting to be really miserable; not just when the others laughed at him, but all the time.

'I'm going off you, Gillian,' he said, quite bitterly, when she scolded him in the playground in front of a great mob of grinning girls.

'That's all right, I went off you a long time ago,' said Gillian, with a superior little toss of the head.

Gillian was looking very pleased with herself, in a cross sort of way, Joseph thought. She was always thinking she was better than other people, these days. Grace was bad enough, but Gillian was a real pain, and Joseph was getting to hate her, almost.

He tried a few more times to give the girls the slip, but they were always too quick for him. Once he nearly made it. The children were all collecting their coats from the rack outside the classroom, ready for going home. When Sharon started an argument with Gillian, about whose pencil it was on the floor, Joseph nipped behind the coat rack and stood very still, hoping Gillian would think he had run along the corridor and down the stairs. Gillian began to lament.

'Where's Joseph? Who's seen Joseph?'

'He's gone, innit,' said Sharon.

'Why didn't you watch him, Grace?'

'I'm sorry, I forgot.'

'You're not supposed to forget,' said Gillian, sternly.

'There he is,' said Sharon. 'I can see his feet.'

The girls hauled him out. Gillian and Grace held him by the arms, and suddenly the last vestiges of Joseph's good humour left him. He began to struggle wildly, lashing out with his feet, and digging his elbows into the stomachs of his captors. 'Leave me! Leave me!' He was snarling with rage and frustration, he didn't sound like Joseph at all.

'Ow!' said Grace, letting go.

Gillian was not strong enough to hold Joseph alone. He wrenched away from her but lacked the spirit, now, to make a real bid for freedom. In any case, the mocking faces of a dozen watching girls and boys told him he would certainly be caught, and brought back.

Nobody was on his side. They were all against him, making fun of him. He cowered against the wall, kicking the skirting with his shoes, his head turned away so no one could see he was nearly crying. 'I feel like I'm a animal in the zoo,' he said to the wall. 'I'm just like a animal.' Near his kicking feet lay two wax crayons, a red one and a blue one, spilled that afternoon by someone in too much of a hurry. Joseph picked up the red crayon and scrawled along the wall, in great big letters, I HATE EVERYBODY.

'Look what you done!' said Gillian, scandalized.

There was a swelling chorus of *oohs* and *ahs* and *Joseph you're going to get in trouble now*, which brought Mrs White out of the classroom, where she had been tidying some books. She was absolutely exhausted from trying to be

177

headmistress and 4L's teacher at the same time. The sight of Joseph's addition to the decor of the corridor was the last straw.

'That's it,' she declared. 'No Art for you tomorrow, Joseph Rundell. You can have a bucket of soapy water, and scrub that absurd exaggeration, which I'm sure you don't really mean, off the wall. I expect it will take you a nice long time, but if there *is* any time left over you can write some lines. *I must show respect for school property.* No, you *can't* do it now, you can do it tomorrow during Art.'

It was a mean punishment, Mrs White knew quite well how much Joseph loved Art. But Mrs White was feeling mean that day. Life was hard for her just now, as well as for Joseph.

The following afternoon, having settled the class to some painting, and despatched Joseph into the corridor to do his scrubbing, Mrs White surveyed Class 4L sadly. They were a depressing sight, Mrs White reflected. She observed their discontented faces, and the spiteful little feuds going on here and there, all over the room. They were under control now, but the heart had gone out of them. The only one who could manage them *and* inspire them was the absent Mrs Lloyd, it seemed. Come back, Mrs Lloyd, all is forgiven!

Mrs Lloyd had her faults, of course, like everyone else. She had a bad habit of forgetting to mark the register, for instance, and her Record Book was never handed in on time. But she was a genius in the classroom, and the kids adored her, and Mrs White would infinitely rather be imploring Mrs Lloyd to hand in her Record Book, than teaching her horrible class.

Mrs White looked at Gillian Rundell and Grace Johnson – two of the nicest little girls you could wish to meet, at one time. Now Gillian's manner was quite ill-tempered and shrewish. And Grace looked really unhappy. It occurred to Mrs White suddenly that Grace was trying to go along with Gillian, and not quite managing it. And that Gillian was giving Grace a hard time, as well as her brother. Someone ought to have a word with Gillian, but this was a tricky matter, and needed careful handling, and Mrs White didn't think her own tact was up to it. Mrs Lloyd would have known what to say.

Then there was Sean Adams. Mrs White had never thought the day would come when she would actually feel sorry for *that* nasty piece of work. But the day had come, and she did feel sorry for him. How were the mighty fallen! No longer king of the class, Sean slumped dejectedly in his seat by the window, looking at no one, talking to no one. He had behaved abominably, of course, and deserved to feel rotten. But someone ought to be helping him learn from his mistakes, and get back his self-respect. Come back, Mrs Lloyd!

There were others, too, who were missing their teacher badly. All round the room, their faces showed their need. This had always been a difficult class, and Mrs Lloyd had done wonders with them. She had had them since the beginning of the third year, and it was always assumed that she would see them to the end of their Junior School lives. She *might* come back after the baby, of course, but somehow Mrs White didn't think so. Not soon enough to be Class 4L's teacher again, anyway.

Mrs White thought she had better peep round the open door, to see how Joseph was getting on with his cleaning job. He was being very quiet about it.

He was being quiet because he was not there. There was a nice pool of soapy water round the bucket, and the red letters had turned to pink, but the scrubbing brush was on the floor, and Joseph was nowhere to be seen. 'Richard, go to the boys' toilet,' said Mrs White, 'and see if Joseph

Rundell is there.' Mrs White had already forgotten about feeling sympathy for Class 4L; now she felt only annoyance again. And Joseph was not even in the toilet. 'Go round the school and find him,' Mrs White told Richard and Sanjay, grinding her yellow teeth with rage.

In the first instance, Joseph *had* gone to the toilet. He hadn't bothered to come in and ask permission, because Mrs White might say no, and anyway he wouldn't be long. But when he came out, and saw the long empty corridor in front of him, with no one to see which way he went, it occurred to him that there was nothing to stop him from taking as long as he liked. Without planning it, in fact, he was free!

Freedom, glorious freedom! Joseph's spirits, heavy as lead till now, began to lift. Where should he go? Well, down the little stairs for a start. The little stairs were right by the boys' toilet – nearer, even, than they were to the classroom. Fate had clearly placed them there with just this occasion in mind. Joseph's spidery legs tripped nimbly down the stairs, and round the first bend.

If he could get to the playground, he'd have it made. Once there he could run faster than anyone could catch him, and the liberty of the streets would be his. For the whole afternoon. No matter about afterwards. Joseph was like a starving person who suddenly sees a delicious meal spread in front of him, and can only think of filling his empty stomach.

Just round the first bend, Joseph stopped. His sharp ears had caught a sound from way below – a throat being cleared! There it was again – nearer now. Oh disaster, there was someone coming up the stairs! Heavy footsteps, one of the men teachers, probably. Mr Davis, maybe, his class was having music; you could hear them singing in the hall. Joseph did not want to be caught by Mr Davis, and nagged for being on the wrong stairs, and sent back to his class when he had only just escaped.

He turned, and charged back up the way he had come. He was going to hide in the boys' toilets again, when his eyes lit on something more exciting. Another forbidden staircase – going *up* this time. Joseph knew before that it was there, of course; he passed it every day. But he didn't know where it led; he had never heard anyone mention what was at the top. Since this was his day for having adventures, Joseph ran up the little twisty staircase.

On a small landing was an open door. Joseph slipped inside, and instinctively stood inside the door, just in case. There was a pleasant smell of sharpened pencils, and new ink, and plasticine. Of course, of course, this was the Stockroom! The mysterious Holy of Holies, where only the teachers ever went. The place where all the goodies came from, the paints and the new rubbers, and crayons, and so on. Joseph stood still, breathing the lovely smells.

The footsteps he had fled from in the first place, kept on coming. Too late, Joseph wished he had hidden in the boys' toilets after all. The footsteps halted outside the Stockroom door. Joseph stopped breathing. He heard the throat being cleared again, and then – *someone was coming into the Stockroom*.

The door swung further open, catching Joseph a painful blow on the forehead, which he managed to be very brave about. It was Mr Davis all right, Joseph had recognized the strains of the theme from *EastEnders*. Mr Davis was rummaging through the piles of new exercise books, and humming to himself. Well, that was all right, he would go away in a minute.

He did.

The heavy footsteps tramped out of the room. The door

181

swung away from Joseph's face, and slammed shut. And there was the unmistakable sound of a key being turned in the lock. Joseph said a bad word.

The Stockroom had only one small window. It was quite high up – Joseph had to stand on a pile of books to reach it – and since it was never opened, ever, it had got quite stuck. Joseph strained and struggled, but he could not get the window to open. He was trapped then, his briefly won freedom all gone. More than that, how was he to get out of the Stockroom? He went to the door, and started banging and shouting.

'What's all that banging?' complained Mrs White. 'I can hardly hear myself think!'

'It's Mr King's class,' said Sharon. 'They're having woodwork, I think.'

'Go along and ask Mr King if he can possibly have woodwork a bit more quietly,' said Mrs White.

Richard and Sanjay returned from their expedition around the school. 'Well,' said Mrs White. 'Did you find Joseph?'

'No, Mrs White, he isn't nowhere.'

'He isn't *anywhere*, you mean.'

'Yes, Mrs White, he isn't anywhere.'

'There's a terrible lot of banging going on still.'

'It's Mr King's class,' said Sanjay. 'They're having woodwork.'

'I don't care for that mess, Sharon,' said Mrs White. 'I don't think you've really tried. If a job is worth doing, it's worth doing well. . . . Now, we shall have to have a proper search for that nuisance, I suppose.'

Joseph gave up trying to attract attention. There was no need to be particularly worried, he decided. One of the other teachers would come soon to get some more things out of the Stockroom. Or someone would come up the little stairs, and he would hear them, and he could shout again then.

He moved round the room, looking at all the lovely tempting things. Great sheets of white drawing paper; wax crayons in untouched boxes; packets of plasticine in corrugated strips of bright unspoiled colour; and felt-tip pens, thick ones and thin ones, just asking to be used. Joseph took a sheet of white paper and began to draw, sprawled on the floor, absorbed for the moment, quite happy.

Mrs White had sent two more children to look for Joseph, and she had also sent a message to Mr Jones, the caretaker; but Mr Jones was off duty just then, and could not be found.

'Where can he be?' Gillian fretted. She could take no pleasure in the Art lesson, though usually she enjoyed it too. 'Have you been having any more feelings?' she accused Grace.

'No,' said Grace.

'I don't think you're telling me the truth.'

'I am, I am,' Grace insisted. But she turned her head away, and wouldn't look Gillian in the face.

Joseph had finished his drawing, and coloured it in with the felt-tip pens. He had made a picture of the zoo. There was a row of cages with different animals in them, and in the middle cage was a boy instead of an animal. The boy had spiky fair hair, and spidery limbs, and bore a remarkable resemblance to Joseph himself. All the people who had come to the zoo were laughing and pointing at the boy in the cage. Joseph thought his picture was quite good – it was probably good enough to go on the wall. But then he thought he didn't want it on the wall, because he didn't really want to show his inside hurt to other people. So he crumpled the picture into a little ball, and threw the crumpled ball into a corner of the dusty room.

Nobody seemed to be coming. Joseph had no idea how long he had been in the Stockroom, but surely it must be playtime, nearly. Perhaps it was home time, and everyone had gone. He went to the door, and banged again, but without much hope. Then he went to the window, and struggled once more to get it open.

Joseph thumped the base of the window, trying to loosen it. He pushed again, and thought he felt it move, just a tiny bit. Encouraged, he thumped some more, then pushed with all his might. The window shot open.

Hooray! Joseph's heart beat faster. He stuck his head out of the window, to assess the prospects. They were not particularly good; a ledge just below the window, but after that a sheer drop to the ground. He looked to the left, and there was only a corner of the building: Joseph could not see round it. He looked to the right, and there was another window, and beyond the window a drainpipe. If he could reach the drainpipe, he could get into the playground easily.

Joseph considered. He was frightened, but trying not to be. Well – they did it in films, and on the telly, so it was bound to be possible. The ledge below the Stockroom window continued as far as the other window. It was about ten centimetres wide. Well – what was it there for, Joseph reasoned, if not for people to climb along? He pulled himself on to the narrow window sill, and pushed his legs through the small opening. He had to curl up to get the rest of him out, and that was scary enough, let alone the next bit.

He sat on the ledge outside, and the February wind stung his face and struck right through his pullover. Joseph shivered. His hands were still gripping the window sill behind him, but once he moved into the space between the two windows there would be nothing to grip except the ledge itself. He looked down, and looked up again quickly. He very nearly changed his mind – this was not like climbing into his own house through the upstairs windows, this was something else!

The ground was terrifyingly far below. Don't look down, then. Whatever you do, don't look down. They always said that, didn't they! Joseph inched along, on his bottom, and now was the time to let go of the window sill inside. He took a deep breath, moved his hands to the edge of the ledge he was sitting on, and braced his feet against the wall of the building. He flattened his back hard, upright against the window, and moved cautiously some more. He was sick with fear. Only pride, now, was keeping him going.

Joseph closed his eyes. Not that that helped much. Looking or not, he could see with equal clarity the dreadful sight of the hard playground beneath him, so far, far beneath him. And here he was – it was true, he wasn't dreaming it, perched on a narrow ledge along which he must move, and keep on moving, if he wanted to come out of this escapade in one piece. There was no one to help him, he must do it himself. Bit by bit, Joseph shuffled himself along the ledge.

Castle Street School was going out to play. Class by class they filed down the stairs, or through the hall, and tumbled into the playground with the usual shouts of joy. Mr Davis was one of the first into the yard, because he was on duty that afternoon, and he was conscientious about being on time to supervise.

'Sir, sir, look sir!'

The theme from *EastEnders* was cut off in mid-note, and Mr Davis's eyes followed the pointing arms. 'Oh my God!' Mr Davis could hardly believe what his eyes undoubtedly saw: a small figure, nearly at the top of the tall school building, perilously perched on a ledge between two windows.

'It's Joseph!' 'Joseph Rundell!' 'Joe! Joe!'

'Shut up, you fools!' said Mr Davis. 'The worst thing you can do is shout at him. Do you want him to fall?'

'What *can* we do, sir?'

'Pray,' said Mr Davis, meaning it.

In fact, Joseph was hardly aware of the sudden outbreak of noise in the playground below. All his mind was concentrated on one objective; the drainpipe, the drainpipe, the drainpipe. He pictured it, he willed it nearer, he imagined the sweet, hot sting of it against his hands, when he should grasp it, and be slipping down it safely at last, into the playground.

Nearly there, nearly! The wall behind was no longer wall, it was window. Joseph could feel the ridges of the frame as he moved slowly, slowly, eyes still tightly closed, hands gripping the ledge, feet tight against the bricks beneath.

The end of the ledge at last. The fingers of Joseph's right hand splayed out against the wall, groping for the drainpipe he knew was there. It was there, it was there, he had it! One more thing to do, and that was almost the worst of all, with his insides like mashed up jelly from fear. He took another deep breath, and he did it. He did it. He swung himself round, and off the ledge, and he had made it! Both hands were grasping the drainpipe, the knuckles grazed raw, but who cared? His knees and his toes dug firmly into the wall, and he was coming down.

13

Joseph is missing again

Dear Mrs Lloyd (*wrote Gillian*)
Thank goodness you have born your baby at last. I am sorry your baby is a boy but we cannot always have what we want. Did you know that Joseph has been very naughty? He climbed out the stockroom window and Mrs White said she nearly had a hart attack when she heard about it. I nearly had a hart attack as well and so did all the class and Mr Davis nearly had a hart attack in the playground. Grace and me are being more stricter with Joseph than before and he is moaning because we are so strict with him but he has to learn his lesson and it is all for his own good isent it.

Sean has still got the hump.

Grace knitted something for your baby and she wanted to send it to you but I said she couldent send it because its dirty and too much rong stitches. If a job is worth doing its worth doing well.

I hope James is being good.
                    Love from
                        Gillian X

Joseph was quite certain that he had never been so miserable in his life. The Stockroom episode could have made him a celebrity in the eyes of the school, only Mrs White made sure it didn't. She was so angry, and frightened, to think how Joseph could have been killed, that she quite forgot Joseph had feelings too, and she held him up to ridicule in Assembly, in front of everyone. She was only making certain nothing of the kind ever happened again, but when she had finished wiping the floor with him, Joseph just wanted to crawl into a hole and disappear.

And when he got over feeling like that, there was being a prisoner to contend with. It wasn't only Gillian and Grace now, either, who were guarding him. At least half the class, it seemed, had come in on the act. They were outside his house in the morning, they made circles round him in the playground, they surged in front of him, and behind him, and each side of him as, head down and silent, he scuffled despondently homeward. Their grinning faces were everywhere; he could see them in his mind even when he wasn't looking. Their taunts were in his ears and continued to be so, long after he was home, when he was in bed even, waiting to go to sleep.

The other children did not know they were being cruel. It was all a lark to them, something to liven up the depressing affair school had become. To Joseph it was a torment that became more unbearable as day followed day. If he couldn't escape just once, and have some fun, he thought he would die. He tried, desperately, to think of ways and means.

Before and after school were no good, because his guards were always there. In school then, perhaps in class time, when the others were safely in their seats, and couldn't get at him, to stop him. Joseph tried asking to go to the toilet in the middle of a lesson, but Mrs White was wise to that one.

'You're supposed to remember these things at the proper time. All right, if you *must* be so babyish, Sanjay and Richard can go with you.'

'I changed my mind.'

'Please yourself.'

He tried, though with no real hope, volunteering every time there was a message to be taken, or a job outside the classroom to be done. But of course, Mrs White never fell for *that* one; she never chose *him*.

When his chance came, it was without any planning at all.

They were going down to Assembly; down the stone staircase to the hall, walking in single file with Mrs White at the head. Gillian was in front of Joseph, and Grace was behind him, and Joseph was thinking he just could not stand another day of captivity. His feet itched to be running somewhere, and the fingers of one hand plucked restlessly at the sleeve of the other. The wristband of the knitted wool pullover was coming unravelled. Joseph's fingers plucked and pulled, until it hung down in loops. 'Leave it alone,' Gillian hissed at him, turning round to check. 'You're making it worse.'

Going into the hall there was a muddle. One of the classes whose room led off the hall started coming out before their teacher said. It was a rude class, with a lot of ill-mannered children, and their teacher was cross with them for doing it, but before she could stop them, they had pushed through the 4L column, and scattered it. Joseph found himself separated from the rest, and by the time he had stopped concentrating on not being knocked off his feet, he discovered that he was squeezed between the wall and Class 4D, just entering the hall from the vestibule.

Joseph ducked. Class 4D surged past, not interested. Joseph slipped along by the wall, under cover of the rest of 4D, and out into the vestibule. The vestibule was empty, but the clatter of footsteps announced another class coming down the stairs. Joseph slipped out of the door, and into the front playground. He hardly dared hope that his scuttling figure would not be noticed by someone, as it charged the short distance from door to gate. But everyone was in Assembly, or on their way to Assembly. There was no one in any of the front classrooms to look out of the window and see him.

Joseph was free!

Although it was March, and the second half of the term, there was an icy wind and little flurries of snow, and Joseph was wearing only indoor clothes. Well, he could hardly go back for his coat! He would have to jump about to keep warm. The only thing was, someone might be looking out of one of the houses and think it funny to see a boy without his coat. Mrs Jones might be looking, and *she* would tell on him for certain, the interfering pig. Joseph made a face at Mrs Jones's front windows to test if she was looking. Oh, he was lucky, he was lucky! Now what should he do, with this lovely lucky day?

There was no one in the street. Yes there was, someone had just come. Oh look – it was Dippy Dora! Toe-heel *down*, shuffle shuffle. Toe-heel *down*, shuffle shuffle. She was wearing slippers today, and the hat with the flowers on it. Silas was in her hand, and he was all wet again, and she was cracking him. Round and round he whirled, in Dippy Dora's hand, then *crack* – oh, it was a wonderful sound. Joseph pranced behind Dippy Dora, mimicking her steps.

What *should* he do, with this lovely free day? He thought, and he thought, and suddenly he knew.

'Where's Joseph?' whispered Gillian, to Grace.

'I dunno. He ain't here, is he!'

Both girls looked anxiously up and down the reassembled line.

'Do I hear a voice at the back?' said Mrs White, from the platform.

'He's *not* here,' said Gillian, as the school began to sing. The news travelled along the class. *Joseph Rundell's missing.*

'Sir,' Sharon hissed at Mr Davis, who was sitting at the end of his line. 'Sir, Joseph Rundell's missing!'

'Be quiet and sing,' said Mr Davis.

'But sir, we supposed to mind him!'

'You can mind him after Assembly.' Privately, Mr Davis thought Class 4L had gone much too far in their persecution of Joseph Rundell. The poor lad wasn't getting any space at all. If he had escaped the clutches of these ghouls now then so be it. He couldn't come to much harm for half an hour or so. Clearly there was a good angel watching over him, or he would have come to grief the other day, over that Stockroom business. Mr Davis opened his mouth and sang, with feeling, 'Glad that I live am I.'

After Assembly, as Joseph still hadn't turned up, Mrs White organized a search for him round the school. She wasn't worried yet, just annoyed. Gillian was worried, and said so over and over.

'Don't fret, Gillian,' said Mrs White. 'We'll find him.'

'But perhaps he run out of school.'

'Without a coat? In this weather? Come along, Gillian, use your common sense.'

'He might have, he's silly enough.'

'Then he'll soon be back, won't he!'

But by playtime, Joseph had not returned, neither had he been found in the toilets, the cloakrooms, the sports cupboard, the caretaker's room, or any of the other possible hidey holes anyone could think of.

'Is your mother at home?' Gillian was asked.

'Not in the morning.'

'I'll ask the secretary to phone, anyway. In case he's gone home. I think he must have, Gillian, it's snowing quite hard now. We'll see if he answers.'

Joseph was not at home.

'He might have gone to the shops,' said Gillian to Mrs White.

'Then he'll be all right, won't he,' said Mrs White. 'Nice and warm. Stop *worrying*, Gillian.'

'He might be climbing somewhere.'

'I don't think so,' said Mrs White grimly. 'Not after last time.'

'Couldn't you have a feeling, Grace, about where he is?' Gillian begged.

Grace tried very hard, but nothing came.

It was dark, where Joseph was. There was just one slit of light, but pale, so pale it was only a little bit lighter than the darkness itself. He could not stand upright; he could just about *sit* upright, but when he did that his head touched a hard wooden surface. If he moved, his knees and his elbows pressed into things with sharp edges. Something sharp and pointed was sticking into his ankle. He tried to reach down to move the sharp thing away, but his head struck metal, and made him see stars, and he could not reach the sharp thing sticking into his ankle anyway, because something else was in the way.

For the hundredth time he shouted, 'Let me out, let me out!' But his voice sounded all muffled, because there was only a tiny space to shout in, and he knew, anyway, that no one was going to hear.

He tried to push against the door, where the chink of light was, but he was too cramped for the push to have any power. And in any case there was a strong bolt on the other side. Joseph knew there was a strong bolt because he'd undone it himself, earlier that morning, when he was still free.

He still believed he would be set free again some time

because – well, no reason really except that was the way things were supposed to happen. But he hoped it would be soon.

By dinner time Gillian was in tears.

'Don't worry,' said Grace. 'Somebody going to find him. *Somebody* going to find him.'

Gillian wept salt tears into her dinner, and couldn't eat any of it.

'Oh, pull yourself together,' said Miss Campbell.

'Her brother's missing,' said Stephen, unexpectedly coming in on Gillian's side.

'Yeah, her brother's missing,' said Paul.

'Well, crying won't help, will it!'

'We'll help look for him after dinner,' said Stephen.

'Yeah,' said Harjit. 'We'll all look.'

'But I been *horrible* to him,' said Gillian, in a fresh bout of sobs.

'Never mind,' said Grace. 'We'll all be nice to him when he's found, to make up for it.'

The boys had a few good ideas. Harjit, for instance, thought Joseph might have crawled into the space under the stage, and got stuck. Harjit crawled into the space under the stage, and nearly got stuck himself, before Mr Davis found them in school, where they were not supposed to be, and shooed them out. The snow had stopped, and fresh air was good for them, Mr Davis said.

Then Stephen remembered the big rubbish bins and a crowd of children trooped across the front playground, where they were also not supposed to be, to look. Paul climbed on to Stephen's shoulders, and peered into each of the three huge bins in turn, but Joseph was not in any of them. Disappointed, the children trailed back to their own playground.

During the dinner hour Miss Campbell, grumbling a

bit, took her car to the High Street and combed through the big shops. Joseph was not in Woolworth's; he was not in Sainsbury's; he was not in MacDonald's; he was not in the Public Library.

Mrs White phoned Mrs Rundell and discovered that no, Joseph was not at home. Mrs Rundell was more put out than anxious, and vowed to give him what for when he did turn up. 'It's broad daylight, innit,' said Mrs Rundell. 'He can't come to much harm.'

'Your mother's not worrying,' said Mrs White to Gillian, who was still crying. 'She says Joseph will come home when he's hungry, and she's going to let us know the minute he does.'

'Will you tell me?' Gillian begged, and Mrs White promised she would.

'I let Mum down though,' Gillian wailed, in a new outburst of self-reproach. 'I promised her I'd watch Joseph, and I let him get away!'

'For heaven's sake, Gillian, stop dramatizing yourself!' said Mrs White, irritably. 'You're only human, like the rest of us.'

By home time Mrs Rundell had not phoned to say that Joseph had arrived, and Gillian, in spite of all the comforting, was quite distraught. 'I can't go home without him, I can't go home,' she insisted.

'Yeah, but you don't want your mum worrying about you as well,' said Grace, sensibly. 'Come on, we best take Joseph's coat home, so he'll have it for tomorrow. Here it is. . . . It is a *mess* now, isn't it?' The grey anorak with the bright stripes was still blotched and stained, and the tear had been inexpertly cobbled together.

'That used to be a really smart coat,' said Stephen.

'He brung it home like that after he went missing the other time,' said Gillian, through her tears. 'It was wet as well. We never found out where he went.'

194

'I just had a idea,' said Paul.

'That makes a change!'

'Ha, ha, ha!'

'Nah – don't muck about,' said Paul. ''Member we see Joseph when he run away from Gillian that other time? 'Member where he was going?'

'Down Jubilee Street.'

'*Could be going to the canal*,' said Paul.

'Oh yeah, that's how his coat got wet!'

'I bet he went to the canal this time. I bet that's where he went!' said Paul.

'Actually,' said Sean, speaking in a stiff, tight voice, 'actually I know somewhere by the canal he could go.' He wasn't really bothered about Joseph – he had troubles of his own, after all – but he knew something the others didn't, and this might be his chance to get back in the gang.

'Where's that?'

'There's a old hut, where we was going to keep our bike,' said Sean.

'What bike?'

'Oh, nothing!'

'I know, I know,' said Stephen. 'Let's go down the canal and look! See if he's there now!'

'What about me?' said Sean, embarrassed.

'What *about* you?' The other boys were embarrassed too, not knowing how to respond. Sean had made himself the king and he had made himself *not* the king. Now the others didn't quite know *what* he was.

'Shall I come?' said Sean, half afraid to ask.

'If you like.'

'Yeah.'

'Yeah, all right, come on!'

'Sean's coming. . . . Come on, let's go!'

'Let's us go too,' said Gillian, to Grace.

'It's a long way,' said Grace, doubtfully.

'Let's go, though – to find Joseph.'

Stephen, Paul, Harjit, Sean, Gillian and Grace ran all the way to the canal. Gillian and Grace got left behind, because they were not used to running, and they had to keep stopping to ease the stitches in their sides. By the time they caught up, the boys were clustered already round the little hut.

'It's padlocked,' said Harjit. 'He couldn't have got in there.'

'Perhaps somebody shut him in,' said Sean. 'Perhaps he's a prisoner, and can't get out.'

The children tried to peer through a crack in the shuttered window, but the interior was too dark for them to see anything. A group of big lads from the High School passed, and Harjit thought of asking if any of them had seen Joseph. 'Nah – haven't seen no kids. There's an old guy walking his dog back there, no kids though.'

The children turned back to the hut. 'Joseph, Joseph,' they called – but there was no answer.

'Perhaps he's unconscious,' said Sean.

Gillian began to cry again.

'I don't think he's in there,' said Stephen, losing interest in the hut.

'He might be,' said Sean, trying to keep it going.

'I want to go home,' said Gillian. 'I want my mum. My mum's going to be worried about me.'

'Told you,' said Grace.

The man walking his dog appeared just then, and the children asked if by any chance he had seen Joseph. The man started to say that no, he hadn't, when his eyes lit on the anorak over Gillian's arm.

'Is that his coat then?'

'Yes. Have you seen him?'

'Has it got a tear on the arm?'

196

'Yes.'

'Is he about your age? Thin legs, yellow hair, sticking up?'

'*Yes*,' said Gillian. She stopped crying, and began to be excited.

'Are you his sister then?' said the man.

'Yes, I am. Oh please, have you seen him?'

The man shook his head. 'Nah – never clapped eyes on him in me life.' And he walked on, chuckling and whistling to his dog.

Gillian burst into tears. 'He was *t-t-teasing* us.'

'He knows something though,' said Sean.

'He's a nasty mean *t-t-teaser*,' wept Gillian, too upset to think straight.

'But he *knows* something,' said Sean.

'I want to go home,' wailed Gillian, not hearing him. 'I want my mum. I want to see if Joseph's got home yet.'

'Come on then,' said Grace, who was beginning to worry about her own mum.

'Lets us follow that old guy,' said Sean. 'Come on, boys.'

'I think Joseph's home already,' said Gillian, as the girls hurried along. 'Do you think so, Grace? *I* think so. I think we wasted our time going to the canal. I wish we never went. I don't want my mum to worry about *me*. I think Joseph's home now though, don't you?' If Grace couldn't have a feeling about it, *she* would have one. She tried very hard, all the way home.

Gleefully, the boys followed the old man along the towpath. It was considerate of Joseph Rundell to provide all this fun for them. They hoped Joseph would be all right in the end, of course, but meanwhile this was great!

The stalking had to be done properly, that went without saying. The boys made a great performance of diving into the bushes every time they thought the man might be going to turn round. Which, to their disappointment, he never actually did. When he turned out of the canal and into a little side street, the boys ran swiftly and were just in time to see him disappear into one of the small terraced houses. A light went on in the front window, but it was not dark enough yet for the curtains to be drawn.

'He must have got Joseph inside,' said Sean.

'You mean a prisoner?' said Stephen.

'Yeah, a prisoner.'

'What for, though?' said Paul, who had enjoyed the stalking, but didn't really understand what it was all about.

'You know, like the police film. That man might be a Stranger.'

'Oh yeah, so he might.'

'Shall we tell the police?' said Paul.

'Dum-dum! We got to have proof first!' said Sean. He was scared then, that he might have made a mistake, speaking to Paul like that, but Paul only said, 'All right, you're the boss.'

Sean was exultant. 'You're the boss,' Paul had said. So Sean was going to be king again. Good – he'd soon get this lot into shape! 'We'll have a look through the window first,' he said.

'Suppose he catch us,' said Harjit.

'We can run,' said Sean.

'I don't like it,' said Stephen.

'Who's the boss then?'

'. . . You are, I suppose.'

'And don't you forget it!' said Sean.

The boys crouched low, to enter the tiny front garden. They spread themselves out below the window, and Sean raised his head cautiously, to peep into the room. 'It's empty,' he said, disappointed.

'What you kids doing in that garden?' said a sharp voice, behind them. 'You trying to break in?'

'That old man got our mate a prisoner,' said Paul, to the indignant middle-aged woman who was glaring at them from the road.

'Rubbish!' said the woman. 'Alf Jennings don't have prisoners in his house. Clear off, the lot of you, or I'll get the police!'

The boys scampered back to the canal entrance and clustered in a group, wondering what to do next.

'I'm going home,' said Stephen, suddenly. 'Else I'm going to get in trouble for being late.'

'Yeah, me an' all,' said Paul.

'And me,' said Harjit. 'Wonder what story I can tell my mum.'

'Go on then,' said Sean. 'Little boys go back to your mums. I'm staying here!'

They went, muttering but not very much. Sean was on top of the world. He was king again, and now he was going to be a Very Important Person as well. Now the others had gone, he was going to have all the glory of finding Joseph to himself. He would watch the house until the old man came out, then he would break in and rescue Joseph. Good old Joseph! Good old Joseph, for being the means of so much triumph for Sean.

Time passed, and darkness fell, and with it more flurries of snow. Sean was stiff and cold, waiting for something that didn't happen. He began to think that perhaps enough was enough. He didn't really need to rescue Joseph, he was all right without that. He was the king again without that, wasn't he? Everything was turning out well for him – it was poor old Joseph who was down on his luck. *He* was all right, though, Sean was all right, and that was the main thing. . . . What about that silly dum-dum Joseph, though? Couldn't look after himself, could he? Couldn't keep himself out of trouble no way! . . . Yeah, well, might as well wait a bit longer. *He* was all right, so he might as well wait a bit longer to help that silly daft booby out of his mess.

Joseph was cold. And hungry. And very, very frightened. It was all dark now, even the pale little slit had disappeared. Joseph had freed his ankle from the sharp thing. He thought he cut the skin when he did that, because it hurt a lot and afterwards there was something warm, trickling over his foot. But that was a long time ago and the trickling had stopped. The ankle still hurt, but not as much as when he cut it. Joseph lifted his leg once more, and kicked feebly sideways. There was a dull thump against the door but Joseph had no hope, really, that anyone would notice. He'd already kicked till he was tired and he had no strength, he thought, to kick any more.

For the first time it occurred to him that perhaps he wasn't *ever* going to get out. Perhaps he was going to be trapped here for always and always. Perhaps he was going to – oh, no! No! That couldn't be! That couldn't be true, could it? Oh no, not that, not that!

Panic swept over Joseph and he began to cry, great gulping, helpless sobs. He struggled desperately for a moment, and then went limp. The nightmare went on, and on.

14

And still missing

The police had come to the house. They talked a long time to Gillian and her mother and father. The police still thought Joseph would turn up safe and sound somewhere. Missing children usually did, they said, and clearly Joseph had only run out of school for a lark. He had played similar pranks before, it was unlikely that he had gone far.

'He's got no money, and no coat,' said Mrs Rundell. 'He'll freeze to death out in this weather.' Her face was drawn and anxious, and she looked quite old.

'His coat!' said Gillian, suddenly remembering. 'That man recognized his coat! How did he know it was Joseph's coat if he never see him before?'

'What man was this?' asked the policeman, interested.

'The man down the canal, this evening.

'You never said about no man down the canal,' said Gillian's father.

'I forgot,' said Gillian. 'I didn't think, before.'

'Tell us now,' said the police, before Gillian's father could bawl her out for forgetting. Mr Rundell was looking quite old this evening, as well. His face was twitching with the effort of trying to keep calm and his fingers tapped rapidly on the side of the chair, as though he were playing the piano. There was a smell of fried onions coming from the kitchen, but the supper on the dining table had congealed into cold unappetizing lumps, because no one had been hungry enough to eat it.

'He was a ordinary man,' said Gillian. 'But he seen Joseph's coat before. And he knew about the tear.'

'What tear?' said the police.

'He come home with his coat all tore one time,' said Mrs Rundell. 'Here Gillian – it wasn't that Kojak man you saw, was it? With the scar?'

'Nah – Joseph made that up.'

'He might not have, it might be true, we might not have believed him and it was true all the time. That Kojak man might have got our Joe, and shut him up like he done before, only Joe escaped!'

'He never, Mum. He made that up, I told you!'

'Oh you're so clever, you know everything, don't you? But somebody's got Joseph, and I reckon it's that Kojak man. You got to go and look for him,' she begged the police. 'You got to catch him, and make him give back my boy!'

'Hold on, hold on,' said the policeman, patiently. 'Can we go back a bit? Now, Gillian, tell us what you can about this man on the canal. The one you actually saw. What did he look like?'

'He was old, and he looked nice only he laughed, and he had a dog. Sean was going to follow him, I think, and the other boys.'

'Sean?'

'Sean Adams. I know where he lives.'

'Is this a school friend?'

'Not a *friend*,' said Gillian. 'He's a horrible boy.'

'He might turn out to be a friend,' said the police, 'if he can help.'

They found Sean, still at his post by the canal. They had been to his house, and found his mother distraught because he had not come home. 'You've worried your mother half to death, stopping out like this,' said the policeman to a cold and hungry Sean.

Sean was annoyed that the police told him off, when they should have praised him. 'Somebody got to watch,' he said, defensively. 'I think my mate's in that house. Somebody got to watch if the old man comes out.'

'You've done very well, lad. Now it's time to go home. Hop in the car, my mate'll watch the house.'

That was more like it! Sean went home, well pleased with himself. He would tell his mum what the police said. That would show her! That would show her he could do other things besides beat up little kids for money. Anyway, he wasn't going to do that sort of thing any more, was he? It was much better, helping the police to find missing people. 'You've done very well, lad,' they said. From now on, he would concentrate on helping the police to find missing people.

Ten minutes later the police knocked at Alf Jennings's house. They learned the story of how Joseph had fallen into the canal, and been dried off, and safely escorted home. Alf was clearly telling the truth, there was no reason on earth to suspect him. So the police were as far from finding Joseph as when they had started. Unless. . . ? But the police didn't think that likely. They didn't think that *really* likely.

Joseph did not know how long he had been in the dark place. He thought it was night, because everything was so still, and anyway it felt like night. But he couldn't be sure. Perhaps it was really tomorrow. Or the next day. He supposed they would be looking for him, all those people in the ordinary world. How would they know where to look, though? How would anyone ever think where he really was? Without knowing he was going to do it, Joseph began to pray. 'Please God, please tell somebody where I am, *please*. I won't do no more wrong things if you let me get out and I will let Gillian nag me if she wants to, and Grace. I mean it you know. Amen.'

Probably be all right now, Joseph thought. In the morning, probably. Uncomfortable as he was, he even slept a bit.

Joseph slept more, in fact, than did any of the rest of his family. His parents sat up all night, listening for the phone and making cups of tea. Gillian went to bed, but whenever she closed her eyes she saw in startling detail the long dark ribbon of the canal, gleaming in the murky light of a winter's evening, hiding who knew what secrets beneath its scummy surface. The police had come back to tell what they had learned, and it was reassuring at first to learn that Alf Jennings was an ordinary, decent person, and not a Stranger at all.

But the thoughts that came after that first reassurance were terrifying. Joseph had fallen into the canal once – perhaps he had fallen in again! Perhaps this time he had drowned! Perhaps his body was even now lying under the cold water, limp and pale, in the slime and the muck at the bottom of the canal. That would not be the case, the police said firmly. Joseph had had one ducking; he'd be particularly careful not to let such a thing happen again. Whatever had become of him, the police insisted, he would *not* have fallen into the water.

All the same, they would be dredging the canal if Joseph

didn't turn up. They didn't tell the Rundells, but that was what they were going to do.

Early next day, Grace knocked at the door to see if there was any news, and to see if Gillian was coming to school. There was no news, and Gillian was not coming. Gillian's cheeks were white and hollow, her eyes red-rimmed, with dark shadows under them. She was past crying. A sort of numb despair had taken the place of fear and grief, and now she was quite sure the worst had happened. She would never see Joseph again.

'I ain't never going to be able to make it up to him. I was horrible to him, and now I ain't never going to be able to make it up. He's got drowned, I know.'

Grace was deeply distressed. 'Don't say that, Gillian. Don't say that!'

'*And* it's all my fault. I was horrible to him, and that's why he run out of school. To get away from me. It's *my* fault he's drowned!'

She had worked that one out at some time during the night, and there was so much truth in her reasoning that Grace did not know what to say. Her kind heart was torn with pity; furthermore, her own conscience was not entirely easy. *She* had been horrible to Joseph, as well. Gillian had made her do it, but still—

'You could have another try to have a feeling, Grace,' Gillian suggested, faintly hoping. '*Please* try.'

Grace tried, and tried, but still nothing came. She screwed up her eyes, and clenched her fists, and tried. Nothing. 'I can't,' she said miserably.

All by herself, Grace trailed to school.

That morning, Mrs White held a special Assembly. She explained to the whole school, in case anyone hadn't heard, that Joseph Rundell was missing, that yes, it was no use pretending otherwise, there were fears for his safety, so they were all going to say some special prayers, and afterwards the police were going to ask them some questions, to find out if anyone had any information which might help them discover where Joseph had gone.

The questioning took up quite a long time, and produced no result whatever. When Joseph had run out of school, yesterday morning, the whole school had been in Assembly. As bad luck would have it, no one had been coming along late, so there had been no one to see Joseph in the street, to see which way he went. No, he had not confided any secrets to anyone. No, there had not been any suspicious Strangers hanging about the neighbourhood, as far as anyone had observed.

After the children had been questioned, the police tried a house to house investigation the short length of Castle Street. Here they had a bit more luck, but not much. One lady did think she remembered seeing a boy without a coat in the street, at about twenty past nine, but she wasn't paying particular attention. Well, which way was he going? Up or down the street? Oh – up the street – oh yes, she remembered something else now: the boy was dancing behind poor Miss Dipper, making fun of the poor old thing behind her back. It was a shame, wasn't it, the way some of the children tormented that poor mad creature?

The police knocked at Dippy Dora's house, but there was no reply. They knocked again, but still no answer. The police shrugged, and went away. It was unlikely she could tell them anything sensible, anyway. She lived in a world of her own, that one.

In the school, the classes were filing back to their rooms. They were all very thoughtful, and Class 4L was particularly subdued. Jennifer was crying. She cried easily, so no one took much notice of that, but Mrs White was anxious in case it set the others off. Satibai and Minaxi were already looking distinctly watery-eyed, and Mrs White didn't want a class of weeping children on her hands, on top of everything else, so she decided to set them lots of very hard work, and grind their faces into that.

The back row were in no danger of weeping, of course. They were thoroughly enjoying the drama, the little beasts! Nevertheless, Mrs White thought she detected real concern on their faces as well. So they had hearts after all – well, in a manner of speaking. Even Sean Adams. Even objectionable louts like Stephen and Paul.

Today, Mrs White liked Class 4L just a little bit more than she had liked them yesterday.

Which did not mean that she was going to give them any rope. Harjit, for instance, tried to start a red herring about how Joseph *could* be under the stage, after all. Mr Davis had dragged him out yesterday, before he had a chance to look properly. Would Mrs White like him to go and look again? But Mrs White slapped Harjit down, because she thought that, mainly, he was trying to get out of doing his maths.

Sharon had another idea, and she put up her hand to tell it. 'Perhaps he's run away to London,' she said. 'Like on the telly.' Jeers, and a spate of unkind laughter. 'Don't be silly, *this* is London!' 'We're *in* London, you silly stupid fool!' 'How can he go to London, when he's already there?' 'Ha, ha, ha!' Sharon went very red, and Mrs White changed her mind about liking Class 4L after all.

'Be quiet!' said Mrs White. 'How dare you make this noise! Get on with your work, all of you. I don't want to hear another sound until playtime.'

Mrs White had had enough of people's ideas. Now she wanted the room to be quiet so that she could worry, in peace, over and over and over, about the boy who had gone missing while he was in her care. There was no way Mrs White could be blamed, of course; everyone said that, including the boy's mother and father. Joseph had run out

207

through sheer naughtiness, and whatever had happened to him outside was nothing to do with the school. All the same, if he were not found soon, and brought back safe, Mrs White did not think she would ever get over it. Mrs White pretended to be studying some papers on her desk, but really she was worrying, and worrying, and worrying, about Joseph.

A restless silence hung over the room. And suddenly into the silence came a voice. Sean's voice, loud and excited. '*I know where he could be.*'

'Be quiet, Sean,' said Mrs White, irritated at having her worrying interrupted.

'But, Mrs White, I got a idea where he could be.' Sean was on his feet now, and everyone turned to look.

'We don't want any more ideas,' snapped Mrs White. 'We only want facts.'

'Well, *this* is a fact. He been there already.'

'Been where?'

'In Dippy Dora's. I mean – in Miss Dipper's. I bet she got him prisoner!'

'Sean, really! I think you've got prisoners on the brain. And we've surely heard enough about that poor lady. Sit down, if that's all you've got to say.'

'But you don't understand—'

'SIT DOWN!'

'No.' The class regarded Sean with some awe, for daring to defy Mrs White. 'You got to listen, Mrs White. There was a horrible smell.'

'I don't know *what* you're talking about.'

'Well I'm telling you, aren't I? There was a horrible smell. In Dippy Dora's. Joe sneaked in, and he was nearly sick when he come out.'

'Serve him right. What on earth possessed him to go prying in the first place?'

'I dared him. To see what she got in her house, behind the curtains.'

'You nasty little boys! It's none of your business what Miss Dipper has in her house. Anyway, if he found the experience so disagreeable I can hardly see him wanting to repeat it.'

'But he was 'shamed he run out! And I took the mickey, didn't I? I bet he went in again. I bet! I bet she got him prisoner in there!'

'Sean Adams, use your common sense. An elderly lady, and a strong young person like Joseph? Now, if you have anything *real* to tell us. . . .'

Sean slumped back in his seat. Silly old cow! Silly old know-all cow! What did she know about it really, anyway? Dippy Dora was old, but she was strong. You only had to see her whacking her broom to know that. Anyway she might be magic, like the girls thought, some of them. She might have *magicked* Joseph. Sean went on brooding, and muttering, and glowering at Mrs White when she wasn't looking.

All right, he made a mistake about Alf Jennings. But it wasn't a *silly* mistake. The police didn't think it was silly. 'You've done very well, lad,' they said. He would like very much to hear the police say that again, if only he could think of a way.

Besides, it must be horrible for Joseph, being a prisoner like that, in Dippy Dora's house.

In his dark place, Joseph was losing heart. He was tired of struggling to thump and kick at the door. He had no strength to thump and kick any more, and anyway what was the point?

It was a pity God hadn't told anybody yet, about where he was. 'Come on God, hurry up,' Joseph pleaded. 'It's horrible here.'

Really, Joseph thought, he didn't know how he was going to stand the horribleness of it much longer.

15

Fire!

At playtime, Sean found himself the centre of attention. The whole of Class 4L, without exception, surrounded him in the yard and clamoured to tell him what a good idea he had had, about Joseph being in Dippy Dora's house. Sean was greatly excited by everyone saying that. The feelings inside him bubbled and boiled and struggled to burst into action. 'Let's go and see,' he said.

'What, now?'

'Yes, now! Let's run out of the playground, and go to her house, and break in, and see if we can find Joseph. Come on, let's!'

'All right,' said Stephen.

'Yeah, all right,' said Paul and Harjit, together.

'*I'll* come,' said Grace. She was terrified at the very thought, but it was all for Gillian's sake. She would be brave for Gillian.

'I'm coming too,' said Sharon, not wanting to be outdone.

In the end, everyone wanted to come. Even Jennifer and Satibai and Minaxi, weeping steadily on the outskirts of the group, were caught up in the fever, and decided to join in.

There was the minor problem of Mr King, of course, on playground duty and at that moment warming his hands round a cup of tea, his eyes gazing dreamily into space. But Mr King was a long way away. Too far away to stop them.

The heavy gates into Bridge Street swung open, and Class 4L streamed into the road. A few busybodies from other classes rushed to point out to Mr King that Class 4L had run out, but by the time the news reached Mr King, Class 4L were already halfway round the block, going past the Infants School and coming into Castle Street.

Miss Robinson, on duty in the front playground, saw them coming but at first did not realize that they were unescorted. They were going to the Public Library, or somewhere, she supposed. It was unusual for a class to be *running* to the Public Library, but Class 4L were a wild lot, lately. Perhaps they had another supply teacher now; anyway, there would be a harrassed teacher of some sort, bringing up the rear of the rabble, Miss Robinson presumed. By the time she realized there was not, Class 4L had swarmed into the front garden of Dippy Dora's house, and were battering at the door and the downstairs windows.

Horrified, but unable to leave her post, Miss Robinson sent a frantic message for Mrs White to come *at once*. Then she, and the whole of the first and second year, peered helplessly through the railings, at the outrage going on across the road.

Some of Class 4L were getting quite carried away – you could hear their shouts all up and down the road. 'Where's Joseph?' 'We know you got him there!' 'You old hag, let Joseph out!' Even the timid ones were doing it. The whole class had gone mad, Miss Robinson thought, there could be no other possible explanation.

'She ain't coming,' said Stephen.

'Shall we break a window?' said Paul.

'Let's go round the back,' said Sean.

Most of the class poured through the side entrance, and began hammering on the back door and windows as well.

'Come on, you old witch, we know you're in there!'

'We know you got Joseph!'

'Look!' said Sean.

The curtains were drawn at the back too, and all the windows fastened. But one of the windows had a pane missing, with cardboard tacked over it. And in the cardboard was a jagged tear, as though someone had stuck a fist through. The edges of the tear had come together again, more or less, but when Sean put *his* hand through, they parted easily.

'I bet Joseph done that break, I *bet*,' said Sean. He was choking with excitement, almost, as he fumbled with the catch. 'Who's coming? Who's coming in?' Sean climbed on to the window ledge, and put one foot into Dippy Dora's kitchen.

'Me! Me!' 'The rescue squad is coming!' 'Out the way, there!' 'Get out of it, you!' Paul and Stephen and Harjit elbowed each other, and fought to be next.

'What's this?' said Grace, finding something caught on the splintered window frame.

'Only a bit of wool,' said Satibai.

'I think it's off of Joseph's pullover,' said Grace. She and Satibai stood aside from the rest, to consider what Grace had found. Everyone else was watching the rescue squad, squabbling about who should be first after Sean to break into Dippy Dora's house. 'Hurry up,' said Sean, from inside. 'Don't matter who's first!'

'How do you know it's Joseph's though?' said Satibai, to Grace.

'His sleeve was all coming undone, I see it yesterday. He

212

was pulling it off. This is a bit of it!'

'Tell the police.'

'Yeah.'

'Tell Mrs White.'

'Yeah, I will.'

Just then there was the shrill, piercing sound of a whistle. 'The police!' said someone. But it wasn't the police, it was Mrs White, blowing a whistle which she had never been known to do before, and looking very, very angry.

'HOW DARE YOU!' Mrs White's face was all red now, from the effort of blowing the whistle and shouting at Class 4L, and the veins were standing out of the poky neck. 'PAUL AND STEPHEN, COME OUT OF THERE THIS MINUTE!'

Meekly, the rescue squad climbed out of Dippy Dora's kitchen. Everyone tried to hide behind everyone else. 'Sean's still in there,' said someone.

Mrs White put her head, on the end of the long neck, through the open window. The stench in the kitchen caught her full in the face, and she gagged a bit. 'Sean Adams, come here!' she ordered him, bravely ignoring the smell. Sean was halfway across the kitchen, and he stopped from force of habit when Mrs White called him by name. He hesitated.

'I'M WAITING!' said Mrs White, in a very terrible voice.

Sean was excited, and all set to carry on, to race through the house and look in every room, every cupboard. His heart demanded that he do these things, but his legs obeyed Mrs White.

'GET BACK TO SCHOOL, ALL OF YOU, AND WAIT FOR ME IN YOUR CLASSROOM,' said Mrs White.

'Mrs White—' Grace began, trying to tell the head-mistress about the piece of wool from Joseph's pullover.

'NO EXCUSES!' thundered Mrs White.

'It's not a excuse,' Grace tried again. 'It's—'

'I DON'T WANT TO LISTEN.'

Grace gave up. She put the piece of wool in her skirt pocket, and joined the shamed and subdued procession going back to school.

Inside the house, Dippy Dora crouched, terrified. Would the banging never stop? First the police – she knew it was the police, because she'd peeped through the curtains. Well, she wasn't going to answer to *them*, oh no, no, no! Not those dirty saucepans, she knew better than that!

But what was happening now? A moment ago she thought the house was falling in. Thumping and banging and demons screeching – she was too frightened to look, but it was certainly demons because what else? She could picture their horns and their tails and their wicked, grinning faces. They were coming to get her, coming to get her! There was no one to help her and she was all alone. Oh what should she do? What should she do?

But they were gone now, the demons were gone. Dippy Dora unwound Silas from her face, freeing her mouth to give a great trembly sigh. 'We ain't done for yet, Silas,' she told her friend. 'Not yet, not yet.' She squatted on the floor, rocking backwards and forwards amid the piles of rubbish – unwashed clothes, rotting food, and her treasures! They were a pathetic collection, the things she called her treasures, gathered over the years from gutters and dustbins all around the area. There was a child's doll with both arms missing, a broken teapot, a clock that didn't work; the pitiful list went on and on. There was nothing of value anywhere in the house, and precious little furniture. Anything that would fetch money had been sold years ago, to pay the bills, and for having a go at the bottle.

Now the rubbish took the place of the things that were sold, and often for her they were all mixed up in Dippy Dora's mind – so the doll with no arms was the doll she played with, years ago; the clock that didn't work was the one that stood in her own parents' bedroom. She browsed among her treasures and relived her memories until the past and the present got muddled too, and Dippy Dora chatted out loud with the ghosts of the past, who came alive in her imagination.

Then the past would fade, and it would be now again, and there was the frightening muddle she was getting into. It was all around her, and she couldn't seem to stop it – that was when she wanted the bottle. The bottle made the muddle not so frightening. But it made her feel ill afterwards so she always said she wouldn't do it again. She always did though; she always did. And the muddle got worse, and the litter piled up, and often there was no money for the bottle anyway.

Money: there was her pension now, and that was all. The lady she went to about not paying the rates said she should ask the Social for more help, but she wouldn't do that. The electricity man said the same thing when he came to cut the meter off. 'Before the winter comes,' he said. But she wouldn't do that. Oh no, no, no, no, no, she knew better than that! If you asked for help they came to see. The electricity man had seen, and that was bad enough, but he wasn't no blabber-mouth – she didn't think so – and that was a long time ago and she'd got more muddled since then. Them others would poke and pry and say she couldn't manage, and take her away to a Home. *She* knew their tricks, she knew! This was her house, and she'd lived here all her life, and they weren't going to take her away from it. No, no, no!

Perhaps they wouldn't even let her keep Silas in the Home. Dippy Dora clutched her friend, and moaned, and rocked him to and fro in her arms, now. Years, he had been with her; through the good times and the bad ones. 'You and me'll stick together, Silas,' she reassured him.

She gnashed her gums, and the tooth and the beard went up and down, up and down. The movement soothed her, just a little bit, and the panicky feelings began to subside.

The house was very still. Dippy Dora frowned, struggling to remember something else. That other banging. The banging upstairs. What happened then, about the banging upstairs? Gone away. The banging had gone away. Of course, of course, because it was a long time ago. That dirty saucepan was gone now because it was a long time ago, and anyway he wasn't banging now, so he must be gone away. In the cupboard upstairs. She went up to see what the noise was, and she was frightened to go, but she had her broom and she whacked it on the stairs to frighten the thieving saucepan and he was in the cupboard already. 'Let me out, let me out,' the saucepan shouted, but she wouldn't do that, oh no! A little saucepan with a squeaky voice. She bolted him in the cupboard before she knew it was only a little one. But she couldn't let him out because he might tell – about the dirt, and the muddle, and then the Social would come and put her in a Home. Anyway it was a long time ago, and he was gone now. She couldn't remember how, but he must have gone, because he wasn't banging any more.

Suddenly panic gripped her again. He had told, the saucepan had told! They were coming to get her, the Social were coming. The police were coming. The demons were coming. She trembled, and two cold tears trickled from her bleary eyes. What about them bottles then? Perhaps they weren't all empty. Dippy Dora shuffled through the piles of debris towards the bottles stacked in the corner. Perhaps there was still a drop that would make her forget how the Social were coming to take her away.

Just a minute though, just a minute, just a minute. The police were gone away, weren't they? The demons were gone away. Ha, ha – they were all gone away. She was still safe, still safe with her treasures all around. *She* didn't want the bottle, she didn't want that! What she wanted was a nice cup of tea. A nice cup of tea then, a nice cup of tea! It took a long time for the kettle to boil, perched on top of the smelly old oil stove. Dippy Dora wrapped Silas round her neck, and rubbed the end of him against her face while she waited.

'Silent Reading and not a word, NOT A WORD,' said Mrs White. Grace took the scrap of wool from her pocket, and held it up, her lips obediently together for Mrs White to see.

'Put that away, whatever it is.'

'Please Mrs White. . . .'

'AWAY – NOW!'

Mrs White's face was pale now, except for two high spots of colour burning on her cheeks. The veins stood out on her neck still, and she was biting her lips with rage. Frightened by so much anger, Grace put the piece of wool in her lap.

Satibai turned round and whispered something to Sharon.

'SATIBAI!'

Satibai cowered in her desk. Sharon's face was pink with excitement. *She* wasn't afraid of Mrs White. *She'd* make the old cow listen. 'Grace got something important, Mrs White. . . .' Sharon's voice trailed off – she was a bit frightened of Mrs White, after all.

Mrs White glared at Sharon. 'All right, stand up Grace Johnson, and it had better be something worth listening to.'

Grace stood up and everyone looked at her. To her horror she felt the smile, the smile of nervousness and confusion, coming unbidden just when it was most not wanted. She made a great effort to control it, and a giggle bubbled up in her throat.

Mrs White was furious. 'You silly little girl! Sit down!'

Sean thought he was going to burst. He was already angry with himself. Why had he been so silly, coming out of Dippy Dora's when Mrs White called him? Mrs White made him be silly. He *hated* Mrs White. He stood up, and shouted at her, 'You should listen to Grace, you know!'

There was a sharp intake of breath, all round the room. No one ever spoke to Mrs White like that. 'When I want your opinion I'll ask for it,' said Mrs White grimly, glaring at Sean.

'But you *should* listen to her! How do you know what it is, if you won't listen?'

'THAT'S ENOUGH! I have eyes, Sean. How am I supposed to take anyone seriously with *that* silly look on their face?'

'But that's just her face, innit! That's just Grace. She always does that. You don't have to take no notice of her face.' And suddenly they were all joining in, all the class.

'That's right.'

'Grace can't help smiling, she don't mean it.'

'You want to listen to her, Mrs White!'

Mrs White regarded the shouting mob with tightened lips. For one moment, she quite loathed them. How dare this pack of eleven-year-olds know more about human nature than she did? Mrs White resented it – but only for a moment. She knew she sometimes made mistakes, and she usually came round to admitting them, in the end. 'What is it then Grace?' she said. 'And try to tell me without looking like Simple Simon.'

Grace held up the piece of wool. It was lovely to have all the class supporting her. That made her feel warm, and brave, and she spoke without smiling at all. 'This came off Joseph's pullover, I think.'

Mrs White took the clue from Grace's hand. 'It's navy

blue,' she said. 'Approximately one hundred and fifty children in this school are wearing navy blue pullovers at this moment.'

'But Joseph's sleeve was coming undone. And this was catch on the window, in Dippy Dora's back,' said Grace.

'But you've *all* been in Miss Dipper's back garden. And how many of you are wearing navy blue pullovers?'

'This bit's all wet though, from the snow last night.'

Silently, Mrs White marched out of the room, holding the little piece of evidence very carefully. The class surged to the window, pushing and shoving to get a good view of Dippy Dora's house. It was going to be good now, they didn't want to miss anything.

The kettle was taking a long time to boil; Dippy Dora gnashed her gums, impatiently. Cup of tea, cup of tea, cup of tea! Or what about something to eat? Something to eat, something to eat! She wasn't sure, but she didn't think she'd had any breakfast. Toe-heel *down*, shuffle shuffle; Dippy Dora danced into the hall, where the smell of rotting food mingled with that of the mildew on the streaming walls. She danced into the filthy kitchen, to look for a piece of bread.

It was cold in the kitchen. The window was wide open, and an icy draught was cutting across to the door. Dippy Dora stared at the open window in dismay. She shut it though, didn't she, after that saucepan came in? That little one up in the cupboard? Anyway, that was a long time ago. Wasn't it? But what was now, and what was then, and what was a long time ago really? The muddle was frightening her again. Back to the front room. Back to the bottles.

A drop, a drop, a big drop to make her feel better! She swallowed, coughed, spluttered and swallowed again. Oh, *that* was good! Never mind she was going to feel ill presently, never mind she couldn't see very clearly, or walk straight. Just for now she felt warmed, and comforted. She began to sing 'Daisy, Daisy', in her wavering voice.

The kettle was boiling. What for? What was the kettle boiling for? The kettle was on the old oil stove and the steam was just beginning to come, feebly, out of its spout. A cup of tea, a cup of tea, she would have a cup of tea. 'Tea for two, for me for you,' sang Dippy Dora as she lurched across the room to where the oil stove was, and the kettle. She was too unsteady to dance, too unsteady to avoid the rubbish in her path. She tripped, she sprawled against the stove, she landed on hands and knees. The stove tipped over and tongues of flame began to lick at a pile of old newspaper.

Dippy Dora staggered upright, retreated into the kitchen, and screamed, and screamed, and screamed, as she tried to fill a small leaking bucket with water to put out the fire.

In the cupboard upstairs, Joseph heard the screams but paid them little attention. It was just Dippy Dora screaming, wasn't it – singing, and screaming, and talking to herself like mad people do. And sitting on her rubbish, behind her curtains. Her dirty old curtains, that weren't hiding anything interesting after all!

He was dying to tell people the real secret about Dippy Dora's house – but he wasn't going to have any chance to tell people, was he! It was going to happen, wasn't it! The unbelievable, impossible thing was going to happen, to Joseph Rundell, not quite eleven, all alone in this dark place!

'I found it out,' he was going to boast. '*I* was the one that went in, ME! I found a window with all cardboard over it, in Dippy Dora's back, and I broke it, and I got in, and I held my breath so I didn't have to breathe too much in her smelly old house. And I looked in all the boxes and there was only rubbish. And all the cupboards, I looked in them. And there wasn't no money, and no jewels. All there was was disgustingness, and pong!

'And I went upstairs but I heard her coming back. And I tried to open a window and climb out, but they were all stuck, like in the stockroom. And I heard her coming upstairs and she was shouting, and whacking her broom. And I got in the cupboard but there was dust in the cupboard and it made me sneeze, so she knew where I was, and she put the bolt over and she said, "I got you now, you dirty saucepan!" '

Well, she *had* got him, hadn't she! And he couldn't get out, no way. And he thought he didn't have any more tears to cry with, but he had. They rolled down his grimy cheeks, and trickled into his mouth, and he wanted his mum.

Through the crack, and under the door, drifted a faint whiff of smoke.

Mrs White had not come back, and the children were still crowded at the window, watching Dippy Dora's house. Any minute now, they thought, the police cars would arrive and Dippy Dora would be arrested for keeping Joseph prisoner. Joseph would be rescued, and Dippy Dora would be taken away, and serve the wicked old thing right. It was going to be great, and Class 4L didn't want to miss a second of it.

'There's smoke!' said Sean, suddenly.

'Nah – it's just fog,' said Richard.

'It's smoke, it *is* smoke,' said Sharon.

It's fire, look! It's all burning, look! In the window!'

'Oh yeah! Behind the curtains, you can see!'

'Dippy Dora's house is on fire!'

'Oh quick, quick, Joseph's going to get burned!'

They streamed out of the classroom, all of them, and pelted down the corridor yelling, 'Fire, fire!' All along the

221

corridor doors opened, and astonished teachers put out their heads to see what the uproar was all about. Most of the children in the other classes, and some of the teachers too, thought the fire was in the school. There was panic, and pandemonium – but fortunately the school secretary kept her head, and phoned for the fire brigade, just in case. She said she thought the school was on fire, but then she changed it because Sean was at her elbow, jumping up and down with excitement and saying, no, no, it wasn't the school! It was Miss Dipper's house across the road, and somewhere inside that burning building Joseph Rundell was trapped.

Mrs White had just finished talking on the phone, telling the police about the piece of wool from Joseph's pullover.

They missed the best bit, after all. Miss Campbell, with admirable presence of mind, rang the fire alarm to be on the safe side. Anyway, they could all do with a fire practice. The whole school had to assemble in the back playground so they never saw the fire engines, and Mrs White and the school secretary running into Castle Street to meet them, and tell about Joseph being inside the burning house.

They didn't see the ambulance, and Dippy Dora being put into it. They didn't see the firemen with their ladders, breaking into an upstairs window because the stairs were on fire already; and Joseph being brought down over the fireman's shoulder, just like on the telly.

'It's funny He picked Sean to tell,' said Joseph. 'I didn't expect He'd pick *Sean*.'

'Who picked Sean, love?' said his mum.

'Oh, nothing,' said Joseph.

'I'm sorry I was a pig to you,' said Gillian. 'I won't never do it again.'

'You can if you like,' said Joseph. 'I don't mind.'

'Oh Joseph,' said Gillian, bursting into tears, 'you are kind.'

'That's all right,' said Joseph, grandly. 'Any time.'

16

A very good teacher

Dear Mrs Lloyd
Did you know that Dippy Dora nearly burned Joseph to
death and herself as well. Dippy Dora thought Joseph
was a burglar and she shut him in the cupboard and
Mrs White says Dippy Dora probably forgot all about
Joseph was in the cupboard. Because she is not very
well. Anyway Joseph is not so silly now he nearly got
burned to death he has improved. The only thing is he
keeps having nitemares about hes still in the cupboard
but Mrs White says he will get over it in time and we
must all be pashent and kind. Mrs White has improved
now Joseph nearly got burned to death.

Sean was the best one for saving Joseph. I use to hate
Sean but I dont now he is not too bad. He has improved. Sean found Silas outside Dippy Doras house
and he took Silas home for a sooveneer Silas is quite
boring now Dippy Dora doesent make him come alive.
Sean came to our house for tea and Grace came and we
all had a game of scrabble and I injoyed it. Did you
know that Dippy Dora was not really wicked she was

fritend and all muddled up. And nobody loves her in the world. And her house was dirty and she dident want anybody to see and that was all the secret was in Dippy Doras house. Dippy Dora is in the hospital and Mrs White says she will go to live in a Home because her house is all burned now and she didnt really want to go to a Home but Mrs White says she will be better off in the Home and they will look after her there and give her a bath.

Please give my kind regards to your husband Winston and all the children in his school and a big kiss for James when are you coming to visit us in school and show us your lovely baby.

Love from Gillian X X X X X X X X X X X

Dear darling Mrs Lloyd

Yesterday was the best day in my hole life. I was walking in the hall and I saw this black lady with a baby in her arms and she had her back turned and I just thought it was somebodys mum. But it was YOU. And I saw James and you let me hold him and I couldent believe it. He is so beautiful and small and so much hair. I think he is the beautifullest baby in the world. Do black babys always have a lot of hair?

I use to want you to come back and be our teacher but now I dont because James is too little and you must not let anybody look after him only you. Promise you will not give him to anybody else to look after. Not till he is much, much bigger. Dont worry about the class we will be all right.

Me and Grace are going to do what you said. We are going to go and visit Dippy Dora in the hospital to cheer her up because we must all be kind to elderly people. Who are not very well. Sean is going to let us take Silas and give him back to Dippy Dora in the hospital to cheer her up.

Love to you and James and Winston from Gillian.

X X X X X X X X X X X X X X X X X X X X X X X X X X X X

Dearest Mrs Lloyd

When you came to school was not the best day of my life after all. Today is it. Mrs White told us the wonderful news this morning. She said do you all know Mrs Lloyds husband who is a teacher in a nother school. and everybody said Winston. Mrs White said no not Winston MR LLOYD. And everybody said yes we know him because he came to the summer fair last summer and the Xmas concert and he is nice. And he makes us laff. And Mrs White said there are too many teachers in Mr Lloyds school and it must be the only school in London that has too many teachers and Sean interrupted Mrs White and he said I know hes coming to be our teacher. Mrs White said yes Mr Lloyd is going to be your teacher thank goodness so you will be his problem now. And everybody began to cheer. And Mrs White said you needent sound so delited I understand he is a very good teacher and he WONT STAND ANY NONSENSE.

And when Mrs White said that they all cheered more. They cheered and cheered and I thought the ceeling would fall down and Mrs White said if you make any more noise the Queen will hear you in Buckingham Palace and wonder what all the exitement is about. But the thing is we are all so happy because we are going to have a very good teacher who WONT STAND ANY NONSENSE.

Love and happyness from Gillian and all of Class 4L.

X X X X X X X

226